Victim

An Emily Taylor Mystery

Catherine Astolfo

Poetry • *Merci Fournier*

Cover & Chapter Illustrations • *Carly Smith*

Footprint & Map Illustrations • *Helen Duplassie*

Moe Publications
24 Shenstone Ave. Brampton, ON L6Z 2Y8

This book is a work of fiction. All names, characters, places and incidents either are the product of the author's imagination or are used fictitiously, and any resemblance to actual persons living or dead, events, or locales, is entirely coincidental. Burchill and its inhabitants are fictional. However, some of the street names are similar to those you will find if you visit Merrickville — one of the most beautiful towns in Ontario.

Note for Librarians: A cataloguing record for this book is available from Library and Archives Canada at www.collectionscanada.ca/amicus/index-e.html
ISBN 1-4251-1546-2

Printed in Victoria, BC, Canada. Printed on paper with minimum 30% recycled fibre.
Trafford's print shop runs on "green energy" from solar, wind and other environmentally-friendly power sources.

Offices in Canada, USA, Ireland and UK

Book sales for North America and international:
Trafford Publishing, 6E–2333 Government St.,
Victoria, BC V8T 4P4 CANADA
phone 250 383 6864 (toll-free 1 888 232 4444)
fax 250 383 6804; email to orders@trafford.com
Book sales in Europe:
Trafford Publishing (UK) Limited, 9 Park End Street, 2nd Floor
Oxford, UK OX1 1HH UNITED KINGDOM
phone +44 (0)1865 722 113 (local rate 0845 230 9601)
facsimile +44 (0)1865 722 868; info.uk@trafford.com
Order online at:
trafford.com/06-3297

10 9 8 7 6 5 4 3 2

This book is dedicated to my beloved father, James, and sister, Candace, whose spiritual energies continue to guide us; and to Agnes Lake, a true shaman for her family.

Acknowledgements

———

My husband, Vince Astolfo, truly the wellspring of my creativity, as well as the love of my life, edited and did the lay out for this novel. My daughter, Kristen, gives me constant support, love and inspiration. None of these books would be complete if it were not for her encouragement and marketing skills. My son-in-law-and-heart, Kelly, has supported us through all of our dreams, even when it has meant sacrificing his own. Some day soon, Kelly, it will be your turn. My son, James, and my daughter-in-heart, Meredith, continue to be my champions. They have given me so much love and affirmation in pursuing this writing obsession. My mother, Maureen, has always believed in me and in *Sisbro*. Her faith and support give me a determination that I would otherwise not possess.

My niece, Carly, did the cover and the chapter pieces. She is an amazing, intelligent young woman whose personal charm is matched only by her talent. She will very soon take this world by storm.

Thanks to Sandy Duplassie and his siblings for the use of their mother's name, Agnes Lake, and for their counselling on Ojibwa folklore. Agnes was the motivation for my interest in Native history, ever since that trip into the woods!

My friend, Merci, who wrote the wonderful poetry, is a part of my heart where dreams and creativity arise and flourish.

My VBFITWWW, Helen, whose art has blossomed so quickly it was obviously just waiting there to bloom after retirement. Thank-you for your map and for bringing the footprints to life, but most of all, thank you for your enduring, necessary presence in my life.

My sisters and brothers-in-law and my wonderful nieces and nephews give me such positive energy, true love and happiness. My stepsons and step-daughters-in-law-and-heart, and my mother and father-in-law give Vince and me their love and support, something we never take for granted. Our grandchildren are a constant delight, a source of pride and faith that keeps us young and joyful. In all the good ways, they are the inspiration for Book Three.

Maire and Mary Jo not only edited both my books so carefully, but they always listen to me, love me, and are more of a source of joy and confidence than they can know.

I wish I had the space to list all of my friends, whose love is a constant wonder and inspiration for me. I am so very fortunate! Many of them read this manuscript and offered advice and assistance, too, especially my beloved Bosco Bunch, the outstanding Four Seasons and the Fifth, and the incomparable Other Mary Jo.

Trafford Publishing for their advice, the wonderful product that "Victim" has become, and for their support of Canadian writers.

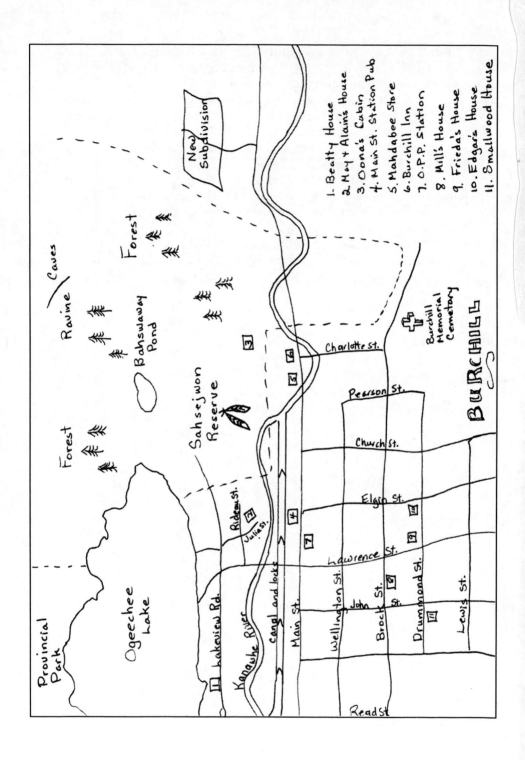

We, like the birds, fly in a certain direction,
and in spring, the jackrabbit starts his way.
Through the hare's eyes, I see.

Frieda waited until the police had finished searching. She did not even make the journey up the road until all the sightseers and relatives had drifted back to their homes. By the time she began walking toward the house, the woods had gone back to their natural quiet.

The sun made diamond patches on the crisp snow as she trudged up the hill. Overhead, several birds circled, silently searching for mice indiscreet enough to take a run through the leafless trees. Frieda's breath came in puffs of white clouds and the cold tingled her nose into a reddish blush. Crunching across the brittle ground, Frieda's eyes and ears told her countless stories about life in the forest.

Just to the side of the road, a small rabbit had been seized by an owl. Frieda spotted the frantic tracks racing to the trees, the sweep of the bird's wings as it grazed the ground and then flew off with its prey. A little further on, Barry Mills' son had destroyed a sparrow; she could see the boy's footprints and then a smattering of feathers and blood, which had once been a bird. Frieda smiled at this. Bobby Mills was learning to be a real hunter.

The thrill of the hunt shivered through her body. She could picture the huge deer she had caught last week, flattened against the snow, eyes bulging and fearful. Waiting, felled by the pain, the victim was at Frieda's mercy. It was left up to her to end the misery, to decide between life and death. At that moment, she was the one in control; she was the god; the arbiter of fate. For Frieda, the power of those moments was the reason she loved to trap and hunt.

The native woman prided herself on her keen powers of observation. She had spent most of her life in the woods, first trailing after her father, the man whose quiet aloofness had taught her to be silent and watchful. Her mother, frail and self-pitying, always lay pale and sighing in her bed when they arrived home, scrutinizing her daughter as though Frieda were an object of great perplexity. Frieda would spend hours in the woods alone, too, or in the shed out back, abiding by the stern lessons that her father had taught her about skinning and drying animal carcasses.

Later, when she was almost a grown woman and her parents had died, Frieda followed in Oona's footsteps. At the thought of Oona and the traps, her heart swelled with pride. Oona had shared her knowledge with anyone she thought worthy of it, and Frieda had proven her best pupil. Together, Oona and Frieda had travelled and camped in these woods several thousand times. They knew it the way most people know their living rooms. The two women had similar builds – strong and stocky, muscular and round from walking and hiking through hills and forest. They could scale walls and ford streams, build campfires from scratch, and create wooden structures that withstood most storms.

Frieda stopped at the bend in the road and sniffed the air. She might have been a bear whose den was being threatened, for only when she did not hear the saw whining in the distance or smell the dust of a fallen tree did she relax her stance. Her round, serious face was creased with sun lines and now, worry and curiosity. Her small brown eyes were inquisitive, almond-shaped, overshadowed by thick eyebrows. Her gaze was disconcerting to most; she had the ability to freeze conversation with her stare. As far as anyone knew, due to the woman's irascible and detached nature, Oona had been Frieda's only friend.

The layer of ice that had fallen over the snow yesterday must have thwarted their efforts to build again today. Frieda smiled maliciously. Along with other Ojibwa natives and Burchill residents, Frieda hated the encroachment of the new subdivision on their communities. As most of the villagers did, Frieda dreaded the increased population as an intrusion on their quiet way of life. But she had other reasons for her reactions. Although the threat of competition in the trapping business was very real, Frieda was also secretly energized by the idea of a more modern life; she had her own secret agenda and the guilt made her uneasy and filled with anger. She knew, however, that the subdivision was not destined to last. Not if she could help it.

The winter this year had not lent its sympathy to those opposed to the construction; instead, it had been unusually warm, with very little snow, allowing the contractor to continue building. Over the last three days, a blanket of snow had coated everything, and then a sheet of ice had fallen on top. It was probably the first time in history that the Burchill Village residents, native and non-native alike, had welcomed the snow and cheered an ice storm.

By the time she came within sight of the camp, Frieda had warmed to the hunt. Her breath was steady, the blood pumped excitedly through her veins. She went first to the little house. The door was open as always. Frieda stepped into the quiet warmth and waited until her eyes adjusted to the dim light.

Everything was as Oona had left it. The rusty kettle sat abandoned on the black pot stove. Her cup, crusted with tea stains, perched nearby, a withered bag curled forgotten inside. Oona's gun, shining and ready, gleamed from the corner.

Frieda went in slowly, touching everything, drinking in the silence of the cabin. She thought she could see the outline of Oona's body on the thin mattress of the single bed. The cupboards were simple and few, constructed of raw wood that had never been finished, although each cup and plate and foodstuff had been organized neatly inside. There were utensils for only three; a small, aluminum table with two uneven and unmatched chairs; one rocking chair with the stuffing held inside by duct tape. Even as she took in every object in the small room, Frieda found herself thinking of her own new home, and of how foolish Oona was to live this simply when she could be living in comfort as Frieda was now doing.

She pictured Oona sitting here, smoking the wooden pipe that had been in her family for centuries, avidly reading whatever book she'd been given or borrowed, her face barely illuminated in the light of the kerosene lanterns. Slightly taller than Frieda, broader at the shoulders and hips, her face wide and open, her eyes impossibly large and disingenuous, only Oona had been able to defrost, at least temporarily, the frigid gaze that Frieda turned on the world.

The real friction had stemmed from her guilt, Frieda knew. She had betrayed Oona's friendship, taken advantage of her innocence and trust. Her eyes flitted involuntarily to the old cupboard, its marred wooden surface spotted with age, sagging against the crooked floor. She remembered what she had done and conflicting emotions darted through her mind; misery, pride, joy, fear, guilt—all struggled to reopen her closed heart. She blinked and turned away from the little room.

Pulling on her mittens, Frieda plodded back out into the cold, following the tracks carefully. The sheer layer of ice covering the snow had molded the prints clearly into the ground, as though they had been painted there. Despite the dozens of footsteps made by the police and others, Frieda was able to find the ones she wanted. Straight and sure, the tracks proceeded emptily in a straight line away from Oona's camp on the edge of the reserve toward the forest. Just before the big rock, the prints stopped abruptly. It was here that Henry, out looking for his sister, had found Oona's old brown coat. Covered with snow and ice, it had been abandoned and flung in a heap next to the rock. A small distance to one side, Henry had discovered her mittens.

Frieda paused here, studying the efforts of the police and the others from the village. It took several minutes of careful observation before Frieda could sort out the correct prints and take up the trail again. They headed directly toward the forest, further apart now, obviously running. Frieda followed them quickly, feeling the pace, imagining some fear that would have made Oona run.

When they reached a huge pine tree standing alone at the forest edge, the tracks suddenly veered to the right. Frieda stopped and stared, amazed at what she saw.

The prints raced around the tree, not once, but exactly twenty times, in ever-widening, almost precise, circles.

H. Duplassie

I

May received the call at 10:30 on a Monday morning. It's a testimony to our friendship that she ignored my obvious, selfish reaction when I found out she had to leave. Somehow, Monday mornings at Burchill Public School are always hectic, unpredictable, and well, as the song goes, rainy days and Mondays always get me (the Principal) down.

This particular Monday was packed with events—a raging, purple-faced parent who absolutely refused to even listen to anything I had to say (luckily, we don't have many of those in town, and, as the villagers would say, they tend not to be Burchill-born); a child languishing in the health room with a suspected broken arm, but whose parent seemed to be taking the long way here; three students who'd been caught throwing snowballs onto a neighbour's property (at a fiercely barking dog) and who were currently writing out their sins at the table in the office; two classes who were being temporarily watched over by other staff while May had begun scrambling to find supply teachers; our caretaker busily deciding between mopping up a leaking toilet and checking the temperature gauge in the gym, which was even too cold for running. Not only that, it was one of those frigid, damp days on which central Ontarians expected their babies to be kept indoors, which had prompted—already—several frantic calls to the office. Not being Burchill-born myself, I am sometimes seen as far less knowledgeable about things like weather than I ought to be.

So when May Reneaux, my only office assistant, got the call telling her that Oona had disappeared, my first reaction was to dismiss the news as another of her aunt's prolonged hunting trips. However, I knew in my heart of hearts that Edgar would not have called May at work if he thought Oona had simply gone off on her own.

Edgar Brennan is in charge of the Ontario Provincial Police detachment in our area. His official title is Chief Superintendent, but we have always just referred to him as the town's police chief. The detachment serves our village of Burchill, the First Nation community adjacent to the village, and the provincial park on the other side, as well as the highways that lead into the area. Edgar is Burchill born and raised, and has worked all his adult life here, so he knows his people very well. If he thought Oona was on a hunting trip, he would never have sounded the alarm by calling May away from the school.

It was not easy to hide my displeasure from May; she has become a very close friend in my four years in Burchill, especially over the last two. She knows me extremely well. However, she was too upset to notice my mood and luckily, when I realized the depth of her distress, my selfishness dissipated, and I made her exit fast and easy.

I spent the entire morning soothing ruffled feathers, checking the weather station, escorting the supply teachers to their classrooms while giving them a quick course on the school's policies, assisting the injured child until her parent strolled in, eliciting apology letters to the neighbour from the snow-throwing boys, calling the school board about the broken gymnasium heaters, and answering the telephone. Two of our most reliable Grade Eight students came down to the office to help over the noon hour, but even with their eager assistance, I was unable to take a breather until later in the afternoon.

I sat at my desk, contemplating this school Principal job. Never had I felt so dissatisfied, even though, on the surface, everything was going well. I began to drift in my reverie, wondering about the source of my unhappiness and bitterness lately, and actually flinched guiltily when Dominic, one of the office helpers, told me Mrs. Reneaux was on the line. I realized that I hadn't thought about May all day. When I heard her shuddering intake of breath after my hello and inquiry about how everything was, I knew the news couldn't be good.

speak, speak to me, all the air, land, water,
speak to me while the earth
locks us together

Frieda shook herself and began to follow the tracks, her heart racing uncontrollably. She pushed the fear to one side, taking deep breaths of the cold morning air. She began to concentrate on the skills needed to follow the tracks. Definitely, she found that the prints wound around the tree twenty times, very close together, obviously at great speed. Yet they were precisely made so that they created wider and wider circles. Frieda was puzzled. On the last trek around the tree, the footprints raced off to the left and disappeared into the forest.

For a moment, the native woman stood absolutely still, listening, thinking. Her round face, framed by long, straight hair that refused to turn grey, looked mesmerized. Suddenly, she bent down and took an object from inside her coat. Digging with her knife, the exercise difficult in the semi-frozen ground, she eventually made a large hole alongside the tree. Frieda placed the object inside and carefully put the dirt and bits of debris back where they had been. Straightening, she was pleased with her work; no one would know that anything had been placed here; the searchers were finished with this spot and would never think to come back. Somehow, Frieda knew that she should not take the treasure into the woods with her. Her decision had been made – she was going to follow Oona – and if she found her former friend, she did not want the burden of that object to hinder their encounter.

Mixed with the tracks of the police and villagers, Frieda almost lost Oona's prints several times. Slowly, keenly, she followed them into the trees right up to the edge of the large pond. Here they stopped abruptly, as if Oona had stepped off into the murky water and disappeared through the thin layer of ice, which had closed like scum after her. The police and villagers had spent much time here, tramping off in every direction, wading into the shore of Bahswaway Pond.

Frieda stood and sniffed the air, staring around at every tree and bush, feeling the atmosphere. It was deathly still, as if every animal and bird were in hiding. No breeze stirred the lifeless limbs. Though she stood silent, Frieda's mind was racing.

There had been talk by the villagers that Oona had been frightened by Walking Bear; that he had found her trapping and had chased her into the icy water.

Frieda did not believe in Walking Bear, but an ancient fear gripped her anyway, as she surveyed the scene. Ojibwa children of Frieda's generation were still taught the lessons of the past; she had been raised with stories of spirits that existed in every animal and in each leaf of every plant. She knew the legends of the various clans; she had been ingrained with the notion that sorcerers could arrange with the spirits of the earth to bring punishment upon humans who disobeyed the laws of nature. As an adult, Frieda had rejected many of the native ways and beliefs, but now, in the hush of a winter forest, the little girl in her still shuddered.

Quietly she inched along the edge of the pond, studying every twig of every bush along the way. Her feet slid over the ice without a sound; her lithe body brushed against nothing as she maneuvered through the trees. A short distance along, Frieda found the first evidence. It was a small bit of fur, drenched with dried blood, caught on a twig of one of the bushes. The fear grew larger and pulsed through Frieda's head. It was the fur of a bear that she held in her hand.

II

"It looks as if she might have drowned." May's voice shook as she fought off the tears that threatened to silence her. "Henry found her coat and mittens strewn all over—and her footsteps headed straight for Bahswaway Pond and disappeared. But Em, get this—the footprints wound around a tree twenty times in these weird circles before she ran off into the water. You should hear the stories that are going around. Our people are still very superstitious during a crisis, it seems. I haven't heard some of these legends since I was a little girl."

I sat back in my chair, stunned, thoughts racing. "My God! But isn't Bahswaway just a pond? Wouldn't it be frozen up over the last couple of days?"

May gave a rueful chuckle in spite of herself. "I keep forgetting you're not Burchill born, my friend! That's why it's called Bahswaway—the Echo. The story goes that it was once a huge well that the natives had dug and then abandoned after several children disappeared into it. A pond formed around the well, but it's still very deep where the hole was. It doesn't actually freeze all the way down, apparently, even in severe winters. The legend could actually be true—or maybe it's not, but at any rate, the pond IS very deep in the middle. . ." The enormity of what she was reciting suddenly caught in her throat.

I jumped in with another question. "The footprints racing around like that—it's so strange, May! What does Edgar say?"

"He doesn't know what to make of it. Everybody's puzzled as hell. Oona's house looks just like it always does—pretty neat and tidy, almost like she's going to come back at any moment. It doesn't look like she'd planned any kind of trip, especially a hunt—her rifle is still there. And anyway, she always lets me know if she's going to be gone for very long."

Although May's mother had been a wonderful, caring person, she had not wanted her daughter to grow up in the "old ways". It had been her mother's sister, Oona, who'd taught May to hunt, fish, camp, and cook in the traditional native ways. May has always felt very close to her aunt, especially when her mother suddenly died at fifty-eight (an age that was feeling more uncomfortably young to us every day). Oona is now seventy-five years old, although she looks and behaves more like a woman in her fifties. She is still active and spends a great deal of her time in the forest around Burchill. May and I had enjoyed more than one camping trip with her, enthralled by her tales of nature and native lore. Oona is a fascinating person; quiet but powerful, able to captivate an audience for long periods of time with her Oral Traditions.

May looks a lot like Oona—long, hooked nose, oval face, straight black hair, light brown skin, large black eyes, all in a short, compact frame. At first glance you might think that Oona and May are overweight, until you notice the hidden power of their hands and arms and the muscles in their shoulders. Her people had been built for carrying water and wood and dead animals, May would laugh; too bad she'd been born when she had. Her self-deprecating humour is just one of the many things I love about May Reneaux.

"But the footprints go right into the pond—and her coat and mittens being abandoned—it just doesn't look good, Em. Edgar is organizing a search party right now. We've got lots of volunteers among the reserve and the town alike, which is really gratifying."

"Everyone loves and respects Oona. She's a towering presence in this community. If something has happened to her. . ." I trailed off, aware that I was not doing much to cheer up my poor friend. "And if something hasn't, she's going to be really pissed that there's a whole bunch of people coming to find her!"

May laughed at that one. "Won't she be, though? I can just see her face!" She sighed. "Thanks, Emily. You can always make me feel better. I just hope we find her and that she's still alive."

"May, don't come in tomorrow. I can ask Gillian to fill in for you. You're going to want to join the search."

"Are you sure? I hate to leave you in the lurch like this."

"You're not—really! Gillian will be fine," I assured her, hoping that it was true.

I could hear the relief in her voice as she thanked me. We hung up, after I'd promised to see her tonight. As soon as we'd done so, I got on the phone again and called Gillian Hubbard, one of our amazing, generous parents, who sometimes helps out in the office. She was quick to say yes, having heard about Oona, and wanting to support May.

The rest of the afternoon flew by, with far fewer problems. By the end of the day, I felt almost normal and had decided not to quit my job after all. I waited until the building was mostly deserted, and then headed home on foot. Most days I do walk to and from the school—in the warm weather I actually jog!—but today I'd had no choice. My husband, Langford Taylor, is a painter of some note in the region, and he had left very early yesterday morning for a showing in a nearby town. In a place like Burchill it would be unforgivable to have two vehicles, and since I didn't expect him until late tonight, I was stuck with my own feet as transportation. I planned to return home, change, feed the dog, and head over to May's house, but it didn't quite turn out that way.

*my horizon is the power of the wild
land, sweet with our ancestors, the natural*

Summoning her hunter's courage, thinking only of the challenge of the chase, Frieda tightened her grip on her gun and forced herself to go on. There were no interfering prints now, as the police and others had not come this far. They must have assumed that Oona had met death in the swamp. Three more times, along the edge of the pond, Frieda found pieces of bear's fur. Every time it was caught on the twig of a bush, buried from the view of ordinary human eyes, and each time the fur was covered with dried blood. She was quite far into the thick of the forest, well past Bahswaway, when Frieda saw the first print.

Catching her breath, she reeled slightly at the sight of it, and sank down to steady herself as much as to study the track. It was huge, one of the biggest prints she had ever seen. Molded into the ice, it leered at her, as if to test her senses. The track was of a huge bear's paw, perfectly set in the snow, the claws outstretched to grip the frozen ground.

Walking Bear. Protector of Innocent Animals. Half man, half beast. Capable of great strength, of strange powers. Could it be true? Could the legends be right? Frieda lifted her head and stared at the trees towering to a peak near a patch of sky. Everything was still, waiting. She watched her breath coming in small clouds of fear. She was a hunter, a believer in real things, in the senses, in the tangible. She could not be fooled by stories. There was something here that she had not seen.

If Walking Bear were true to his legend, Frieda reasoned, he would not have attacked Oona. Oona was a protector of animals herself, using only the smallest of traps, catching a minimum quota of furs. She barely made enough money to provide the simple necessities of life. In this case, Frieda thought, the pupil had outdistanced the teacher. No, it would not have been Oona that Walking Bear would have been after. Unless—had Oona been holding out on Frieda? Was her innocent demeanor merely a cover? On those long, solitary hunting trips, was Oona doing a lot more than communing with nature?

Frieda straightened up and shook her head fiercely. Walking Bear was a story, made up by frightened and superstitious people to explain things they could not understand. And if Oona were holding out on her, why did she live so meagerly? Frieda was going to understand this mystery; she was going to hunt the truth.

Stealthily, Frieda continued her slow inspection of the area. The sun had been hidden by snow clouds and in the shadow of the trees, it was difficult to follow the trail. Still, Frieda was able to find evidence of the animal's presence . . . a footprint here, a bit of bloodstained fur there, a crushed branch, a clawed tree. Slowly she tracked through the woods, deeper into the forest where the intertwined branches overhead nearly blocked out all light. So fascinated was she by the hunt that she did not realize that she was shivering with the cold, dampened by the sweat of fear. When the trail ended, suddenly, without warning, in a darkened section of the forest, Frieda felt the cold pass through her entire body like an electric shock.

All at once the silence, the aloneness, the fear, closed in and gripped her in an iron fist. All evidence of the bear had disappeared. She could find nothing; no prints, no fur—nothing—nothing. Frieda stood shivering in the semidarkness, unable to think or feel, unable to move.

It was the sudden crunch of a branch that jerked her into

motion again, an instinctive, rabbit-like movement, born of fear and helplessness. Gone was the cool hunter's objectivity. Frieda turned and ran like a frightened animal. She got no more than a dozen feet when she was flung heavily to the ground. Her body skidded and bumped on the ice, crumpling in a heap. Her gun flew from her grasp, scuttling across the icy surface. Writhing with a pain for which she could find no centre, Frieda saw the trees begin to sway before her. Darkness surrounded her, her stomach lurched, and her mind closed.

III

Wrapped in scarf and hat and mittens and my big wool coat, I was fairly warm in the bitter cold, but I also managed to maintain a fast pace despite the icy surface. The snow was hard packed, crunchy and crackly beneath my boots, and quite slippery. Two nights ago it had snowed, then last night the precipitation had turned to freezing rain, and now the sky looked full of snow clouds again. I slipped, slid, and shuffled as fast as I could, up and over the bridge toward Lakeview Road, my breath forming puffs of crystals above my head.

Whenever I approach our house and see it clearly from a distance, a mixture of emotions bursts through me like adrenaline—it's a combined feeling of relief, pride, excitement, disbelief. I can't describe it except to say that my heart actually pounds and a grin comes over my face almost every time I come up over that bridge and see its rooftop.

My husband and I live in what is known in the village tourist brochure as the "Beatty House". A turn of the century frame house, it has two beautiful verandas at both the front and back doors, overlooks Ogeechee Lake and is surrounded by lovely old trees. Painted a light blue with white shutters, the house was meticulously and lovingly restored by the former owners. They were careful to maintain its original grandeur, but cleverly modernized it at the same time. I have loved Beatty House since the moment I saw it; it is my dream home come true.

On this most unusual Monday, I had another surprise waiting for me. When I rounded the side of the house, I saw my husband just beginning to unload some frames and paintings into his studio, and my heart began to pound even harder. Langford Taylor is tall, loose limbed, and lanky; his dark hair is shot through with grey and his brown eyes are wide and expressive.

I know that my husband is deemed by many to be very eccentric. Until he is comfortable with people, he tends to be somewhat reserved and quiet; he has a very direct way of looking into your eyes that causes some to shy away from him at first. There is a certain tilt to his head, a way of widening his pupils, a habit of straightening and towering over you with muscles tensed, which can actually frighten anyone with a secret to hide. For those who get to know him better, he has an unusual, attentive way of listening that inspires loyalty and affection.

Many have attributed his eccentricities to the fact that he is a talented artist. I am aware, however, that most of his current habits were learned through hardship. I alone knew the hopeful, friendly, trusting young man who was almost obliterated in a prison cell.

He turned at that moment and saw me, his face lighting up with a huge smile, deepening the crinkles around his mouth and illuminating his expressive brown eyes. Propping the load he was carrying against the studio wall, he hurried back out the door toward me. In the cold air our lips were hot and steamy, our kiss long and delicious. We stood there in the yard, oblivious to the ice and snow, focused only on each other. Langford and I hate separation—any hours away only remind us of when we were apart for many, torturous years. We moved away from each other by a few inches and, after locking the car and the studio, we made for our front door arm-in-arm. If anyone had come into our house a few minutes later, they would have seen coats, boots, hats, scarves, and mittens abandoned in a pile in the hall and, up the stairs, a mess of slacks and sweaters and underwear next to the bed.

"I love you, Emily," Langford whispered in my ear and I returned his murmur, using his real name in the privacy of our bedroom, "I love you, too, Will."

His lips were soft and warm against my neck, my breasts, my legs. I sighed over and over again, running my fingers through his thick hair, across his wide smooth shoulders, down his silky back. His tender mouth, his expert fingers, the touch of an artist whose hands convey layers of emotion and passion on canvas, played my body like a musical instrument. Strings taut, quivering, then bursting into waves of physical release and pleasure, the sounds of ecstasy escaped from me as I gave myself entirely to the orgasmic pulse of my body. When he entered me, whispering and breathing in my ear, I pushed into him as though I could melt into him, become part of him. Holding him so close, moving so slowly and deliciously, feeling his body inside me, I was lost in a sea of passion and desire, all thought gone except of loving him so deeply. I could feel him gathering his excitement, his love, like a milkweed exploding from its pod, and I intensified my response. Soon I could feel him pulsing inside me, his body throbbing with each burst, moans and ecstatic breathing mingling with his endearments. Our hearts pounded against one another when the movement of our bodies had quelled, but for a long time we stayed cuddled close, letting the sweat trickle off; dry, warm and comfortable in each other's arms.

A few minutes later, we were forced to turn over and separate, as our small brown and white dog jumped up on the bed, her beautiful brown eyes full of excitement at seeing "Daddy" at home. We had acquired Angel two years ago under very strange circumstances, but there had been an instant rapport on both sides, and we could now not picture life without her.

I sat up and, one hand propping up my head while the other petted Angel, I told my husband all about Oona. "That's the damndest thing I've ever heard," Will responded, concerned but intrigued, too. "Ed's got a search party out tonight?" I nodded. "Should we go help May keep vigil?" I nodded again, so all three of us got up, two of us showered, and two of us dressed.

We hated to leave Angel all alone again; she looked so forlorn, her tail thumping sadly on the hardwood floor, but we were afraid she might not be welcome in such circumstances. Because of the extreme cold of the evening, we took the car over to May and Alain's place, so we were there in about two minutes.

May and Alain Reneaux are our only real friends in Burchill. Our past has not exactly caused us to be very trustful of our fellow human beings, but May and Alain are special. May, a full-blooded Canadian native, descended from a group of Ojibwa who, about three hundred years ago, had defended and settled among the Hurons and Ottawayans in this area. Although there had been intermarriages among most of the tribes, May's mother had learned the Oral Tradition from her mother, who swore to being "pure" Ojibwa. May had been taught that they were descended from the Bear Clan, whose members were the strong and steady 'police' and legal guardians.

Traditionally, Bear Clan members were said to have spent a lot of time patrolling the land surrounding the village. In so doing, they learned which roots, bark, and plants could be used for medicines to treat the ailments of their people. Oona's skills in healing, based on her inherited herbal knowledge, and her defense of the environment, were much admired.

Alain Reneaux was descended from the legendary "couriers du bois" and was still strongly French Canadian. Alain's family life as a boy had been harsh and often cruel; it was the reason he and May had decided on remaining childless. Alain was terrified of his own temper, afraid he'd repeat the sins of his father literally. Langford and I had never seen any sign of this infamous temper, however. Alain is quiet, but once he was comfortable with us, we have seen only a serious, intelligent person, not someone quick to judge or lose control.

Although May had had some initial doubts about never becoming a mother, she once told me frankly that she'd put all those regrets behind her years ago. However, whenever I watch May with a hurt little one at school, I sometimes privately mourn both our unborn children. Langford and I had been denied the experience because of a hideous mistake that took twenty years away from us. Thus despite our outward appearances – May rounded, almond eyes, dark-skinned; Alain French speaking, wavy brown hair and green eyes; myself blond and short with a waist that I work hard to keep small; Langford tall and lanky—the four of us have much more in common than might be obvious from observation alone.

The Reneaux live on Julia St. in a home that has been here since 1815. It is a hodgepodge of architectural designs, as various portions were added over the decades. Peg and beam, clapboard, stone, wood frame and shiplap, brick veneer—all combined to create a fascinating, if incongruent, structure. May and Alain have a flair for decorating which has transformed the interior into a warm, rich environment, one that pays homage to both their traditions and ancestry. If it had been later in the spring or in the summer, we would also have seen their gardening skills in full display.

Will squeezed the car into the driveway beside Alain's Dodge truck, avoiding the street where numerous other vehicles had taken up most of the space. Shaking off snow and ice, we removed our boots in the crowded front hall and followed the sound of voices to the living room. Frances Petapiece, Doc Murphy, Ruth McEntyer, Kathy Mills, and Teddy Lavalle were all seated in the large, high-ceilinged space, listening intently to Edgar Brennan outline the efforts to find Oona Nabigon. May sat in a huge armchair, her uncle Henry Whitesand at her feet, while Alain stood in a small circle with Basil Fisher, Peter Smallwood, and Chief Dan Mahdahbee. Langford and I joined the group silently; most of them nodded solemnly at us; May gave me a weak smile.

"So, it looks as though there might be two of them missing now," Edgar was saying. "Frieda Roote apparently went out this afternoon to look for Oona and has not returned, according to Scott Ashkiw, who was supposed to meet her at her house around five o'clock to discuss decorating plans. But she could still be searching—Frieda is an experienced trapper and hunter and I'm not ready to say that she's missing just because she didn't show up for dinner. However, we will keep an eye on the situation as night closes in."

"Speaking of dinner," May inserted, sounding tired and sad, "there's food on the table in the kitchen for everyone. Just help yourselves when you're hungry. The neighbours have already started supplying all kinds of goodies, so make sure you eat it. Don't leave it to go to my waist!"

We all smiled back at her and my stomach rumbled in response. I realized I hadn't had anything to eat since early this morning, so I quickly went and filled up a plate of vegetables and crackers and cheese, which Langford helped me nibble on as we continued to listen.

"There's still a bunch of volunteers out searching in the forest around Bahswaway, using some dogs and searchlights. Chief Dan, you've got more info on that, they're mostly your team."

Chief Dan Mahdahbee is a formidable presence in our joint

communities, yet he stands only five feet tall, and perhaps as wide. His pudgy brown face is always wrinkled up—sometimes with frowns and often with smiles. He is a true symbol of the mixture of Burchill, with his First Nations colour-weaved shirt and his Gucci watch.

Dan owns a highly successful department store at Main and Charlotte, just on the edge of the First Nations Community, which is known as the Sahsejewon Reserve. He lives on the reservation and has added a great deal of prestige, political persuasion, and hope to his peoples' lives. It is his influence, as well as that of his father's and grandfather's, that has contributed to the stable, mutually beneficial partnership between native and non-native interests. As a result, there is a complete amalgam of first nation and white cultures.

The village of Burchill has remained largely as it was envisioned in the 1800's—a waterside community, quiet tree-lined streets, preserved architecture and wide-open spaces. There is a canal and a system of locks that provide a by-pass over the wildest sections of the Kanawhe River, which slices through the town and the reserve. Sahsejewon, in fact, means "rapids" in Ojibwa, referring to the tumbling, turbulent waters that race off to the St. Lawrence River and into Lake Ontario. Lake Ogeechee, which graces Burchill's outer edges and lies next to our own house, is still clear and calm, with soft sandy beaches and healthy fish.

The provincial park spans one side of the lake, native land another, so Ogeechee's shores remain somewhat private. For years now, the provincial government, Native Council, and Town Council have agreed on a ban of motorized boats. Thus the lake is dotted with sails and canoes, while the ships and motorboats use the locks and the river. North of the lake, stretching all the way to Ottawa, are over a thousand hectares of beautiful mixed forest.

Burchill is an artists' town. In fact, the name of the village was given in honour of a local sculptor who became famous in the 1800's. There are many artists who make their homes here, which are more often than not combined with their workplaces. The old mill has been converted into the Burchill Inn, which also has an excellent restaurant. In the summer the town is inundated with tourists, who arrive by boat, car or bus. They stay at the Inn or various bed and breakfast accommodations, spend money on crafts, gifts and souvenirs in town, and eat in the restaurants and pubs. Even the edges of the reservation are dotted with beautiful shops, which boast of the artistry and creativity of the native peoples. Many in Burchill make a good living from the tourist industry.

There is a museum that provides testimony—factually, respectfully—to both native and non-native histories. While the street names and homes demonstrate a largely British influence, the lakes and rivers and natural settings proclaim proudly native roots. Many people take the walking tour, from the museum to the locks, to the historical homes, and to the reservation sites. It's a kind place, peaceful and pretty, a place that welcomes tourists and the occasional new villager (like us) alike.

On the outskirts of town, just to the east of Sahsejewon, along Main Street (which turns into Highway 54 just shortly outside the village limits), there are several subdivisions being proposed. This is the most contentious political issue in our town at the moment. Both the Chief and the Mayor and their respective Councils have been campaigning to stop the encroachment of this "civilization" on the surrounding forests and farmland. The entire eastern area is largely crown land, while a small number of acres are privately owned.

There has been very little the collective council members have been able to do about the latter areas. These parcels of land are under federal law, which has allowed them to be zoned for housing. Demonstrations, petitions, and legal wrangling have slowed construction, but not stopped it, although the "crown" seemed to be responding more favourably of late. Cynically, we have observed that a federal election is due next fall, which may explain their reluctance to cause a huge problem right now. Given the history of broken agreements between the aboriginal people and the government, most of our First People do not trust the federal representative's promise that the issue will be handled carefully and consideration given to halting some of the sale of the land to contractors.

One builder who has purchased crown land has been very aggressive about sticking to his own time lines, regardless of the spirit of unwelcome emanating from the village. In addition, he has been rude and belligerent with anyone who has attempted to explain the "other side". While I could understand his point of view from the business outlook—he had, after all, purchased the land in good faith—I was too fond of Burchill the way it is to feel much sympathy. After all, it's been this way for about a hundred and fifty years, and existed as a native settlement far longer than that. It is pretty tough for someone to insist that change is a good thing, when all we could see were the wide-open spaces and the majestic rise of the forest being eaten up by noisy machines.

Victor Reeves' subdivision, therefore, was the only site currently plowing ahead—literally; with trees careening to the ground and dirt flying in filthy clouds everywhere. Except for the last three days, this winter has been unusual. We have had very little snow in comparison to most years and the temperatures have been oddly warm. Throughout January and February, the moist, cool weather caused all kinds of influenza and colds throughout the village, especially in the school. It also allowed holes to be dug and trees to be felled. Burchill residents were suffering from a double dose of depression and anger.

Chief Mahdahbee was speaking. "The search teams are going to have to stop by dark. Plus, the wind is whipping up and it looks like more snow is on its way. We'll continue early in the morning, with as many volunteers as we can get. So far, we've been fanning out in straight lines on either side of the Pond. But there is a great deal of forest to cover and the snow is coming. There has been no sign of Oona so far."

Edgar took up the tale. "The OPP in Ottawa have an Underwater Search and Rescue Unit. If we find nothing in the surrounding area, we might actually be able to get them to do some searching in the pond." He looked over and saw May's face. "Sorry, May. I. . ."

"You're just telling the truth, Ed, and I appreciate that."

"Is there any possibility that Oona would go on a trip without telling you, May?" Frances Petapiece asked.

May smiled fondly at the young blond woman who was seated next to Edgar. Frances, an Ontario Provincial Police Constable, had come into Edgar's life two years ago when she was investigating the murder of our school caretaker. Since then, she had transferred to Burchill, where Edgar had become both her boss and her significant other. So far, they seem to be very happy with the situation, and are planning on marriage.

Frances is a warm, giving person, hidden behind a cool, intellectual front. May and I have often mentioned that there seems to be an "at home Frances" and an "Officer Frances". She looks too tiny to be a police officer (she is only a couple of inches taller than I am), until one notices the muscular frame and the solid way she has of walking toward you. Perhaps her size is one of the reasons she assumes a tough, aggressive exterior when she is on the job. Her small, thin face and lovely grey eyes form an attractive, though not quite beautiful, picture. She has become a good friend of May's, despite the fact that Frances is twenty years younger.

"It's possible, I keep telling myself, but it's so improbable that I can't imagine it. I haven't much hope that she would do that to all of us. She would at least have told Henry, or Agnes, or Frieda. And she hasn't gone on many trips lately; she's become more of a homebody than I've ever seen. Besides, the footsteps around the tree and into the pond. . ." May stopped abruptly, unable to continue without breaking.

"I agree that it's improbable. But I still think we should keep hope alive on that count." Frances shifted to face everyone better. "I have a couple of contacts with Ottawa, so if we don't find her in a few days, I think I can make a case for a search of the Bahswaway by their USRU. In the meantime, have we questioned all her friends and family?"

Henry spoke up. He resembles his sister so much in appearance that I wondered how May could look at his face. "We interviewed the entire family and no one has seen her since Saturday afternoon, when she delivered some food to our Mary." Mary is Oona and Henry's oldest sister, who has been in a wheelchair for several years now. They all take turns bringing her food and companionship, since she refuses to go into a health care facility. "As for Frieda, I hadn't seen her in a while before this happened. I have a feeling she and Oona had a falling out, though Oona didn't say anything really. It's just that Frieda stopped being her constant companion. I know she's supposedly out looking for Oona now, but I never saw her."

"I saw Frieda at the initial search," offered Basil Fisher. "She was just standing at the edge of the crowd, listening. She never came into the forest with the rest of us. I agree that she's probably out searching now, but not with the team.

Frieda likes to do things on her own."

This last statement was not made with admiration; Basil's voice was thick with derision. I wondered briefly what had caused him to dislike the woman. I don't know Frieda Roote well at all, having met her very briefly at community activities. She too is from the Ojibwa Bear Clan—or so tradition says, as May would add! Frieda is a compact, wiry person, not quite as stocky or tall as Oona; she often wears her straight, black hair in a loose pony tail, frequently tied with colourful bobs, and her clothes look expensive. May has told me that Frieda is an accomplished hunter, that her small frame belies great strength, that she was Oona's protégé, but this is all I know about her.

A few months ago, Frieda had purchased a small home inside the village and outside of the reserve. It's a lovely stone house on the corner of St. Lawrence and Drummond, and must have cost her a fortune. I remember wondering where she might have gotten the money for such a move, and I do remember some talk in the village about Frieda's choice to live outside the native community. Perhaps that explained the disdain in Basil's voice and the rift between Frieda and Oona.

"I saw her, too," Ruth McEntyer spoke up.

This statement surprised no one; Ruth is our town busybody and know-it-all. She works part time as a waitress in the Burchill Inn and probably gets most of her gossip and news from the customers. Ruth is tall and very beautiful; her long red hair and flashing green eyes are extremely compelling. Her looks, combined with her friendly attitude and keen powers of observation, combine to make her a wealth of information about the latest gossip or event. However, despite her constant thirst for knowledge about everybody's business, Ruth is a kind, jovial person whom most people (myself included) quite like.

"Just as Basil has said," Ruth continued, "she was watching and listening, always on the edge of the crowd. When the search teams split up, she didn't offer to go with any of them. She just trudged back in the direction of her home."

"Maybe she's just too upset," Peter Smallwood offered, to which Basil grunted and Ruth shrugged. Peter is a very tall, thin man whose grey-blond hair is thinning and whose mouth is always, it seems to me, formed into a line of condescension. Most people find him hilarious, but to me his sarcastic wit and humorous anecdotes belie an attitude of superiority. However, I seem to be the only one who does not think well of him. In this room, he towered over everyone except Langford.

Henry broke the uncomfortable silence that followed. "If anyone would know that Oona was on a trip, it would be Agnes. And Oona has not been to see her in several weeks. Agnes is on a Vision Quest, but she came back to Mary's house to speak with me."

The mention of Agnes Lake seemed to energize the group. Once again, I must admit that I know very little about Agnes, except that she is famous throughout the community and beyond. Even more than Oona, she is the most recognized and respected native woman in Burchill and Sahsejewon. She is similar in build to Oona and Frieda; fairly short and stocky. Her long straight hair is completely grey and she always wears it flowing over her shoulders. She has a kind, well-worn face, from which the beauty of her youth still shines through; she looks almost stereotypically wise and peaceful. Her light brown eyes are direct and seem to look right through you. Agnes Lake is, in fact, one of the few remaining female Ojibwa shaman, and certainly one of the last of her generation to practise her craft. Her Vision Quests consist of fasting, prayer, and, I think, offerings to the spirits. But I am ashamed to say that I have not spent a great deal of time learning about what these rituals entail.

The conversations kept going around and around, in small groups, across the room, between couples. Peter Smallwood kept the whole group mesmerized and even laughing out loud once or twice, with his tales of following his native friends through the bush when he was a child. We waited until well after ten o'clock before news finally came from the search teams, who had all given up and regrouped to report to Edgar. No one had found any sign of Oona. They were all heading home for a good night's sleep; many intended to assist again the next day. When Langford and I left May and Alain's place, there were still a few people lingering, but all seemed to be in the process of going home to bed. Langford was going to join the search tomorrow, while I—feeling, I must admit, frustrated and ineffectual—was going back to work.

It is strange to be going about your regular duties when a crisis is swirling all about you. With Gillian Hubbard's cheerful assistance in the office, and lots of indoor recess due to the weather, the week began to pass more quickly than Monday had. As events continued to build in the community, my school soldiered on as usual, the little details of every day life managing to seem as important as always. We were heading into March, with spring break scarcely three weeks away, and winter had decided to arrive at last.

The promised snow thudded in around us later that first week, making continuing the hunt for Oona next to impossible. The search parties, Langford included, had done their best each morning, trudging through the fields and forest, bundled yet still frozen, for hours in daylight, but were forced to give in long before dusk. At the end of the week, a couple of divers arrived from the Ottawa USRU, due mostly to

Frances Petapiece's influence, but they were driven away by ice and snow. The water of Bahswaway turned into an icy sludge, too chunky and dark for a successful search, and the snow kept piling up, forming treacherous hills all around the pond.

By the second week, the snow had stopped, but the air had turned absolutely frigid. Warnings were posted over the weather advisory channels and students had to keep huddled inside the school for a couple of days in a row. It wasn't until the following Sunday afternoon that the sun shone through, increasing the temperature to more pleasant numbers, bringing people outdoors again, to face the fact that not only was Oona Nabigon still missing, but her friend Frieda Roote had never returned from the search either.

my earth, my fate, my woe

When Frieda woke, she first felt the sweat pouring down her skin through the parka. At the same time, the icy cold crept into her mind and sent uncontrollable shivers through her body. She stared up at the trees and saw a patch of night sky through the thick branches. It was then that the pain hit her again.

Somewhere near her right foot, she felt gnawing, pounding agony, coming in waves that threatened her consciousness. With tremendous effort, through gasps and cries, Frieda pushed herself up on her elbows and looked. At first it was hard to believe; it seemed that she was gazing down at someone else. And then pain rolled in; her head thudded back onto the ice. Her foot and part of her leg had become a tangled mass of blood and bone, gushing between ripped boot leather, snapped in the jaws of a huge bear trap.

Frieda's mind began to swim. She pictured the animals—the large, gentle-eyed deer, the small mink, the little cub—all writhing in her bear traps, waiting for her to end their misery. She saw her garage, full of skins, hanging, drying, smoking, brushing, ready for the buyers. She saw their eyes when they looked at the skins, hungry, admiring. She saw the money in her hands.

Frieda's body jerked spasmodically with pain and fear. She had only wanted the good things she saw other people enjoying. She had only desired that little stone house on the corner, to live among the others, to go for lunch at the Inn, to have nice clothes. Her guilt coursed through her with each wave of pain. She saw the little packet hidden in the dusty corner; she imagined the man's eyes as he lit up with his greed; she felt again the power of knowing that she could, when or if she chose, answer his craving.

There was no one here to end her misery. She was now the victim, without a deity who could decide her fate for her. Frieda squeezed her eyes shut, felt the tears crystallizing in the cold. She tried very hard to reassert control, but she had never felt such agony and she could not regain any sense of the cold objectivity needed to think her way out of this situation. She allowed herself to drift again, welcoming the waves of darkness, the dulling of the pain. Somewhere in the back of Frieda's mind, in the files of her hunter's training, she knew that lying here would bring death, but she was unable to force herself to care.

She could not tell whether she had her eyes open or closed when she saw him. Semiconscious, she was not frightened or surprised by his appearance; she was unable to feel any emotion. She lay blank, waiting, ready to be used.

The figure seemed very tall, standing above her, shaking that bear head. Not completely covered in fur, part of a red parka showed through. The claws were clamped over boots and mittens. Walking Bear, Frieda thought, half human, half bear. The legend is real and I have been caught. I am now victim. The pain shook through her as Walking Bear bent to investigate the trap.

"I am sorry this happened to you, but now you know how it feels. You are as helpless as the hundreds of victims you have caught here in these woods." A pause. "Caught you on the big bone; you are fortunate."

Frieda's mind ached at the sound of Walking Bear's words. The voice penetrated her consciousness, so familiar, the words of the ancient ones, of her father, of her aunts and uncles as they sat around the fires, as they spoke of important issues.

"There are four orders in creation," the legends said.

"First is the physical world; second, the plant world; third, the animal world; last, the human world. Never attempt to put the last first, or you will destroy the harmony of our existence." The Legend of Walking Bear had spoken of moments like this one, Frieda thought.

The human bear walked around her body, investigating, pulling and tugging at her. "You will recover," the voice intoned. "I will help you. You will recover in every way. It was known that you were doing evil all along. But no one could stop you. The greed had filled your spirit."

The voice droned on and on, pushing through the pain, pounding through Frieda's agony. "How does it feel now, to be a victim?" Walking Bear bent and began to work at the trap.

The pain seared up Frieda's leg, burning through to her mind. The legends of the old ones, told to her as she sat by the fire at night, continued to swirl past her eyes and ears. Each lined face would be serious and fierce as they told of the punishment that a hunter would suffer if he or she broke Walking Bear's ancient laws.

"Remember the words of the old ones," Walking Bear said gently in her ear, as if Frieda had spoken her thoughts aloud. "I, too, am an old one now and I tell you again, 'the forest is given to us to use for need, not for greed'. If you break the ancient law, you must be punished."

Frieda's eyes no longer focused. She felt, rather than saw, her body being lifted onto a sled.

"Sometimes the spirits choose the punishment; sometimes we are conduits for it to happen. I think this punishment will be enough. You will heal, but the time with me will be long. You will stay here in the woods where you will be able to think about and see the stories of the old ones, where you will learn to live the truth."

Shock and misery squeezed more tears from Frieda's eyes as she was dragged through the woods, each bump and movement a wave of pain.

IV

As has been the rule in Ontario over the last few years, there are no constants in our weather. We no longer appear to have four distinct seasons, but can, in fact, have all four climate patterns in one day. Our newest joke is "Don't like the weather? Wait fifteen minutes", which used to be reserved for other parts of the country. Thus when it suddenly turned very warm that Monday and Tuesday, no one was greatly surprised. This winter had been a hodgepodge of temperatures, precipitation, and extremes. Dire warnings from environmentalists that these changes are going to become the norm have largely gone unheeded.

In Burchill, an even greater symbol of danger to the environment was the new subdivision. Our residents constantly complained about and lamented over the encroachment of new homes and roads into the fields and forest. For the last couple of weeks, both the weather and the facts about the native women's disappearances had served to divert everyone's attention. But by Wednesday of this week, the sun had melted most of the snow and ice in the field where the subdivision was being plowed. The area looked bald, scraped of its vegetation, scarred by ribbons of dirt that marked the future streets. Victor Reeves, anxious to fulfill promises to home buyers, and perversely determined to defy the villagers, had his excavators in full swing by Friday, when two days' worth of unseemly sunshine had melted the surface freezing of the ground. Thus, the villagers were once again consumed with talk about the subdivision.

Oona and Frieda had been missing for nearly three weeks; most of the searches had been abandoned. The USRU from Ottawa was scheduled to arrive next Monday to search Bahswaway Pond. A rumour had gone around Burchill that had led many to expect that both bodies would be discovered, drowned in some kind of weird suicide pact. Lately, however, their disappearance was not the main topic of conversation, and I was glad some of the talk had subsided.

I knew the rumour had hurt May deeply. She had insisted on returning to work last Monday, stating that she couldn't stand being at home just waiting and listening to idle talk. Whenever we had a chance, we sat in my office and discussed the situation in detail, trying to come up with all kinds of theories.

"Oona would never kill herself," May said firmly, struggling against the tears filling her eyes. "She is so strongly religious, in her own way. She believes in the sanctity of life. I can't imagine she would ever do that. She and Frieda used to have a strong friendship, but there was nothing destructive about it, in the way that some people seem to be implying. They'd fallen out lately, which would seem to prove that they wouldn't be involved in some mystery that led them to a suicide pact."

I agreed with May to make her feel better, but I must admit that I had my doubts. I have learned the hard way that people wear many masks. On the surface, they go about their lives in ordinary and even boring ways, while underneath a whole other world seethes. I considered my husband and myself, who respectively held positions of admiration and trust, who appeared to be a couple whose lives served as models to the community, yet who'd both so far led a life that sounded like fiction. I thought of the police officer in Vancouver who had hidden a burning hatred for and jealousy of the young man who was now Langford Taylor; an officer who'd seemed in every way to be understanding, empathetic, and objective, when in reality he'd plotted, schemed, lied, and resorted to extreme violence. I remembered clearly—the hurt and shock still fresh to me—the murder of Burchill's bridgeman and our school caretaker, the discovery of hidden lives filled with depravity, perversion and abuse.

Could Oona have been hiding a pact or a relationship with Frieda that led them both to suicide? Could they both have some other secret that had caused them to run away or drown themselves in the pond? I thought it was entirely possible.

Of course I expressed none of this to May. She was suffering and I would never add to that hurt. May loved Oona fiercely, and it was my friend's loyalty that so endeared her to me and to everyone else. I could only silently hope that her loyalty in this case had not been misplaced. I could not imagine what a discovery of some terrible secret might do to her. Each day I responded to her with words of encouragement, sympathy, and belief. Plus, although I had taught myself to avoid outward, physical signs of affection, I had learned from my loving friend over the last four years to once again give a hug or touch a person's hand as ways of lending support.

The last week before spring break went by fairly slowly in the school, mostly because we were all anxious for the holiday, but also due to the unseasonable weather conditions. Mud appeared in the yard, temperatures caused students to shed their coats prematurely. The influenza virus resurfaced, causing coughs and sneezing throughout the halls. Behaviour deteriorated as the children became impatient for freedom and in response to the spring-like wind that blew in from the south.

These factors contributed to a busy office. May and I were active all day long, cleaning dirty hands and faces, lending clean clothing from the lost and found, calling parents to come and get sick little ones, or dealing with discipline issues. Since these were not exactly intellectually challenging tasks, the hours appeared to crawl by, and the staff was physically exhausted by the end of the week.

On Thursday evening, I suggested that we adjourn to the Main Street Station Pub to celebrate only one more day to go. Nearly the whole staff responded—twelve of the fourteen of us—and I almost regretted saying I'd buy the first round. Even May, with not too much urging from Alain and myself, decided to join us. Any vehicles that had been brought to school were left in the parking lot and the entire group of us walked up Read Street to Main, talking and laughing, the late afternoon sunshine buoying our spirits.

Our staff is a cohesive bunch, but they welcomed me into their fold almost immediately, and over the last four years we have grown to be a true family. We have our problems, as all families do, but we are always able to talk it out or come to a compromise. There are some villagers who believe it unseemly for the staff to gather in the pub, but we have grandly ignored them until they have been silenced. We are a team that likes to celebrate and we're always careful not to drink and drive. It's fairly easy to do in a village this size, because one can always walk home and pick up the car the next day.

Only Lynda McLeay, our Grade Eight teacher, Paul Granmercy, the French teacher, and Diane West, Kindergarten Assistant, live outside Burchill. Neither Lynda nor Diane could join us today, and Paul usually only has one drink. (I secretly suspected that, if the first round weren't free, he wouldn't even have one.)

By the time we reached our destination, the group was in high spirits, and I could tell we were in for a night of humour and letting loose. I was glad I'd warned Barry and Kathy Mills that we were coming.

Constructed in 1848 as a general store when the village

was a hive of activity and industry, the Main Street Station Pub was built of rubble stone covered with stucco. Since then, of course, it has been modernized both inside and out, but the front door and outer wall of the building still have a warm, traditional character that is reminiscent of old pubs in Ireland.

Barry and Kathy Mills, both Burchill-born, are the latest owners. Their good humour, creativity, and Kathy's ability as a fast-food chef have contributed to its huge popularity among the villagers and the tourists. On weekends, we can enjoy a variety of musical groups, many of them local, and during the week, there are munchy specials to tempt every after-work appetite. Thursday is Nacho Night—spicy meat, huge dollops of sour cream, mounds of tomatoes and peppers and lettuce—my favourite.

We tumbled through the door, cheerfully greeting Barry, who stood behind the bar ready to fill our orders, and called hello to Kathy, who waved from the kitchen archway, already piling nachos onto enormous platters.

Their son, Bobby, who is fifteen and a graduate of Burchill Public School, greeted some of his former teachers. Bobby now attends a private school—the prestigious OBA—Ottawa Boys Academy. From what I'd heard, Bobby Mills had gotten himself involved in a few predicaments—probably nothing in comparison with the trouble I'd seen with some city boys, but his parents had decided boarding school was the answer.

Kathy and Barry work long hours, so I'd guessed that a troubled boy might act out for attention. In addition, he is a small, thin boy, and appeared to want to continuously prove that he was strong or smart or tough. Maybe a strict private school was a good solution for their situation, but, as Bobby was proudly telling some of the staff, he had two weeks spring break instead of our paltry one. More time for trouble, I thought.

Barry directed Bobby to help us get settled. We shifted small tables and chairs in the area that usually serves as a stage and is large enough for all of us to be seated in a circle, where every face could be seen and enjoyed. A big picture window allowed the sun to follow us into the pub. Very shortly after dealing us napkins and utensils, Bobby Mills disappeared with some friends into the afternoon.

Everyone shared pitchers of cold beer, or litres of wine, and platters of steaming food and crisp nachos. Conversation was loud, funny, and irreverent. Margaret Johnston, our Resource Teacher, is retiring this year, and I swear her enthusiasm and wit have actually increased as the school days have fluttered past. She began a litany of jokes and anecdotes that had us all clutching our stomachs from laughter.

Before we knew it, dinnertime had approached and a round of French fries and burgers was ordered. Several people began to drift home, mindful of the fact that we did have one more day to get through, or of family obligations that beckoned. May, Margaret, Duncan Otiquam and myself were the only four left at seven o'clock. We had wound down some—even Marg—and had moved into one small corner of the staging area. Several other patrons had entered the pub as the hours progressed, including May's uncle Henry, Basil Fisher, and Peter Smallwood.

The topic of conversation for our little group had turned to Oona and Frieda's disappearance, the impending search of Bahswaway, and the mystery in general. Duncan agreed with May's belief that the two women would never have committed suicide. For half the week, Duncan is our Native Studies/Second Language teacher; for the other half of the week, he works with students at the Sahsejewon School.

"Those two have been raised in the Oral Traditions, which teach that you must never harm another, and that includes yourself. They believe strongly in the spirits that reside in all living things. You would go straight to some kind of hell or be condemned to live between earth and heaven if you killed yourself," he was saying now.

I chimed in, wanting to get my guilt off my chest. "I have to admit, even though I've been in Burchill for four years, I haven't done much research into the native traditions. I know the kids we've got at Burchill Public, but their parents have chosen to live away from the reserve, and don't really practise the rituals of your culture or seem to believe in the so-called old ways. Of course Oona has taken me on some camping trips, and I learned a lot about the land, but I didn't really pursue the history or the cultural associations. I feel badly about that—it's something I plan to remedy, maybe this summer when I've got more time."

"I'll help you, Em," May said, sipping more white wine. "I think you'll find it's really interesting. When Oona comes back, I'll get her to take us on another camping trip, and this time she can teach you about the traditions." No one seemed to notice May's hopeful projection about her aunt's return, or if we did, we didn't have the heart to contradict her.

"The Oral Traditions are deceptively simple at first," Duncan added, as if he were about to begin a lecture. "But they're many-layered. I agree with May, I think you'll find the study fascinating, Emily. Besides going camping with Oona, I would say you should also spend some time with Agnes Lake."

"I've been around Burchill for thirty years," Margaret chimed in, "and I've only been in Agnes Lake's presence twice. But both were very memorable occasions. Somebody said she's on a Vision Quest right now. What exactly is that?"

"It's like a religious retreat," Duncan told us. "Except the native people who practise it, do so in the forest, away from civilization, usually alone, not in a church or a retreat house. They fast until they induce a vision that tells them what they must do. People go on Vision Quests for many reasons—maybe they or a loved one has an illness, or they've lost their job, or they're having trouble handling some problem. Sometimes, when there is a difference of opinion between two people, they will both go on separate Vision Quests and then come back and try to solve their differences peacefully. In the old days, people would go and try to make peace with the spirits, especially in situations where the hunting was scarce or the weather was particularly harsh.

"The Ojibwa believed—and we still do really—that a spirit exists in every living thing. Thus if the animals stayed away, it meant that the spirits must be angry. Most of us don't believe in that part of it any more—science has quashed that, but we still hold to the idea that every thing on earth contains a spirit, a soul; some extend that belief even to rocks."

"I like that concept," Margaret said. "Too bad everyone didn't adhere to that belief; think of the death and destruction that might have been avoided."

"Why is Agnes on a Vision Quest right now? Is it a form of prayer to find Oona and Frieda?" I asked.

May answered this time. "It's my understanding that she went on the Vision Quest a few days before they both disappeared. She returned to talk to Henry and Mary, but hasn't been seen since. No one is worried about her, though; she specifically told Henry that she was going back to her Quest, that she hadn't yet fulfilled its purpose. She cautioned them that she may be gone quite a long time and not to fret. She promised she'd reappear from time to time, even if her quest wasn't finished, just to reassure them. As far as I know, Agnes didn't tell anyone why she was on this particular Quest."

"She's been known to be on a Quest for a couple of months," Duncan said. "She disappears into the forest and doesn't come back until the vision, the solution to the problem, is clear. Agnes has had amazing success with some of the greatest dilemmas facing the community. She comes back thin but inspired, and serves up the solution ready-made."

"Maybe she's trying to solve the problem of the subdivision," Margaret ventured.

It couldn't have been better timing. At that very moment, Victor Reeves and three other men entered the pub; their dark business suits way out of place, their loud voices unwelcome and intrusive. An immediate hush fell over all the other patrons, including our little table.

the seeds of knowing are in the night
Big Bear, my transition to adulthood

Frieda's nostrils filled with the acrid smell of a fire, mingled with the odours of meat cooking. She was lying on a small, straight bed, made soft with furs or blankets. She forced her mind and body to relax, first emptying her thoughts, concentrating only on the pleasant odour of the meal on the fire, conjuring up peaceful, happy associations to calm herself.

Then she began a mental and physical search of her body by tightening each muscle, beginning in her feet, up her legs, her arms and hands, through to her face and head. With each tightening, there was a corresponding release, until her body lay relaxed and her breath was controlled and deep. In her slow climb through her bruised body, she was able to take inventory of the damage: her foot was bandaged and still extremely painful; her right leg, in response to the injuries of its lower extremity, was trembling and tight; it felt as though other bones in her lower leg had also been broken. Most disconcerting of all, Frieda's eyes were filmy and dark, swollen nearly shut.

Though Frieda was unable to see whether or not it was daylight, the lack of sun heat told her that it was probably evening. Under the smells of the fire, she could sniff out that she was lying on an animal skin; that the floor of the shelter was bare earth; that the roofing was likely some kind of rock, perhaps a large cave. The bed upon which she lay could have been a rock shelf, carved out long ago by ancestral hands. She could tell that the camp fire probably lay several feet to her left, both by the sounds of the crackling wood and the strength by which the smoke drifted toward her. There were other sounds as well—someone was preparing dinner. Large feet scraped the ground with every movement; utensils clicked against a pan; water thudded into a pot. A knife slapped up and down, slid back and forth, squealed against a rough surface. It was being sharpened.

Frieda's heart began to pound, her breath responding with quickened gasps for oxygen. She forced away the fear by considering what she had heard: Walking Bear was obviously as much human as animal—the cooking was being done with some modern conveniences. She forced a sarcastic rumble from her dry lips, which would have been a laugh or a chuckle if her throat had been able to function.

The sounds of the knife sharpening stopped; there was a stillness that told her Walking Bear was listening. Frieda only knew the figure was suddenly there right beside her by the smell; Walking Bear had approached soundlessly, hot breath on her cheek and in her ear making her flinch involuntarily.

"You awaken. Your consciousness took a very long time." The voice was low, half growl, half mouthed.

A trickle of cold water scorched her lips and tongue, stinging and relieving at the same time. Her head was lifted carefully and gently; her throat coaxed open with small amounts of water that eased into her parched body. Frieda's mind became focused only on that life-giving drink; she lapped and swallowed, her tongue darting to pick up every drop.

When she was completely sated, Walking Bear tenderly placed her head back onto the bed, brushing her hair back off her face with soft, furry fingers, deftly scratching and massaging her itching head. Frieda's eyes filled with tears at the empathy of that touch, at the kindness she had not felt even from her family but which now emanated from her captor. Somewhere inside her tired brain, she knew that her emotions were making no sense, that she was in terrible danger from the very one who touched her so sweetly, but the tears came anyway.

Now she was offered a small, juicy piece of the meat that she had smelled earlier; her body was ready for the nourishment and though she tried to chew slowly, she snatched it from the outstretched hand into her mouth at starvation speed.

Walking Bear was silent; breath almost imperceptible; patience alive between them. Frieda could feel herself drawing toward a figure she could not see, pictured herself crawling into huge arms, her head against soft fur, wanting to be protected and touched and never let go.

Once again the thinking side of her scorned the weak emotional part; what kind of hunter are you, giving into your captor so easily? Are you a deer, your wit and strength crushed by one blow? Are you a bird, your tiny pea brain flying into the light of your captor's weapons? But in her needy, vulnerable, soft state, Frieda could only feel a strong aura of love from the being who had trapped her.

As she was fed, the strong fingers continued to give her relief from the itchiness of her dried scalp, and the furry hands rubbed softly over her limbs, gently bringing her circulation back. Frieda imagined this was how an animal felt when it was being stroked and petted.

Finally, once she was lying peacefully and much more comfortably on the bed, Walking Bear spoke again, the strange voiced muted and low.

"Your body continuesits healing. You have been unconscious for a long time. Now that you awaken, you will begin in earnest. Do not be afraid. You have begun your Quest." The fingers continued to massage. "The fever has caused your eyes to be blinded, but soon you will see. You will see everything, my friend."

And Frieda, too exhausted to explore her feelings, believed; her heart beat in a steady, satisfied rhythm; the throb of pain became a burning sensation that did not spread agony throughout her body; she closed her tortured, glutinous eyes.

"I leave you now, for only a short time. Sleep, sleep."

Immediately Frieda fell into a heavy sleep, her snores muffled by the trees and rock that made up her shelter.

Walking Bear moved swiftly through the forest, the sure steps a testimony to knowing your home well. If anyone had been there in the twilight, they would have seen a huge head bobbing past the trees, dipping and swaying as though too heavy for the rest of the body. Indeed, Walking Bear felt a heaviness in that head and a raging chest pain, but these were borne of anger, not illness. The feet made large tracks in the damp earth, but Walking Bear knew they could be covered up on the return journey—and that would be shortly. There was only one small errand on this trip.

Walking Bear was able to hear them long before they came into view. Young, loud voices, raucous laughter, filthy words, stung the air. Cans of beer, its liquid spiraling onto the ground, were flung mostly empty among the trees. Four young boys sat around an earthen campfire, where the remains of a rabbit, several birds, and a tiny fawn lay bleeding into the earth. The left leg of the small deer twitched, indicating that its life was still ebbing away, slowly and painfully.

One of the boys, a small, thin boy with bony shoulders—the one Walking Bear had targeted on this foray—had a gun lying casually across his knees; his face was suffused with the afterglow of murder; just by looking into his eyes, you could tell that he had the blood lust, that the thrill of the hunt had consumed him. He was completely unaware of his helpless victims, totally ignorant of the deer suffering at his feet. Instead, he was laughing the loudest, king of this empire, celebrating his mastery over the animals of the forest.

Walking Bear was almost overtaken with the rage that had propelled this race through the forest. A short rest brought back that control; breath eased; heart returned to normal. Walking Bear began calculating distances, planning for the greatest effect. This would be the only chance and that meant it had to be used well.

Suddenly Walking Bear crashed into their circle, snatching the gun from the boy, dangling him from one paw, roaring in their faces. At first the other boys stood in silent shock, staring through the dusk at the apparition before them, unable to react. Terrified, one by one they raced away like rabbits, screaming and hollering, falling, jumping, hopping over logs and tree branches and bushes. Walking Bear turned a huge head and flashing eyes toward Bobby Mills.

V

Victor Reeves and his cronies didn't seem to notice that the rest of the patrons of the Main Street Station Pub had grown completely quiet at their entrance. In fact, it seemed to me that Victor was louder than necessary. He grinned at everyone, made a show of shaking hands with most of us (especially the Principal of the local school), and ordering piles of food. In general, he behaved as though he were an accepted and celebrated member of the community. Victor Reeves was tall and muscular, his blond hair touched with just the right amount of grey, his face tanned and reflecting that perfect blend of experience and youth. Though I didn't like to admit it, I found him exceedingly handsome.

The contractor was accompanied by three other men, who were all dressed in the same expensive suits, varying shades of dark blue or black, with bright ties and shirts. Their collective heads of hair had been expertly dyed and cut; I couldn't see their finger nails from here, but if they were anything like Victor's, they too were shaped and polished. One of the men parted from the group, which had thankfully settled at a table on the other side of the pub, and came toward us.

"Hi, are you Emily Taylor?" he asked, looking directly at me.

Wondering if the criterion for working for Reeves Construction was good looks, I nodded my head at the sandy haired, blue-eyed man before me, giving that reserved Principal look that I've been able to cultivate so well. He took it as encouragement to continue, however.

"My name is Evan Fobert." (He pronounced it the English way.) "I'm crunching some numbers for Victor, which I'll be happy to share with you at any time. I think I can give you a pretty accurate projection of the increase your school population will experience once the subdivision is fully committed."

Now, the thinking side of my brain told me two things: one, this information was not only useful but also necessary; two, Burchill Public School was declining in enrolment and could certainly use the infusion. My emotional side, however, told me a whole bunch of things to counter those thoughts—the way he delivered the information was pompous and condescending, I can get those numbers through the school board planners, I am retiring in two years any way so what do I care, Burchill Public is fine the way it is and the villagers will add enough new kids to keep it functioning very well, thank you very much.

What I did say was, "Thank-you, Mr. Fobert. I appreciate your offer." At which, he proffered his business card. And yes, his nails were beautifully shaped and polished.

Conversation pretty much died after that intrusion, although Margaret made a valiant effort to divert our attention with some humorous tales about her past lives. Very soon, however, Duncan cajoled her into letting him walk her home, and May and I were left to finish our drinks alone.

"I know logically that Oona's being gone has nothing to do with that man," May said to me in a low voice, swirling her white wine and dabbing at the last vestiges of food. "But he makes my skin crawl and somehow I just have this feeling that the subdivision is the root of all evil in the village right now."

I grinned at her ruefully. "I know what you mean. Ever since those excavators came, it seems that Burchill has been on edge. And now with Oona and Frieda. ..."

Just then, Bobby Mills came tumbling into the pub and flung himself into his mother's arms.

Everyone looked up, stunned by the transformation from cocky, confident teenager to blubbering child. Out of force of habit, May and I instinctively moved toward him, hovering to see if there was anything we could do. Kathy gently led him to a chair in the kitchen, her arms around him the whole time, dabbing at his face with a tissue, talking softly and soothingly to him. Were it not for the largeness of her eyes, the slight shake of her hand, she would have been the picture of calm.

Bobby moaned and muttered, sobs erupting like spurts from a broken water main, as he clutched onto his mother.

"Are you hurt anywhere, son?" Barry asked, squatting down in front of him, tenderly turning his arms and hands, feeling his legs and feet, looking for cuts or bruises or any tracks of injury.

Bobby shook his head, drew in a shuddering breath, looking up wildly at us all. His eyes caught sight of May and he fairly shouted at her, "It's you Indians. You created it. You brought it on us." Then another round of sobs burst from him.

Kathy and Barry stopped suddenly in their ministrations and stared at the boy; May and I cast bewildered glances at one another. Bobby had never spoken to May this way; in fact, she often talked about how helpful he'd been in the office despite his reputation as a wild child. Kathy spoke up.

"Bobby, that's Mrs. Reneaux you're talking to," she said, as if he had become blind or stupid, as if his remark about "you Indians" wouldn't apply somehow to May and therefore excused it.

"What happened, son? Tell us what happened," Barry pleaded, his frustration and fear obvious in his tone.

"It's . . . it's . . . I know you won't believe me . . . but the other guys, they saw it, too." Bobby's voice shook and his words were muddy with tears.

We waited silently while he took several breaths, his shoulders shaking as he attempted to regain control.

"It's Walking Bear. It's real. And it told me if I ever hunted again. . ." The boy's fragile control slipped again and he buried his face in his mother's shoulder.

The Great Spirit led the Chief to the land that was
thick with forest and animal life.
"This land," Manitou said, "is given to the People
to be protected and nurtured.
For every vegetable or tree you pull from the earth,
Nanna Bijou," the Great Spirit warned,
"you must plant a seed.
For every animal you hunt, you must nurture its young.
All spoils of the hunt must be used even to the very bone.
The forest is given to us for need, not for greed."
The good Chief agreed that this was the way of things.
He went back to his tribe and taught them these lessons.
For many years the brave People
abided by the Great Spirit's laws.

V ery slowly, Frieda became aware of the sound. Someone was chanting, just on the other side of a stone abutment. The voice was muffled, as if spoken through cloth, or with hand clasped over mouth. Frieda could pick out a few words only, just enough to tell her that they were Ojibwa. She had always thought that her parents' language was difficult and stilted; she had rejected it as singsong, childish. Thus Frieda had never learned to speak Ojibwa fluently, though she remembered more vocabulary than she ever wanted to admit.

She thought about her parents' disappointment as she'd grown older and had shown less and less interest in the old ways. Her mother and father had long since died before Frieda had broken ties with their community altogether, though by then, she would not have cared about their reaction anyway. Her mother, confined to a bed most of Frieda's life, had never seemed to understand; her father, cold and undemonstrative, had appeared to have little love for his only offspring. Frieda was filled with a strange, bitter flood of remorse, wishing suddenly she'd gone to her mother's bedside and taken those thin hands in hers. She wanted to reach up and touch her father's cheek.

Unable to move beyond the restraints that limited her, restricted to the use of smell and hearing only, she began to listen. Snatches of words washed over her, low and soothing, like the rippling of a stream, the soughing of the wind. The voice of the chanter was female, though too far away and too muffled to determine if it was someone Frieda knew; her pitch was sad and angry at intervals; her sound guttural and throaty.

Frieda listened to every nuance, frustrated that she could not hear it all, translating automatically when she caught the odd full word that she recognized. Perhaps it was the throbbing of her foot, the pain radiating hotly up her leg; perhaps it was the darkness; perhaps the forced stillness of her limbs. But suddenly Frieda could hear with a clarity she had never known before.

The music of the words blended with the whisper of leaves, the rush of wind, the murmur of birds. They washed over and around Frieda, filling not only the cavity of her ears, but the gaps in her soul. She could tell when the speaker was angry, even if she caught only one word, for the poetry of the language lent cadence and rhythm to the emotions that full paragraphs of English could not.

Yah-no-tum—unbeliever, the voice admonished; Frieda was awash with guilt and with shame. Bah-bah-me-tum—obedience, the stranger told her; Frieda was filled with yearning, with sorrow, with fear, not of giving up her possessions—for this is what obedience would cost her, she knew—but that she would prove unworthy, unable to give back what she had taken. Che-baum—soul; each letter had life, each syllable was drawn wholly and meaningfully; Frieda's body responded with trembles and the roar of her heart pounded with every sound. Let me show you, let me take you, do not fail me, e-nah-kay-yah—the way.

She recalled Walking Bear's low growl like a lover's whisper in her ear. You will recover; I will help you; you will recover in every way; you have many lessons to learn or relearn; the greed has filled your spirit; the forest is given to us to use for need, not for greed; if you break the ancient law, you must be punished; you will be able to think about and see the stories of the old ones; you will learn to live the truth; you are not alone; do not be afraid; you have begun your Quest.

Frieda was no longer sure where her voice began and the Other ended, whether these were her thoughts or those of Walking Bear or the Other, where she ended and the Other began. The sounds mingled and tumbled over one another, under and over, up and down, she or the Other, keening and crying, linking their voices as one.

And the forest responded from the force of their longing, their anger, their fear, their sorrow. The trees bent over and listened, whipped their leaves in sympathy, rain began to hammer on the stone roof, birds squawked in anger, animals ran away, tearing through the bushes, their feet as thunderous as Walking Bear's.

VI

"And then, so the legend says, the White Man came."

"Thank God I'm a white woman," I laughed to May, "we're never mentioned."

She locked arms with me, actually laughed heartily, and then continued with the story. "The white man—not woman—filled the Ojibwa braves with firewater, intent upon taking away the riches from the land. They tricked the natives into hunting for greed. Soon the carcasses of the unused animals were strewn around the countryside, their blood seeping into the earth, their offspring abandoned, their rotting souls weeping and calling to the Great Spirit. And Manitou, upon seeing the animal bodies, stripped of their fur, shining white in the moonlight, came to Nanna Bijou and berated him for allowing this to happen. The kind and well-meaning Chief was shocked and stricken, for he had not known of his peoples' digressions. Manitou was angry, saying that a good Chief would know what his people were doing; that Nanna Bijou had become lazy and had taken things for granted. The Bear Clan was supposed to be strong and steady, the police and guardians. Good Chiefs were expected to spend a lot of time patrolling the land surrounding the village, but Nanna Bijou had spent his time in contemplation, assuming the people could and would sustain the rules without his direction. So the Great Spirit turned the Chief into a half-man, half-bear, and ordered him to wander the land, looking for those who did not respect the animals and their environment.

"Nanna Bijou, now known as Walking Bear, is said to appear to those who hunt too much or pollute the land. He metes out various punishments, depending on the severity of the transgression."

May and I were walking home in the twilight. Before we

left, Bobby Mills had told his story in a halting, tear-filled voice.

He claimed that they were just sitting around a campfire, talking and laughing, though I imagined the innocent picture he was painting wasn't quite so blameless. None of the boys had heard it approach.

"It's huge," Bobby had cried, trembling once more as though he were a baby, his thin shoulders bent over in fear. "The face – I couldn't really see it close up, but it's a bear's head, and the eyes...it looked at me as though it would kill me. It grabbed me in its claws – look, see, Mum, I have some scratches – and turned me around and shook me and made me look at the...there was a deer...it shook me and said it would make me its victim if I...if I ever hunted again. Then it made me sit in the blood where the animal had died. When I turned my head, it was gone, so I ran." He sobbed silently for a moment. "It's so big," he repeated, "and covered in this stiff hair...and all these feathers. I'm never, never going out there again."

Bobby had grown calmer by the time May and I got ready to leave; his mother was able to lead him upstairs to their apartment. He'd even given May a grudging apology, although his father's prompting seemed to be more the impetus than genuine sorrow.

The pub had come alive with talk about the legend of Walking Bear, but May and I were tired and shaken. With unspoken speed, we had said our good-byes and walked out the door. We weren't to know until later that we would miss a most extraordinary event by mere minutes.

The evening was beautiful. Almost all traces of snow and ice seemed to have disappeared from the village streets, replaced by puddles of shiny water that smelled of spring. A beautiful moon floated among the darkening clouds, reminding me of the old poem. "And the moon was a ghostly galleon," I whispered to myself.

The village was peaceful and quiet, at least on our side of the streets. I lifted my head and drank in the wonderful scent of trees, unpolluted air, the promise of warm skies. I listened to the quiet rush of the breezes through the tree branches, the distant sound of humans, the whisper of animals poking around the melting earth.

"I love that story, May," I said. "It has a terrible truth about it. We HAVE as a species done so much harm to the earth. I'm just reading a book by David Suzuki about the environmental damage and it's frightening. Maybe Walking Bear should have come around a lot sooner." I looked up at the stars, smudged as they were by clouds, and remembered how difficult it was to see these magnificent lights in the city.

"Well, you're right, Em, it's a legend, it's not true, but it does have a good moral. My Aunt told me there are at least twenty all about the legends of Walking Bear, all with different morals or lessons to learn." May's voice sounded strangely excited. "But Bobby Mills' story—it started me thinking." She waited until we had crossed over the bridge on Lawrence Street, the sound of the rapids loud in our ears, before she began again. "Did you follow Bobby's description of Walking Bear? I think I was too busy controlling my anger over his Indian remark to pay close attention and he was definitely babbling at times."

"He was hysterical. Hard to believe that that kid could be so scared. Anyhow, yeah, I did listen carefully. He said the thing was half bear, half human—he couldn't tell the gender of the human—but it had a bear head and bear claws. He said it towered over him. It picked him up by the collar and shook him, growling at him to never hunt again or he'd be severely punished. He said he could smell the musty fur and saw teeth glinting at him, but from what I could gather, he was held up and forward, so he wasn't facing the beast. It could easily have been anyone dressed up, I suppose, and maybe some of the description was from Bobby's frightened imagination. Plus, if you think about it, Bobby really is rather small; anything might look huge to him. Though it sounded like Henry and his friends believe it was the real thing."

May gave a mirthless laugh. "Uncle Henry would love that. It would give credibility to all the stories, the Oral Traditions, which he's been passionate about since boyhood. I'll bet he'll spread this incident all over town before morning." We trudged along in silence for a moment, listening to the wind gather strength in the trees, the brittle, leafless branches ticking together like rhythm sticks. "Do you think this Walking Bear could be Oona out there, scaring the boys?"

Her question made me literally stop in my tracks. I looked above her head where the Bridgeman's house loomed in the distance and I remembered that anything is possible. Though it had immediately occurred to me that someone must have been pulling a dangerous trick on the boys, I had never connected it with Oona. Perhaps I really did, along with many other villagers, expect to find her body at the bottom of Bahswaway Pond.

"Would she disappear like that, though, May, without at least telling her family? Wouldn't she be sensitive to how you must be feeling? And she couldn't help but know the whole town has been out looking for her."

I could see the light go out of May's eyes. "I guess you're right, Emily. I'm just grasping at straws, trying to make sense of her disappearance." She struggled to keep the tears at bay. "But who just scared those boys half to death, then? It can't be some half-human, half-bear, I don't care what Henry says.

The form is a symbol used in the story to frighten people into caring about the environment."

"What about Agnes Lake? Doesn't that seem like something she would do?"

May thought about that for a moment as we resumed our walk. "That would make more sense, I suppose. She has told everyone she's going to be gone for a while on her Vision Quest. I just don't want to let go of Oona."

"You don't have to, May. I could be wrong about this Walking Bear business—it would seem to be like Oona to want to teach Bobby Mills a lesson. She's always been a champion of the environment."

We kept walking and then May spoke up again. "I'm not sure about that lately, though." This time her voice was hesitant, as if she wasn't certain how to put her feelings into words. "She seemed to be—I don't know—talking a lot about how others had reaped the riches of the land, why shouldn't she, maybe she ought to be more like Frieda—she didn't say any of this to me, but I heard about it from Henry and a couple of others—she'd been mouthing off in the pub. Which is also unlike Oona—she knows that when she drinks, she becomes the stereotypical drunken Indian and she hates that about herself, so she hardly ever touches the stuff. But over the last few months, she'd been showing up fairly often at the Main Street Station."

We both slipped through the slush on the sidewalk, heads down, contemplating. The wind tugging away from the lake had become cool and damp, causing us to button our coats and plant hats back on our heads.

"We'll probably have a bunch of scared kids tomorrow," I said, suddenly remembering that we had to work the next morning, and deciding a change of topic was a good idea. "That'll make the last day even more pleasant!"

We had reached Rideau St., which led to Julia. I had a short distance to go on St. Lawrence before I turned onto Lakeview. Although May and I had both just now been adamant that the story of Walking Bear couldn't possibly be true, we were suddenly nervous, looking at each other sheepishly as we caught the scent of one another's fear. May threw her arms around me and we stood for a moment wrapped in the warmth of our friendship.

"Walking Bear can NOT be true," she half-whispered in my ear, trying to convince herself and me. "It has to be someone dressed up—maybe even my Aunt Oona."

"I agree. Run home, though, just in case." We both laughed and separated.

"See you tomorrow," May said. "Thanks for tonight – I needed it." And, after squeezing my hand, she was gone.

VII

Edgar had just reached home after patrolling the Highway, when the telephone rang. Thinking it might be Frances telling him that she'd changed her mind and wasn't too tired to come over after all, he rushed to the phone and said a delighted hello into the receiver. He wasn't prepared for Barry Mills' frantic tones and the noise in the background. In a matter of minutes, Edgar had climbed back into his patrol car and had arrived at the Main Street Station Pub. He was surprised at what he saw.

Edgar Brennan has spent his whole life in Burchill. Thus he is not used to angry confrontations or drunken brawls in the street. Contrary to the cities and many towns, Burchill is a quiet, peaceful place, a template for co-operation and citizenship. Or at least it used to be.

Two years ago, Edgar had experienced his first murder and the stain of other unspeakable acts that this little town had reeled over. He'd watched the village and the reserve go back to their normal, friendly, innocent ways over the last twenty-one months, painfully but determinedly putting the pieces back together. It took hard work on the part of the politicians, the law enforcers, and the people to maintain a calm serenity in the face of the potential for unrest and controversy. Especially given Burchill's unique circumstances—a small, conservative village and native reserve, seasonally inundated with tourists, plus a provincial park, a pleasure canal, surrounded by acres of untended forest.

In the last few months, Edgar had felt as if everything were unraveling again—the subdivision had been the first of the troubles, followed by Oona and Frieda's disappearance. Now the scene that spread before him reminded him of an angry, tumultuous wave suddenly rising up on a relatively calm sea. He wondered briefly if it would turn them all upside down in salty water.

Flashing the lights on his car to illuminate and, hopefully, part the crowd, Edgar got out into the middle of a tight knot of people on the sidewalk in front of the Main Street Station Pub. It was difficult at first to see who was in the middle, and then he caught sight of a small old man flailing crazily in the direction of a tall dark suit. Voices were raised in a babble of anger, indistinguishable as the words swirled over one another. Several hands and arms struck out now and then as though to either encourage or immobilize. Edgar shoved his way fairly roughly to the middle of the circle.

Henry Whitesand, his gnarled brown face purple with anger and exertion, was pummeling Victor Reeves' chest with ineffectual punches. The taller, younger man merely stood there, laughing and jeering, seemingly unfazed by the blows, despite a trickle of blood oozing from his lip. Barry Mills was trying to separate them, without much success.

Edgar spoke twice and the second time, his voice penetrated Henry's fury. "Henry. Stop. Now." Loud, forceful, designed to drown out the raised voices around him. It worked.

The native man turned toward Edgar long enough to register through his outrage that the Chief Superintendent of Police was speaking to him. As soon as he had done so, his anger dissipated like a balloon being popped, and he slumped against Basil Fisher. Barry, who had been trying to pin Henry's arms down long enough to calm him, gave Edgar a look of pure admiration.

Hands on hips, Edgar slowly looked around at the small group. Victor Reeves maintained the smirk on his face, but his three comrades stood grim and respectful. In the silence that followed, Edgar studied each person carefully. He noted that the four businessmen looked very much alike: handsome, well dressed, and tall, in varied and attractive shades of grey-blond hair. Their formal state of dress contrasted sharply with the casual villagers—Henry Whitesand, Basil Fisher, Steve McEntyer, and two others whose names escaped Edgar at the moment—who had mostly donned sweatshirts and jeans. (Edgar almost groaned at the sight of Steve McEntyer, for through his wife Ruth, this incident would be all over the village tomorrow.) Only Barry Mills stood out, his white apron glowing in the moonlight.

"What is going on?" Edgar finally said, when he saw that everyone had become calm and silent. "Barry?"

"Henry and Mr. Reeves began to argue in the pub," Barry said, betraying no emotion, reporting the way he would in his role as police volunteer. "They were arguing over Walking Bear. Then Henry took a swing at Mr. Reeves. The other gentleman—" he nodded toward the most blond, and apparently younger of the quartet—"got him to move out onto the street, but Henry followed, and then everyone else got up and went after them, so I thought I'd better call you. Sorry I wasn't able to handle it myself, Edgar."

"See, Chief, the little man swung at me first," Victor Reeves piped up, his tone still light and touched with amusement, "and"—he said this as if he'd just discovered something quite profound and triumphant—"I'm bleeding!" With that, he whipped out an impossibly white, starched handkerchief and began to dab at the corner of his mouth.

A low growling sound erupted from Henry and his arms began to swing again. Barry, having just relaxed his stance, had difficulty getting the man under control again. Edgar put a hand on Henry's shoulder. "Henry, if you don't calm down, things will get much worse. How about we go back into the pub—just you four -" and Edgar pointed to Victor Reeves, the sandy-haired sidekick, Henry and Basil—"and we can work this out, hopefully. The rest of you, please, go on home. And Barry, do you think you or Kathy could brew up some coffee?"

"Coming up, Chief," Barry said with relief and quickly disappeared into his premises.

There was a bit of discussion following Edgar's request, especially among the contractor's quartet, who appeared to have only one car. In the end, though, the group complied and the five men were soon gathered around a table in the silent pub, each with hands wrapped around steaming cups of coffee.

"Okay, I need to hear it all," Edgar said. "And Henry, don't lose it again, or I will take you off to jail, and that's a promise." He sat back in his chair and surveyed the group, trying his best to maintain a casual, country-bumpkin air while at the same time listening to every nuance, alert to every gesture. "Why don't you start, Mr. Reeves?"

"Victor," the man said, making a big display of drinking from the uninjured side of his mouth only. "After the boy came into the pub screaming and crying about Walking Bear, we wanted to know the legend, so. . ."

Edgar held up his hand. "Stop. I think you need to go back to the beginning. What the hell are you talking about? What boy? What walking bear?"

"Maybe I can explain, sir," the sandy-haired man said, smiling and putting out his hand to shake Edgar's. "I'm Evan Fobert, Victor's partner. While we were in the pub, Mr. Mills' son came in, hysterical over an incident that had occurred in your forest." He said "your forest" as if he were accusing Edgar of not being very vigilant. "He and his friends were accosted by a creature that he claimed was called Walking Bear, which people at the bar began to tell us was part of some native tradition. Once the boy had been tended to and left, we asked about the legend and what it meant. Mr. Fisher here", nodding as though Edgar wouldn't be sure to which man he was referring, "was kind enough to explain the story to us."

"At which time," Basil interrupted, matching Evan Fobert's precise speech and condescending tone, "Mr. Reeves began to laugh and make derisive remarks about native folk lore."

"So I socked him," Henry mumbled, his head lowered as though either he'd just realized what a fool he'd been or he was falling asleep.

Edgar was well aware that his own responses to the conversation could have been based on prejudice toward the businessmen, but he was having a difficult time shaking the feeling that Reeves and Fobert believed they were talking to a bunch of illiterates, and could sense their surprised reaction to Basil Fisher's vocabulary. A native man knowing how to use and pronounce 'derisive'? Weren't they still at the 'How' stage? All of this passed through Edgar's mind in a flash, making him uncomfortably aware that he was a small town police chief with emotional ties that could threaten his objectivity. However, just at the point when Edgar was successfully swallowing his biased thoughts, Victor Reeves began to laugh.

"I can't believe you people actually exist in this century! How the hell can you walk around in the twenty-first century believing in some kind of half human, half animal? I knew this was a hick town, but really. . ."

Edgar surprised himself and shocked the little group by slamming his hand down on the table. "That is not helping," he said in clipped, angry tones. "I ask you to keep your opinions to yourself for now. What you are telling me is that Bobby Mills was confronted by something he called Walking Bear and that he ran back here, hysterical?" They all nodded.

"Okay. I'll have to check this out. Next, Victor, you began to insult native lore after you'd heard the story."

Victor, in the middle of a sip of coffee, tried to make some sort of verbal protest, but Evan Fobert smoothly cut in once more. "We apologize for that, Edgar. We were out of line. We'd had a lot to drink, though I know that's no excuse. However, I do think Henry's violence was uncalled-for."

"Do you want to press charges, Mr. Reeves?" Edgar asked, ignoring Basil's look of disapproval and Henry's sharp intake of breath.

Victor Reeves looked straight into Edgar's eyes. The police officer could feel the steely, condescending vibrations from the stare—he knew instinctively that the contractor was calculating whether pressing charges against a respected older member of the Sahsejewon Reserve would seriously affect his business plans. His decision would have nothing to do with human decency, forgiveness or kindness, Edgar was certain of that. Reeves' definition of community included only quantitative factors.

"No," he said finally, putting down his coffee cup. "However, I would like an apology and a promise that the man will stay away from me. I don't want to feel constrained whenever I come in here."

Henry made a strangled noise. "The things you said," he moaned, as though he had been the one bleeding, "are so hurtful, man. How can you live with yourself? How could you insult my people thus and not expect retaliation?"

"Henry, Mr. Reeves is offering a compromise. I'd like to propose one other caveat, Victor." Edgar took a moment to look at all of them. "Henry, you will apologize for striking at Mr. Reeves; Victor, you will apologize for insulting the Ojibwa traditions. Both of you will promise that you will not drink in the same place again—after all, there are other choices. You might find the Burchill Inn suits your purposes much better, Mr. Reeves, Mr. Fobert." He nodded at each of them in turn, reverting purposely to their formal names.

"Fine." Victor Reeves stood, towering over the table. "I apologize for insulting your traditions, Mr. Whitesand. May I go now, Chief Superintendent? I am tired and I wish to put ice on my lip." Though he sounded like a recalcitrant adolescent, Edgar surmised that his apology was likely the best one could expect.

"Not yet, sir. Henry has something to say."

"I apologize for socking you," Henry intoned immediately, without raising his head. Edgar noticed that Basil had poked his friend in the ribs to elicit the recital.

"Now you may leave, Mr. Reeves," Edgar said quickly, "and thank-you for your willingness to end this situation amicably."

"Good night, everyone," Evan Fobert said sweetly, putting his hand on his partner's back and steering him solicitously toward the doorway. "Thank-you for the coffee, Mr. Mills. Is there any charge?"

"Not at all," Barry answered formally from behind the bar. "On the house."

As soon as the door closed, Edgar motioned for Barry to sit down with them. "Tell me the whole story about Bobby," he said, "but first, have you got any more of that delicious coffee?"

Out on the street, Evan Fobert was folding his partner into the car with the other two contractors, who had waited up the street. "I'll take care of everything, Victor," he said quietly.

Victor Reeves looked straight into Evan's eyes, his mouth curled in a grin that managed to convey distaste, scorn, and condescension all at once. "You'd better," he hissed.

"I'm gonna walk," Evan said in response, loudly, for the

others to hear, "clear my head."

He watched carefully as the automobile disappeared around the corner, then took his cell phone out, pressing the speed dial.

"It's working," he said. "I've gone an idea for phase two."

As Evan Fobert strolled up the dark, quiet street, he continued to speak into the receiver. If anyone had seen his serene, smiling face, they might have thought he was simply enjoying the fresh, unseasonably warm air.

VIII

The Friday before March break turned out to be quiet and subdued. It may have been partly because most of the staff was tired from the night before; it may have been the light, mild, springy air; or it may have been the presence of the police chief's car in the parking lot first thing that morning. Edgar, May and I even had an opportunity to sip coffee and talk in the office.

"What did you think of Bobby Mills' story?" Edgar asked, tipping his chair back slightly, looking more relaxed with us than he had in days.

Edgar is very tall, with a compact body that boasts broad shoulders and long, muscular legs. He isn't really handsome; his face is too broad and his nose too long; his black, wavy hair is always unruly and falling across his forehead. Yet his wide brown eyes are so alight with intelligence and interest that he can't help but be attractive. He is the perfect picture of a town "chief" – he has the kind of strength that is apparent not only on the outside.

"At first we didn't know what to make of it," May told him. "But he certainly was genuinely afraid. I've never seen Bobby Mills look that way. To tell you the truth, I still can hardly believe he could be that frightened; it made him seem almost human." All three of us smiled at this; we knew what May meant. Bobby always gave a facade of careless self-confidence that bordered on a superiority complex. It was difficult to remember how he'd sobbed like a baby last night.

"He told us it was Walking Bear, but the details were pretty sketchy—just that it was some very tall creature with a bear's head, fur and claws, and the ability to speak," I went on. "It told him to stay out of the woods and leave animals alone. Which is good advice, overall."

Edgar nodded. "I have to go over to the Main Street Station Pub after I leave here and ask him a few questions. I wanted to get your perspective first. Did you hear about the fight?"

May and I both said, "What fight?" at the same moment, which prompted Edgar to tell us the entire story of the confrontation between Henry and Victor Reeves.

Assured that Henry had not been injured, we asked a few more questions and got all the details. We were both shocked, but also slightly amused. The picture of the little native man swinging punches at the tall, conservative business man made us want to laugh, despite the relative seriousness of Henry's anger and hurt.

"I'm going to watch Henry, though, just to make sure he stays away from that bunch. It's not going to do him any good to remain angry with them. It'll just make Victor Reeves more determined than ever to spread houses all over the place. I don't trust Reeves and I don't like him, but I have to uphold the law, as they say."

"Of course you do, Ed, and Henry knows that, too. He's just upset. I'm sure it won't happen again," May answered him.

"As for Walking Bear, May and I were saying last night that the boys definitely saw something—and it had to have been human. We were wondering if it could be Oona or Agnes, dressed up, wanting to frighten the kids."

Edgar mulled over that suggestion. "I had been thinking along those lines, too, though I hadn't considered Oona." The meaning of his words was not lost on May. "I'm getting the search parties out again tomorrow. We won't just look for Oona and Frieda, we'll be looking for whoever is acting this little charade out, too." He stood up, placing his empty cup on my desk. "Well, I'd better be getting along. I have a feeling it's going to be a busy weekend." Edgar had no idea that this would turn out to be the understatement of the year.

The rest of the day was busy. By the time May and I had waved good-bye to all the staff and students, we were exhausted, and more than happy that we'd brought our cars to school. Even the short walk home today would have been too daunting. Langford and I planned to go on the search tomorrow with May and Alain, so we made a promise to meet at Oona's cottage where Edgar would be gathering the volunteers early the next morning.

I happily spent the night at home with my husband and Angel, watched a movie on television while eating popcorn and nuts, read my book, scratched the dog's back, and cuddled Langford.

Because we went to sleep early, we awoke prepared for the long trek through the woods. It was difficult to know how to dress for the day, so we chose layers of heavier and lighter clothing, and a long leash for Angel.

We reached Oona's cottage on foot and were among the first to arrive. We said hello to Basil Fisher, Peter Smallwood and his wife Ellie, Ruth and Steve McEntyer and Edgar and Frances, then stood around talking about anything but the reason we were there, as other volunteers began to assemble. By the appointed time, there were thirty villagers, mostly couples, who were ready to comb the woods once again.

This time, as Edgar instructed us, he wanted us to look for any unusual signs—and since Ruth McEntyer had already told the Walking Bear story several times over—that included any signs of bear, real or otherwise. We were divided into groups of six and eight and Edgar warned us seriously that we were not to walk in pairs or alone.

"Most of us here know the woods really well," Edgar said, "but we can't let that make us complacent. This forest is a dangerous place at times. Please be on your guard. Use the flare guns to signal to the other groups that you've found something important, or you've encountered danger. Make lots of noise. We're not trying to surprise any one or any thing and noise will limit the possibility of THEM surprising US." He handed out the equipment—flare guns, a hatchet and a weed clipper—to the people in the group who would know what to do with them. Luckily, our group consisted of Basil, May, Alain, Peter and Ellie, so both Langford and I felt safer and less ignorant. Edgar pointed out sectors on his map, and sent us out, with strict orders to return in three hours max.

As our natural leader, May started us off in our sector to the left of Bahswaway Pond walking slowly abreast in a line through the woods. Whenever a weed tangled around one of our legs, Alain would snip it off with the clippers.

It is an odd sensation to be inside the cocoon of a forest, trudging deliberately loudly and slowly, kicking up fallen plants, bark or stones, scaring small animals to a dash through the underbrush. The winter residue remained, especially in the shaded sections; little pools of water were icy and almost frozen; last week's snow still sprinkled the muddy earth; the growth surrounding us was stark and somewhat sparse. Every step felt like walking on top of a mattress—that soft little give, followed by the firmness underneath. Every now and then we'd feel and hear the suction cup our feet made in the muddy ice.

In no way did it resemble the thick richness of a spring or summer forest, yet you could see a patch of green here and there being coaxed out by the unseasonable warmth of the last few days. Many of the trees in Burchill's forest are evergreen; tall furs and pines still blocked out much of the sun, so that long fingers of light pointed to the ground in the front of us. Branches and vines brushed our faces; winter birds screamed their dismay.

Langford and I stayed very close, relative strangers to the country, out of place in this wilderness, our little dog loyally snuffling slightly ahead of her amateur masters. The others talked, sometimes seeming to speak in a language we couldn't understand, especially May, who led the group as though we were on a naturalist expedition, instead of a hunt for missing bodies. She pointed out tree types, bushes, leftover leaves, the Latin names for the vegetation. We all knew she had to keep talking to block out the sound of her thoughts, so we listened politely, and even asked questions to bolster her speeches.

When she grew tired, Peter Smallwood took over, telling his hilarious stories just as he had done at the Reneaux household on the first night of the search. Our laughter echoed through the quiet trees, enough to dispel any thoughts Walking Bear may have had about attacking us. The distraction also served to pass the time. I was somewhat surprised that Basil was so quiet; he seemed to be fully absorbed in the search and disconnected from the rest of us.

Despite turning our heads every which way, down, around, shuffling, observing, examining, searching, time did not move quickly. We trudged, halted, waited while Alain or Peter hacked at some vines or roots, then traipsed along again, stopping each time we thought we saw something significant. I guess it was inevitable that it was May who found the first real clue.

We had been walking and trudging for about ninety minutes when May bent down swiftly, her hand disappearing into the tangled branches of a bush. Straightening up, she gave a small cry, and we all gathered around to look. In her hand, May held a chunk of stiff brown fur.

"Bear," she whispered, looking around at all of us, alarm making her eyes look huge.

The group was deadly silent, even Angel, who darted from one to the other, sniffing, seeking clues about the waves of fear that had suddenly radiated from all six of us. May twisted the stiff, brown hair in her hands, studying it carefully, sniffing at it as if she were a fellow bear.

"It's covered in old blood," she said in a voice barely audible to the whole group.

Peter stepped over and took it from her, studying it as carefully as she had done. "And it was stuck under here. . .?" He bent to examine the bush. "It looks as if it were tossed there. It doesn't seem to be a natural place for a bear to catch itself on." He stayed on his haunches and looked up at the group. "I think we should send out a flare; what do you guys think?"

Langford spoke up. "I agree. Edgar did ask us to look for any signs of bear and this is certainly an unusual one. Maybe the rest of the gang should join us and concentrate on this sector."

The rest of the group assented, unconsciously huddled together near the bush where the find had appeared, while Alain set the flare soaring and hissing into the sky. We stood close together in a patch of sunlight, eyes peering through clumps of evergreen branches or spindles of deadened maple limbs, stamping our feet on broken bits of bark and bush and moss. We listened to the breeze soughing through the forest, to the occasional complaint of an animal disturbed, to the chirp of a squirrel high above us. At that moment, it seemed to me, this was a silent, secretive wood, a place where Bear walked upright and spoke, a yawning chasm that had swallowed up two women.

in sleep we are given wings
the colours of the night are fixed in my mind, offering
sublime peace

She had no idea how long she had been there, swimming in and out of consciousness. Sometimes when she was awake, she was unsure of whether or not she was in her own body, or whether she had entered another dimension. As the hours wore on, she became convinced that she could not withstand the pain any longer. Instead of improving, she felt as though her body were collapsing in on itself, unable to sustain the repercussions of her injury. Her eyes continued to be blinded, filmy with infection. She surmised that some hideous contamination had passed from the bear trap into her blood stream.

She began to hum to herself, a constant moan, a redirection of her concentration away from the source of her pain. Whenever Walking Bear or the Other chanted, she chanted too, as loudly and as pitifully as she could manage, no longer seeking empathy and help, but simply as a way of diverting the throb of agony.

The Other had not returned, it seemed to her, for a very long period of time. Walking Bear had seemed distant, coming to her only with food. Each time she was left alone, she found herself aching for the touch; the faint, reassuring growls; the sustaining water that Walking Bear brought to her. She wanted to be held, rocked, and nourished.

She had drifted into another dream, so she was not sure that the shift in the air, the scent, and the movement were real, until she forced her body to jerk by leaning into the pain, pressuring her injury until it created a twinge that catapulted the rest of her into consciousness.

Now she was certain that Walking Bear was close to her again; she could smell dampness; she could hear hoarse breathing. She lifted her shaking hand to take the wiry stiffness of fur surrounded by the soft padding of skin on a paw; it felt strange yet comforting. "You will be healed now," came the whisper. "You are ready."

She was aware then that The Other had entered her space for the first time. She could smell a human body, unwashed, sweaty; yet an underlying sweetness permeated the air. It was a familiar scent; she realized that this was a person with whom she'd had close contact in the past, but her mind would not allow her to choose a face or a name. Licking her parched lips, she tried to ask Walking Bear who this was, but just then the figure leaned toward her again, and the cool water began to trickle down her throat and chin.

Walking Bear fed her as before, cradling her head, slowly coaxing water and food into her starving body. When her body was released, gently eased into the prone position again, the voice said, "You will not speak" and she was willing to do whatever she was asked.

The first touch was like an electric shock. Heat that came in waves shot up her foot and leg. She was aware of a pressure, light and feathery, as though fingers were trailing over the hairs of her limb. Shivers of warmth radiated from it, flooding her broken bones with a pulsing energy; the vibrations ebbed and flowed all along her body. She could feel her face begin to flush, her fingers tingle, her stomach flip. The hands kept moving, back and forth, all around, not quite touching, yet connecting all the same. Her body responded like a cat's to the gentle stroking of a loving owner, stretching and purring, restorative, cleansing, alive once more.

When the chanting began again, it was low and soothing, humming along with the waves that buzzed through her system like a plug in a light socket. The words came from some primal, womb-recorded section of her brain, from the roots of her native ancestry. The tears flowed freely through the crevices and rivulets of her time worn face. She began to feel the gooey infection loosen and seep away.

Walking Bear moved even closer to her, flesh and fur brushing her body, and gently wiped her eyelids and cheeks. She blinked, eyes sore and tear-filled, as the dim but piercing light filtered in and seared her brain. It took patience and time, opening and closing her lids, before she could keep them open on her own. At the same time, she felt Walking Bear's movement, as something shifted in the semidarkness. As Frieda was given back her sight, as she realized that she could truly see, Walking Bear showed to her a human face.

IX

"I'm glad you sent the flare," Edgar reassured us. "This has to be the right sector, the one Walking Bear is to be found in, at least." He gave an embarrassed chuckle and then stared off into the distance as though trying to see beyond the trees into the future. "Where does the forest end here? I know where we were heading goes straight into Sahsejewon and the centre one begins like an inverted triangle and ends at the Provincial Park. But this one. . . I've never actually been through it, even as a kid."

"Me either," Peter said. "I think it was out of bounds for us as kids. Isn't there some kind of ravine a few miles up that's pretty steep and dangerous? Appears out of nowhere? I think some people were badly injured traipsing through there and thus it became forbidden to Burchill kids . . . and adults, obviously."

"You are right, Peter," Alain added. "My Dad warned us never to go too far and we did not, even as rebellious teenagers. I think it was really impressed upon us how dangerous it is. Did Oona ever take you in here, May?"

May nodded, still looking contemplative. "She did take me through this sector." She pointed back in the direction of Oona's cottage. "Her place is on the edge of Sahsejewon, that way, and not too far from here. She used it a lot for trapping, probably because not many people came through. She once showed me the ravine edge. It would be several hours' walk from here. There are caves on the other side of the ravine that were said to be sacred burial grounds. I think that was part of the reason kids were discouraged from exploring that far."

I wondered if the same thoughts were running through May's mind—bear fur, the legend come alive, Oona and Frieda's disappearance, Agnes' Vision Quest, all occurring at the same time. Did it have something to do with this sector, where few people roamed? Would we discover the three native women bringing the moral tale to life and if so, why? I reflected back to May's observations of her aunt in the last few months, how she'd begun to drink again, the way she'd spoken of being poor while others had benefited from their spoils. How was her behaviour connected to her disappearance or to Frieda's? Was the purchase of an expensive home by Frieda somehow linked? Was Agnes Lake with them, or was her quest completely separate? Perhaps we'd find their bodies at the bottom of Bahswaway after all. I couldn't make sense of any of it and from the look in May's eyes, she couldn't either.

"What do we do now, Edgar?" I asked, leaning down to absently stroke Angel's silky neck.

Before he could answer, there were several shouts and the rest of the search parties joined us. Discussion, explanation, and theories went around for a while after that. Finally, Edgar answered my question.

"Let's continue on for a short while in this sector only," Edgar said. "Most of you can go home. Let's keep about twelve—" he smiled and said, "twelve apostles, okay?—to keep going. May and Alain, I'd like you to stay on if you can. I don't think there's any danger, with all of us together, and I'm damn curious about what is going on. Please, don't anyone stay who is unsure about this, or nervous, or whatever."

In the end, May and Alain, Langford and I, the Smallwoods, the McEntyers, Basil and Aileen Fisher, and Edgar and Frances, made up the twelve apostles—and one dog—who elected to keep going. By this time, the sun had risen nearly to the treetops, so the ground was becoming softer and quite muddy in spots, not to mention the fact that we were now shedding some of our layers. We were even bulkier with sweaters and jackets tied around our hips. The forest was filled with the sounds of our swishing and snapping through the brittle branches and resistant bushes, our feet thudding and slipping on fallen twigs and decomposed leaves. Angel stayed very close, her nose twitching with the various odours that wafted toward us on the wind. It was a slow, tedious process.

At first, we were very quiet, until Frances began asking questions about Burchill, native traditions, and the history of the canal. Frances was raised in Toronto, and although she'd been around Ottawa for the last five years, including her stint here in Burchill, she was like me—enjoying the small town life, but not too well informed about its foundations. Her questions began a whole avalanche of answers, stories, legend and fact, that kept us fascinated and alert while we walked.

It wasn't long before we found another sign of the bear—a huge print preserved in the muddy, icy ground inside a small clearing that was free of vegetation. Incongruently big and grotesque in that space, it looked like a clay model, something deliberately designed to be frightening. Whoever, whatever, had planted it, certainly had done the job well.

I had a difficult time holding Angel back from traipsing all over the print; she strained and whined until Langford picked her up in his arms, from where she stared and panted but did not resist. May, Edgar and Frances squatted and bent their heads over the print, talking in low tones, their voices expressing wonder and bewilderment.

Finally May straightened up. "This isn't an animal's print," she pronounced to no one in particular. "It's not embedded enough. An animal that would make a print of this size -" she pointed to the muddy area still crowded by Edgar and Frances—"would weigh a ton! The print would be a lot lower in the mud. Not only that, there is no heel mark—as if the bear were walking on his toes."

"And bears walk flat-footed, especially if they happen to be standing upright at the time," Edgar added.

"Which they rarely do," chimed in Peter Smallwood.

"There is only one print, too," Frances said, "even though the whole area of this clearing is muddy, not just one little spot. It's not likely that one paw could have landed in the clearing and the other in the grass."

"This was planted here," May asserted. "I think Walking Bear is far more human than it is any other animal." She stretched her back, searching through the trees. I could imagine that she searched for the answers beyond the quiet evergreen branches. "Someone was meant to find this and become frightened." Later, she would tell me that she felt like hollering out for her Aunt Oona, demanding to know where she was and why she was doing this.

Edgar stood up beside May and agreed with her. "I think we'd better get out of here. I'm going to get a picture of this, then we'll mark our way out, so we can easily get back in. Somebody is playing a hell of a bad joke. We need more law enforcement so we can find out who it is."

He withdrew his small, digital camera from his jacket pocket and began to snap pictures all around the print. It was while our attention was drawn to this process that it happened.

Far ahead of us, filtered through sunlight and the skeletons of winter trees, an apparition appeared. The head of the bear reflected shades of light and dark brown, with tinges of yellow from the sunlight fingering down upon it. Shoulders of fur and feather poked through the evergreen tree around which the animal peered. Yet it was clear that this was not quite purely bear, for in addition to the steely stare of the bear's eyes, a human visage, cloaked in animal hair, mostly covered by white and black feathers, glared straight at us.

It was as though bear and human had become one, an angry mixture of instinct, hatred borne of experience and deep disappointment. The feeling that we were interlopers, invaders, enemies, cut through the distance and held us all very still in its spell.

Before any of us could react, Walking Bear turned and disappeared.

X

If the Burchill villagers and reserve dwellers had not experienced the horrors of the "Bridgeman" incident two years ago, the stories that swelled over the homes and businesses might well have caused panic that weekend. As it was, there were very few if any tourists around at this time of year, and, because the subdivisions were not finished, only a handful of newcomers. This occurrence was nothing compared to the Bridgeman incident, so everyone, though they talked and talked about Walking Bear, went about their daily activities as usual. It was Spring Break, though, which meant more children on the loose, and there were some in the village who suspected teenagers to be at the root of it all. As well, many villagers appeared to be amused by the entire incident, while others were charmed and fascinated by the legend-come-true.

Edgar and Frances were kept busy the rest of that weekend, chasing other sightings. The volunteer police officers—such as Barry Mills and Michael Lewis—were recruited to follow up on many of the complaints. There were reports of Walking Bear appearing near the woods, around Oona Nabigon's house, on the shores of Ogeechee Lake, and on the edge of Sahsejewon. In some cases, the police did find evidence of bear fur and prints. Mostly, though, the sightings turned out to be imagination. A fallen tree twisted into a bear leaning menacingly over the pathway, or a dog print morphed into a bear claw.

Edgar felt as though he hadn't had a moment alone with Frances since this whole incident began. As for Frances, she appeared, to Edgar at least, to be finding more excuses to be apart. It seemed to him that his recent proposal of marriage had chased her out of his arms and his bed into her patrol car and her job. On one level, he knew he was being irrational—he who strived so carefully to use intellect rather than emotion. After all, their jobs had become much busier and more stressful over the last few weeks. However, he couldn't shake the notion that the fact that this stress was driving them apart rather than pulling them together was a bad sign. Thus it was that on Sunday evening, Frances was patrolling the highway, while Edgar was meeting with Chief Dan and some of his Council on the reserve.

Edgar had long ago heard the legend of Walking Bear, but he enjoyed hearing it again as he sat around the council table, his notebook spread before him, a ritual whiskey in his hand. Basil Fisher was especially loquacious today, having had more than one ritual whiskey it appeared, and being especially thrilled with his confrontation with the legend. His little round face was alight with possibilities; his lively black eyes danced and it seemed that his short-cropped grey hair stood up even straighter on his head.

"We all stood there in shock while he got away from us," he chuckled, and Edgar had to agree. "We just stood there for the longest time after the apparition disappeared, saying absolutely nothing. Not even Edgar moved."

They laughed and then Edgar said seriously, "You know, I almost hate to admit this, but I was in awe. I have never seen anything like this. You know me well enough to know that I like things that I can explain scientifically or tangibly—so I'm not saying I believe in the legend—but I must say I was ... I don't know how to explain it. I just felt like I was in the presence of something awesome and wonderful."

Basil nodded. "It reminded me of the stories my grandfather would tell. He said that any native who met a bear should greet it with the utmost respect, calling it Grandfather of Us All, and talk to it. He said it was a great sight to see a bear's head and ears moving as you spoke to it."

Several of the others chuckled and someone said they didn't relish talking to a bear at any time, respectfully or not.

"I know you don't really think it's Walking Bear, do you Chief?" Edgar asked, sipping on the excellent whiskey, feeling the warmth calm him.

Chief Dan Mahdahbee sipped on his drink, too, filtering it through his teeth before he swallowed, and then spoke. "No, Ed, I have to admit I don't. The legends were invented to teach, not necessarily to reflect fact. However, I did know a few shaman who constructed large bear shields out of carcasses, then wore it as a headdress."

"What was its purpose?" Edgar asked.

"Sometimes it was simply out of respect," Dan said. "The Shaman of the Bear Clan were known for their knowledge of medicinal herbs, and the headdress – which is also called a diadem—was to honour the wisdom of our ancestors, the most important of which was the bear. Other times it was to teach the people a lesson through fear. The Bear Clan was supposed to protect the environment. If the people were disobeying the laws of nature, Walking Bear would come to reprimand them."

There was a thoughtful silence. "Do you think. . ." Edgar, knowing Chief Dan's respect for Agnes Lake, hesitated before asking, ". . . this could be Agnes, trying to scare away Victor Reeves and his like?"

Chief Dan turned his dark, intelligent eyes to meet Edgar's. "I've thought of that," he admitted. "I think it's possible. It's not something I would have thought she'd do, but if her Vision Quest moved her ... maybe."

No one mentioned Oona and Frieda, perhaps not daring to believe that they could be alive, or maybe it was that they doubted the two women would be participating in something so spiritual, so entirely native.

At the same time, out on the highway, Frances was going through some reflections of her own. She was trying very hard to concentrate on the job, to use all her faculties to note and observe as she drove slowly past rock and tree silhouetted in the patrol car's headlights, but her thoughts kept straying back to Edgar.

She was very irritated with herself, having been proud for so many years of keeping her emotions in check. For Frances, meeting Edgar Brennan had been both a blessing and a curse: she was all at once flooded with both warm feelings and sheer terror. Frances was the product of a childhood spent in the company of a distant, older relative, never feeling secure or completely at home, and though she'd worked it through with a caring psychologist, she knew that in times of uncertainty she reverted to throwing up barriers and icing up against the risk of hurt.

She knew perfectly well that her spontaneous acceptance of Ed's marriage proposal had frightened her badly. Within the baggage of her insecure past, her little suitcase of 'things are going too well, we're going to get burned' had spilled its contents once more. Yet despite knowing all of this in her head, her heart refused to allow her to confide in her newest best friend, her love, the one with whom Frances knew she could spend the rest of her life.

"I will tell him everything, I will," she told herself, even mouthing the words out loud as though to ingrain them on her tongue.

Purposefully she turned her thoughts to the case, to the incredible events that had unfolded in this little town. Frances admitted secretly that she was a superstitious person—she'd relied often in the past on crossed fingers, salt over the shoulder, avoiding black cats, and horoscopes—to make life more certain and reliable. The legend-of-Walking-Bear-come-true had, in her heart of hearts, thrilled her completely. She devoured the stories; delightedly recalled over and over again the image of that bear-human face in her mind; listened to every word uttered by the villagers about the legends and conjectures. Inside her head, a whole drama played out. She fitted different pieces across the imaginary chessboard according to which suspect she selected—the visionary, the thief, the crooked land owner. Frances was enjoying herself immensely, even as she fixed her poker face and forced her trained eyes to zero in on the facts before her.

She would never know later what led her to swing past the subdivision one more time. Perhaps she wanted to prolong her patrol; maybe it was sheer coincidence. Nevertheless, as she rounded the corner from the highway onto the dirt road, Frances Petapiece was the first to see the huge column of smoke and flame that leapt into the star lit sky.

XI

Early on Sunday evening, Langford and I were huddled up in our bed. Despite the warmth of the days, the nights were still seasonably cool and damp, so we had a low fire sparkling in the fireplace. Langford was lying prone, his arms thrown up in complete relaxation, eyes closed and breath even and contented, while half a dozen pillows propped me up so I could read. Angel lay fast asleep in her little bed in the corner.

This is my favourite room in a house full of wonderful, welcoming rooms. It is huge—running the full length of the house—with wide picture windows and a balcony overlooking the lake, a fireplace, and an en suite bathroom. From our four-poster bed, we can hear the rocking of the waves all night long. We have filled it with early pioneer furniture and beautiful Langford Taylor paintings. Our decor is simple but peaceful and comfortable. Each time I cross the threshold here, the love I have for Will and he for me washes over me, calming any storm, freeing mind and soul from any trouble. This room was the main reason I knew I was home the first time I saw Beatty House.

Since we moved to Burchill, I never think of British Columbia as home—especially after the hell we'd lived through in Vancouver. Now that my mother and father are both gone and my brother and his wife live in Ireland, there are no ties out west. Any good memories were long ago obliterated. It took five minutes in this bedroom to give me a vast sense of peace and belonging, of happiness and contentment.

I reached out with my toes and traced my husband's soft hairy leg. A few minutes before, I had lain out of breath and sated across his chest. Our lovemaking is sometimes almost rough, prolonged, our bodies craving one another with such force that we are often left panting and nearly embarrassed by the strength of our passion. I looked over at him, my eyes caressing his soft grey-brown hair, his long dark eyelashes, the five o'clock shadow darkening his strong chin, the soft grey hairs spread over his chest. Langford Taylor towers a whole foot over me at six foot four; no matter how much weight I might gain, I always feel dainty and small when I am beside him. I work very hard at maintaining my petite figure and it's costing a little more each year to keep this blond mane, too.

But our looks have never guaranteed nor strengthened our passion; it has always been a connection that Will and I have, which is there in the meeting of our eyes, or in the electricity of touch. More than once I have heard my husband telling someone of a dream that had actually been mine, and several times a week one of us says aloud what the other is thinking. We laugh often; we are both lusty and irreverent. We may look dissimilar and approach the world from varied perspectives, but our differences only make things interesting. Underneath, I swear that we are the same soul.

In the midst of my reverie, the telephone rang. It is both a testament to my more outgoing nature and to my job that the phone is on my side. I promptly picked it up, trying not to awaken Langford as I said hello.

"Emily, it's Maurice Fournier." Mo Fournier leads the volunteer fire brigade in town, but I have to admit, that didn't cross my mind. "Can I speak to Langford?"

I glanced over at my husband, who had propped himself up on an elbow and was nodding at me. "Sure, Mo, hang on."

"Hi, Mo, what's up?" Langford's eyes began to widen almost immediately. "Of course. I'll be right there." He hung up and swung his legs over the side of the bed. "Holy shit, Em, the subdivision's on fire."

At first I couldn't even picture what Langford meant by

subdivision—and then it struck me. Victor Reeves' new houses, rows of wooden skeletons, dusty roads and piles of dirt and brick. I drew in a deep breath, thinking immediately of the quarrel outside the pub and wondering how the homes had begun to burn.

Langford was pulling on his jeans and searching for a shirt. "I never thought when I signed up for volunteer fire fighting that I'd actually be called to fire fight."

My heart lurched. "Oh my God, I never thought you would either. Can I come with you?"

"Absolutely. I was hoping you'd want to. You can't miss the fun."

In my opinion, Langford was not taking this incident very seriously. I could sense his excitement. It's probably ingrained in every boy-inside-the man who has secretly wanted to be a fire fighter. Angel looked up sleepily from her bed as we rushed around throwing on underwear and sweaters, but she settled back down with a sigh when I patted her head and told her not to worry, we'd be back soon.

The air outside was a shock after the warmth of our bed and fireplace. It was dark and windy, the kind of air that slips right through your clothing with damp fingers. We both shivered as Langford started up the car and headed for the highway. As we turned onto Main Street, we could see the smoke and flames piercing the sky beyond the Mahdahbee Department Store. Its nearness emphasized the close proximity of the subdivision to our little town. As we approached the dirt road leading into the new houses, we could see the dark shapes of parked cars and flash-lit people rushing around in organized clumps.

Langford sprang from the car and I found a spot down the road to park. My flashlight immediately hit upon a familiar red coat bobbing along the edge of the ditch ahead of me.

"May!" I called, thrilled to see her here too.

She turned and waited for me, clutching my arm as soon as we were side-by-side. "Isn't this incredible?" Her eyes shone in the moonlight; she was almost as excited as Langford. I guess it isn't just little boys who dream of fire fighting.

"Look at the flames!" I exclaimed, astonished. The fire appeared to be licking the sky. "I've never seen anything like this."

"I remember once when I was a little girl, the reserve dump went on fire. My dad took me out to watch. I even helped stamp out a grass or two. I think the whole reserve came to watch."

We lurched along the roadway, finally stepping onto the dirt road that led into the subdivision—or what was left of it.

"It looks like all of Burchill has come out for this one, too." Throngs of people ran to and fro; the fire truck sprayed water furiously.

The fire seemed to dance and flit from one group of wooden poles to another, chased by the water. Six or seven of the fledgling homes were stark black, the lumber whittled down to stumps of ash. Shouts, tarpaulins, pails of water, hoses, all flapped at once to squelch the busy flames and smoke. Faces were lit by the orange light and sweat poured down the volunteers' faces. Fire Chief Dave Milne stood barking orders in the centre of everything, his face dusted with ash and concern.

It seemed to take hours for the fire to die out, even under the onslaught of the hoses. The subdivision was perfect fodder for the blaze; orange and blue flames skipped from one dry wooden frame to the other and back again. When it was over, a silence fell over the crowd. The dying inferno hissed through the still night. Smoke continued to hover, as though trying to revive the crumbling embers.

Langford and Alain, covered in sweat and ash, came to stand beside us. It took a few moments before Chief Milne finally turned his round, reddened face toward all of us and signalled for the crowd to come closer in order to hear. It was only then that I could make out faces among the dark shapes: Mo, Edgar, Frances, Peter Smallwood, Teddy Lavalle, Basil Fisher, Henry Whitesand, Chief Dan, Steve McEntyer, and a host of other villagers. The only people I didn't see were Victor Reeves and his cronies.

As if reading my mind, Dave Milne asked, "Does anyone know where Victor Reeves is staying?"

Edgar answered immediately. "At the Inn, Chief. I'm surprised he didn't hear the commotion."

"Okay." A thoughtful pause. "We are going to have to do some investigating now. Thanks to all of you for your help. But we need to clear all the volunteers out now. Please check with Mo on your way out so we can make sure everyone's got his or her volunteer hours logged. We'll let everyone know what's what as soon as we have any information." Dave Milne is a big man and his voice was loud and authoritative in the darkness with only the hiss of the embers as background. "Edgar, Frances, we'll need you to stay."

May went over to Frances, whose face was drawn and tired, and gave her a hug before she moved off with the rest of us, who made do with a wave in the police officers' direction. As we trudged toward our cars, Langford and Alain talked rapidly, the adrenaline that still pulsed removing their usual reticence.

"Why don't you two come over to our place for a night cap?" I asked. "It's not likely we're going to get to sleep yet and we don't have to get up in the morning."

"Speak for yourself," Alain laughed. "I'm the only

working stiff in this crowd this week."

May punched him playfully. "Give me a break. You can get Joey to open up for you."

"I promise not to keep you up that long," I said, not really meaning it, as we drew close to the Reneaux truck.

When Alain finally relented, I suggested that Langford go back and ask Edgar and Frances to join us if they were finished early. Alain was able to do one better—he called Edgar's cell phone and got an affirmative. Eventually we drove off to Beatty House.

through the nervous watch of animals
I have become what I am

The man's head jumped and thrashed from side to side, as though consumed with fear. Negative energy pulsed from his body. Frieda could feel the waves of confusion, anger and hurt flowing from him. He appeared to be weak and unable to walk; his arms curled strangely at his sides, as if he could not lift them. Walking Bear and The Other hovered over him, their ministrations tender and solicitous.

"Aaniin," Walking Bear had said formally, greeting the man as if he had voluntarily walked into their cave home, as if they had some business to transact between them, as though he were not twisted in pain and fear, but could respond with a hearty hello in return.

Frieda's heart had sounded a drumbeat in her ears when she heard the man awakening. She was able to sit up on her bed now, though her leg remained firmly in place in front of her, bound by wooden slats and poultices of healing herbs. Listening in silence as Walking Bear and The Other attended to him, she heard the murmuring and chanting, the grunts of displeasure and resistance in response. It was eerie in the dusk of the cave, smelling their nearness, seeing shadows dance on the walls, hearing the disjointed communing.

Frieda had an odd sensation of jealousy as she perceived the outline of those healing hands as they passed over the man's body. She longed for the fur and skin, the electricity of healing, the proximity of kin. She clung to Walking Bear's promise, "Giga-waabamin," I shall see you—see you for more than the pathetic human being she had become, see her for how she had been born, pure and innocent and beautiful. See her as friend, as sister, as lover.

"Miigwech," she had whispered to Walking Bear, saying more than thank-you; I am unworthy of your friendship, your love, but I will try to show you that I have changed.

Frieda realized in some recess of her brain that she was exhausted, that her sleep was not restorative, that a fever still raged as her body attempted in vain to heal her wounds. A tiny part of her kept insisting she was being duped, she was waawaashkeshi—a trembling, frightened deer, a coward, pliable and usable.

But that voice had grown dim, infrequent, almost silent. Walking Bear had known all of her sins, her betrayals, her weaknesses, and Walking Bear had forgiven her, healed her, raised her up to be proud and strong and hopeful once more.

She lay back on the bed and listened to her saviours, joining their chants, wishing the man would be still so they would turn to her.

XII

We were into our second bottle of wine, having laughed about our heroes, the fire fighters, discussed seriously the origin of the blaze, and laughed again about Angel's insistence on jumping into Alain's lap, when Edgar and Frances came to the door and knocked timidly.

"We weren't sure you'd still be up," Edgar said. "Plus, we're covered in soot and dirt still, but we're in dire need of friendly company."

"Come in, come in," Langford said, grabbing hold of their coats and ushering them into the family room. "There's plenty of friendly company here, and even some friendly wine—not to mention a friendly fire." (Of course, it being the end of the second bottle, we all burst out laughing at that, too, while Frances and Edgar grinned at our silly foursome with something like envy of our condition.) "Don't worry about the soot—we're still covered in it, too, which is why we're all huddled up here in the family room. This furniture is virtually indestructible."

They were soon all resettled in our huge, two-person, fluffy chairs, while I was sitting cross-legged on the floor, Angel cuddled in my lap, leaning against my husband. The fire was golden and blue, crackling and spilling its warmth into the damp night. Langford put some soft music on for background.

As we all sipped our glasses of wine, I felt a finger of happiness and contentment creep up my spine. Along with that tentative appreciation of Burchill, our friends, our home, our sanctuary, came that same shudder of insecurity and forbidding. These are our friends, I thought, but they don't really know who we are. As though they knew what I was thinking, everyone was suddenly more serious.

"Tell us, Officers," Alain urged. "What was that fire all about? Any clues? Did Victor Reeves show up eventually?"

Edgar snuggled even further into the chair, as close as he could get to Frances, who, though she had obviously hastily washed her face and brushed her hair, looked tired and disheveled. They both shook their heads and Edgar answered.

"Victor never showed up. We did find that smarmy little weasel of an assistant, though—Evan Fobert." At Frances' squeal of protest, he smiled and said, "I know, it's not professional, but he's just a little too smooth for me. I can see why Reeves employs him, though. He could probably talk the paint off my car." A round of appreciative laughter ensued; we all felt the same way about Evan Fobert, it seemed. "Anyhow, Fobert said he thought Victor had headed into Ottawa earlier this week so he could be there for a meeting—but he didn't seem very sure of anything. He claims Reeves goes off on his own a great deal and according to his own drummer. Fobert assures us that someone will be able to track Reeves down pretty quickly though.

"Meanwhile, Dave actually sent us away very soon after everyone else. The scene was already trampled enough and if he's to find out what the cause was, he needs some time with just his trained crew. So he asked us to inform someone from the Reeves camp, and then go on home, which we did. But he did say that it looked and smelled like arson to him—I guess he has a real nose for gasoline, which he told me privately seemed to be spread all over the place."

"Who would have done it, though? Kids?" May asked. Her face was pink from wine and the warmth of the fire; with her long black hair pulled forward, I thought she looked beautiful, though her eyes were still tired and worried.

"Dave doesn't think so," Frances said, "though he wasn't

specific. Unfortunately, he mentioned . . ." Edgar's rib poke was obvious to most of us. I had a sudden dreadful feeling that I knew what she had been going to say, but Frances was a quick study. ". . .it could have been someone who wanted the subdivision stopped or at least delayed."

"That could have been any of the villagers, then," Langford said, but I could tell by May's look that she was making connections too . . . Oona? Frieda? Agnes? Henry?

My tentative feelings about the sanctuary in which we live were quickly diminishing. I reminded myself that my friend's beloved aunt was still missing and that her uncle had been involved in violence for the first time in his life. Things were not exactly stable in Burchill when I considered the disappearances, the arson, a legend-come-true stalking the villagers, the hatred brewing against the developers.

"Everything has been so strange for me over the last couple of weeks, starting with my aunt's disappearance," May mused, as though she had been reading my mind. "I keep asking the same questions over and over, trying to guess what happened. Why the twenty circles around the tree? Why did Frieda follow her? Where the hell is Agnes Lake? Who is Walking Bear? It's driving me nuts, not knowing. And now this fire—do you think it's all connected?"

There was a thoughtful silence, then Langford said carefully and quietly, "I really think it must be. My private theory is that it's all being perpetuated by the same person or persons, as they say in the movies. I think it must be a plot to get rid of the subdivisions. Whoever it is must know that Walking Bear would be a powerful symbol and message for our native villagers and that soon all the white villagers would be scared and wondering, too. The next step was to burn the new buildings. What I don't know is how or if Oona, Frieda and Agnes are involved. It just doesn't seem like something Oona would do—deliberately disappear to create havoc. Especially since she knows how worried you would be, May."

"I agree, Lang," May said, her voice stuttered with tears. "But Oona has just not been herself in the last few months. She was acting so strangely, saying weird things—but the thing she didn't seem upset about any longer was the subdivision. It almost appeared that she was questioning her whole life, all the time she had spent on conservation and the environment. I wish I COULD think she was behind this Walking Bear thing. At least then I would know she's alive."

Edgar leaned closer in a gesture of support. "Let's think about this, everyone. If Oona ran off to terrorize the villagers, maybe Frieda followed to help. Maybe Agnes too. Maybe all three of them hatched this plan to get rid of the subdivision. It wouldn't have to be completely altruistic—certainly I can't see any self-sacrifice on Frieda's part. It could be that the greater the population of people, the fewer animals there will be, which would cut down on their hunting profits."

Alain spoke up, his slight French Canadian accent tinting his t-h's. "I think you could be right, Edgar. Perhaps Oona and Frieda had been friendlier in the last little while, but Oona did not tell you that, May. That might explain why she was a little cool and talking crazy things."

"If that's true, then at least she's alive," May said. "But why would they disappear? It makes them look pretty suspicious. They could've carried off this ruse by pretending they were out hunting. Or in Oona's case, she could just claim she was at home the whole time. Again, I just don't think it makes sense, even though I'd like it to."

We all sat quietly again, a little disappointed that our theory had huge holes.

"The Bahswaway gets searched tomorrow," Frances

reminded us. "If there is no sign of Oona or Frieda, then our theory is going to seem more plausible."

"What will you do if and when the pond is found empty, Edgar—which I fully expect it will be?" I asked.

"I'm going to call for a deeper search of the forest. We haven't even covered all the way up to the sacred caves. I'll have to get the Native Council to agree, but I think it will be acceptable."

"Will you take me with you, Edgar?" May asked.

Alain piped up, "Then it will have to include me as well."

Edgar thought a minute. "I don't see why not. There isn't a crime scene as of yet, so I can ask for any volunteers I want. And if we're right, and either Oona or Frieda or Agnes or all of them are involved in some way, they will be guilty of nuisance and not much more at this point. That is, as long as they didn't burn down the subdivision."

"Then count me and Emily in on the search," Langford said, to my delighted surprise.

"It will be good to have all of you there, just in case," May said, and we all knew what she meant—just in case something had happened to Oona. May was not to know for several days just how bad it could be.

*I wander through centuries made wise
with ancestral suffering*

Somewhere in the still and dark of the night, the man had been freed of his gag. Immediately, he had begun poisoning the air with his invective—sharp, filthy, demeaning words that made Frieda shudder with anger. She was fearful, tired, aching for Walking Bear's touch. The man's commanding, insulting voice filled her with disgust and hatred; she wished fervently that she could fling herself at him, claw at his eyes, punch his mouth into silence. Frieda knew the air inside their hideaway was laced with rage and hate, and that she was contributing to it. She tried to join the chanting of The Other, who seemed to be huddled somewhere to Frieda's right, but she knew she was missing some of the words, not concentrating enough, her heart not there; thus her energy was not strong.

Frieda could not be certain when she became aware that there were others present in the cave. Her eyes, still filled with the heat of her fever and pain, could not make out the lines clearly. But her nervous system told her the story in detail— her stomach rolled with shock, her heart pounded, her upper body twitched with fear. Mouth and throat dry, she was unable to call out as she saw Walking Bear swing around toward the silhouettes that loomed up in the recesses of the cave, their shadows thrown by the firelight so that they appeared even taller, the energy of their anger twisting their shadows into menacing specters that leaned into the space and overwhelmed their quarry.

Frieda heard Walking Bear's grunt, saw the strong shoulders fold, heard the sound of scraping and falling on the ground, heard the thunk of a kick or a club pounding into the prone figure.

The man's voice had been silenced, but an energy of expectation had replaced his fear and anger.

No longer could Frieda hear or see The Other; no longer did she care. Frieda's cry was one of grief, of devastation. Her saviour, her friend, her guide—crumpled on the ground writhing in pain, now silenced by the thud of those massive blows—Frieda's face dissolved in tears, her voice rang out in desolation.

Nooo. . .maîlingan. . .glottal. . .stop. . .

She rolled onto the ground, the pain of her injured leg searing up her right side, knocking thought from her head for a moment, sending tremors throughout her body. She continued to shriek and protest as she rolled toward Walking Bear. Once she was there, she forced her screaming body to its feet, rage propelling her upward, until she flung herself onto the back of one of the assailants, pummeling with her fists, screeching Ojibwa threats as loudly as her voice would carry.

The attacker stood up straight, away from Walking Bear, steely eyes turned toward her. Something bright flared and roared from the hand of the other attacker; she was flung backward against the hard earthen floor. The noise filled the cave again; smoke and light and a metallic odour overflowing, sucking out the air.

Frieda moaned and turned onto her side, hugging herself, shaken that the pain could actually be more ghastly than before. A thick, brackish liquid spurted from her stomach through her fingers. Frieda drew in a stunned, ragged breath, and swiftly, the pain shot through her side, her heart, her head. She moaned, but no sound issued forth. She lay still, the darkness filling her.

It was hushed and tranquil in the cave when she blinked her eyes open. Only a dripping sound emanated from the man; he lay on his stomach, his head twisted sideways. The Other was nowhere; the energy of her presence had dissipated.

Frieda saw Walking Bear, crumpled and destroyed, huddled in the corner. She had to touch that soft fur, stroke the head that had bent over her with healing and love, with unconditional forgiveness. Makwa . . . izhichige . . . Bear, I will show you I love you by my action, I will reach you, touch you, give you what you gave me, together our energy, our manidoo, will overcome.

Frieda snaked her way closer, then forced her body to sit up, close enough to touch the silky coat. Walking Bear's breath was low and shallow; the energy of Being was seeping out slowly. Frieda placed her hand on the brown, fur-covered back, feeling the movement. She allowed her energy to flow from inside herself out to her friend, her mentor, her saviour.

"Makwa, izhichige," she said, over and over, until she could feel the heart beating a little stronger, the breathing composed, the body subdued as it invited the healing to begin. "Our manidoo will overcome," Frieda said, her words hardly distinguishable in the silence of the cave.

XIII

We had actually forced ourselves onto other topics when Edgar's cell phone rang. A few brief words on his part and suddenly there was silence in the room.

Edgar looked at all of us and breathed deeply. "Well, that was good old Evan. It seems Victor Reeves' cell phone is not answering and he never checked into the Ottawa hotel he was heading to."

"What the hell?" I couldn't help the exclamation. "Another disappearance?"

"I'm not going to think that way yet," Edgar said, "but I suggest we get on home, old girl." He pulled an obviously exhausted Frances to her feet. "I have a feeling tomorrow is going to be a very long day."

After Frances and Edgar had gone, Langford and May and Alain and I adjourned to the kitchen, where we finished another bottle of wine along with a mountain of cheese and crackers and grapes. When I reflect back on that evening, I think of it in two ways: one, as an outlet for all our fears and musings and theories; and two, as the beginning of our real, solid relationship with the Reneaux. We hadn't yet come to the point where we could talk to them about our past, but if that evening had not developed the way it had, perhaps we would never have moved to that stage at all.

The next day dawned grey and wet and miserable, the kind that makes people want to hunker down under their blankets and forget about the world outside. The weather was not good news for the divers about to enter the pond, nor was it making the search for Oona and Frieda any easier. The only positive was that any residue from the subdivision fire had been completely wetted down overnight.

As a result of the rainy conditions and the early hour, the

umbrella'd group that gathered by Bahswaway that morning was small. Although the temperature was still unseasonably warm, the rain was cold and harsh, which only partly explained why we huddled so closely. Henry, Langford, May, Alain and I stood on the pond-side of the yellow tape, while several other villagers huddled under the trees a few feet away. Oona's sisters had not been able to face the ordeal and were waiting anxiously at home.

The two divers were young men, with the small waists and thick legs that you often see on professional swimmers. Their wet suits were already slick before they descended into the black water, their masks and tanks slowly sinking into oblivion before us. The crowd was silent. Only the pong of the rain drops on the tree trunks and hard ground could be heard and, occasionally, the faint squawk of some official's walky-talky.

I distracted myself from the shivers that began to play with the tiny hairs of my arms by scanning the faces around me. Henry Whitesand looked small and fragile; his usual proud stance had crumpled and he had suddenly become old. All his pain was etched into his face—his fear about what they might find in this icy black pool; the memories of his vibrant, determined sister, who had survived the tragic death of her husband and two children to end up as a cipher in the forest; the worry and anger about how his life in Burchill had been torn apart. I couldn't help but wonder if he had helped to start the fire in the subdivision, but right now all I felt for him was pity.

Barry Mills, Michael Lewis, and Edgar stood silently around the yellow tape, theoretically keeping people on the safe side of the barrier, although no one was really expected to attempt to cross it. They appeared solid and strong, but I knew the weight of these latest Burchill mysteries was heavy on their shoulders.

Steve and Ruth McEntyer stood side by side, their faces mostly covered by hoods and umbrellas. Margaret Johnston smiled wanly at me; Doc Murphy remained grim as befitting his medical role in the search. As I let my eyes and thoughts dwell on each one of the villagers, I realized again that I was slowly beginning to feel that I truly belong in this place.

The last face I searched was May's. Her eyes were huge and round, her broad face pinched and flushed. I leaned closer to her, clasping her hand in mine, and at that moment, the pond filled with bubbles and ripples and the divers surged to the surface. They conversed for a while with Edgar and the others, then suddenly they were gone again—the ice and scum closing over them like a lid. It seemed interminable before they were once more forcing their diving helmets above water, a large tarpaulin between them, obviously weighted down with something.

At the sight of their burden, Henry's legs wobbled, and Alain and Langford had to hold him up. A sharp keening rose from his lips, a sound so foreign from a human, yet so plaintive, that it made shivers of fear surge through me and tears of sympathy rush to my eyes.

We all seemed to lean forward, as if to get closer to the action.

Edgar held up his hand, signaling both for Henry to quiet down and for us to wait. After a few moments of searching through the tarp, which had been spread out too far for us to see, Doc Murphy straightened up and spoke to Edgar. It was only then that the big police chief lumbered toward the crowd, a serious but determined look on his face. When he reached Henry and May, he put an empathetic arm around the old man and a big hand on May's shoulder.

"It's okay. It's not Oona. It's not Frieda, either."

"How can you be so sure so quickly?" May asked, her voice trembling.

"Because most of them are very old bones and all of them are also very young," Edgar said, his voice almost a whisper. "We've found the bones of several children or even babies at the bottom of that well."

"The other legend..." May whispered to me and I knew what she was thinking: if the story of the children in the well was true, what were we to think about the tale of Walking Bear?

As we trudged back to our homes, gladdened by the thought that Oona and Frieda might still be alive somewhere, yet shocked at what had been discovered, we could not possibly know how entangled we would become in the mystery of those tiny bones, just a couple of years later.

XIV

I was barely able to tell that it was May's voice on the phone the next morning.

I had spent the rest of yesterday in a pleasant cocoon, wrapped up in my shawl, Angel at my feet, a fire lit to take away the dampness, and a great book to read. Every once in a while, Langford would come out of his studio and supply me with sustenance, like a giant cookie or a cup of hot chocolate. It was a decadent afternoon and evening, quiet and peaceful, and I felt very much rested.

Guiltily, I realized that I had not thought of Oona or anyone else but myself, whereas I could hear the pain and stress in my friend's voice. "Has anything happened, May?"

"No, and that's the real problem. I can't stand it any more, Em. I have to do something."

"But what can we do? Edgar is doing everything he can."

"I know," May interrupted, an impatience in her tone that I rarely ever heard. "But he's reluctant to go into the sacred grounds and search the caves. I think he should have done that long ago. I know the elders are protective of it, but this is ridiculous. What if Oona is injured and out there somewhere and we are letting her die?"

I left a short silence while May's quiet sobs drifted over the telephone line. "May," I said gently, "Edgar is planning to do a search. He said he would include us. It was just sensible to wait until they had searched the pond. I'm sure he'll call us, maybe even today."

I must admit here and now that I was used to my friend's compliant and easygoing nature, so her response, especially the ferocity of it, took me completely by surprise.

"Fine, Emily," she said, her tone cold and angry. "I'll go by myself." And then the line went dead.

For a moment I held the receiver in my hand, unable to move, listening as the telephone began to whine again, shocked that May would actually hang up on me. It was, however, the impetus that I needed, for suddenly I was no longer relaxed or sleepy; I flung on my clothes and headed out the door.

Although I didn't want to keep Langford out of the loop, I didn't want to spend too much time telling him what was happening either, so I stuck my head into his studio and told him May was really upset, and I was going over to her place, which was, in fact, part of the truth. Her desire to go to the sacred grounds was the part I didn't want to explain to him just now.

I jogged up Lakeview, across Lawrence, cut through Norval Lane, and was at the corner of Rideau and Julia before I realized I was completely out of breath. Leaning back with my hands on my hips, I panted for a few moments and looked up at the grey sky. In my panic, I hadn't realized the wind was so strong, hadn't appreciated the fact that the air smelled of spring, and the darker morning clouds were being dispersed to make way for sunshine. I also hadn't realized that a few weeks had gone by since I'd last jogged. I was sweating and my legs were screaming at me, even though I'd only gone a short distance.

Once my breath was under control, I walked briskly to number seven and mounted the steps of the porch just as May pulled the front door open. When she saw me, she dropped the backpack and toolbox she was carrying and dissolved into tears. I folded her shaking form in a huge hug and we stood there for a few moments while she clung to me, her grief and despair flooding through her. I kept saying softly, it's okay, it's okay, but I knew it really wasn't.

Eventually we sat on the porch chairs, neither of us

minding the winter dust that still clung to them. I held May's hands in mine, as if afraid she would fly away if I let go.

"May, I'm not going to try to talk you out of this. You have to do it," I said, and her tear-filled eyes brightened with gratitude. "If you don't, I'm so afraid you're going to have a breakdown or something. I just want to talk you into going to see Edgar and asking him to come with us."

May sniffed and actually wiped her face on her coat sleeve. "Okay," she said in a small voice, so immediately that I was taken aback, having put several arguments together in my head. "I'm so sorry, Emily, I don't know what's wrong with me."

She started to cry again, so I pulled several crumpled—but clean—tissues from my pocket, trying to save her coat from more damage.

"I do," I said. "You're suffering from shock. You haven't been able to grieve and so much has happened in such a short time. Oona's so close to you it's like losing your mom all over again. Edgar will come with us. I know he will."

I convinced May to freshen up and change her jacket to a lighter (and, I didn't mention, cleaner) one and we headed out to see Chief Superintendent Edgar Brennan.

Small towns in Ontario are policed by a detachment of the Ontario Provincial Police services. A couple of years ago, due to the increase in traffic on the provincial highway surrounding Burchill, not to mention the large influx of tourists, our little detachment had become a regional headquarters. Edgar had been promoted to regional commander and Frances had been hired as one of four detectives assigned to Burchill's station.

The other three detectives lived in the small towns to the north and west of Burchill, so although we would see their vehicles patrolling the area and meet them in the street, we had not gotten to know any of them as well as we now knew Frances. Edgar was thrilled with the help—covering Burchill and Sahsejewon, plus the provincial park and the canals filled with tourist boats, had become more and more difficult to do thoroughly. But he also had more responsibility and was actually less free than before.

The Burchill Regional Headquarters is a fancy name for a very small office at the corner of Lawrence and Main Street (also known as Provincial Highway 54). The station, like a lot of places in Burchill, is old but refurbished, a tall, brick structure that was once a granary and is now split into two narrow, three-storey buildings. The other half has been converted into Robin's Nest, one of those fancy tourist boutiques that sells cute little knickknacks and antiques side by side.

Edgar's office was now on the second floor, somewhat away from the action; he says it is designed to keep him from being curious about what's going on outside and focused on all the paperwork that has been expected of him in the new position.

I didn't share my misgivings with May that he might not be able to get away. As we got closer to Main Street, I also did not share my discomfort at going to the station. I had not been there since being questioned by the Ottawa contingent—one of whom was, at the time, a stranger, Frances Petapiece—two years ago.

In the past, I would often persuade myself that I have left all my old fears far behind. Lately, however, I have to admit that I am still haunted. As I approached the Burchill Regional headquarters, as we swung the door inward to face the counter I had stood fearfully in front of just a few months before, I was suddenly transported all the way back to Vancouver, all the way back to Langford and the bars that separated us. I shivered and swallowed, struggling to hide my reaction from May, who has become very adept at reading my face. But I didn't have to worry this time; my friend was too preoccupied with her own fears and tensions to even look in my direction.

The constable behind the counter was Martin Michano, one of the new additions to the headquarters. Martin is half native and half French descent, but the French features have won out—he has a reddish tinge to his shortly cropped brown hair, his eyes are a deep blue, and his face is thin, ending in a long dimpled chin. There is something very attractive about Marty; perhaps it's his grin and the sparkle that reaches his eyes every time he says hello.

I was impressed that he knew our names, too, even though he had only met us a few times. Perhaps that is an advantage of being the school principal, or maybe Martin Michano is just good at names. I felt better immediately after his cheerful, warm greeting.

When we explained that we wanted to see Edgar, he didn't question that at all; he lifted the intercom phone and almost immediately, we were invited to go on up the stairs. The steps creaked under our combined weight, reminding us that this building, despite its modern facelift, was still old.

We found Edgar behind his desk, signing what looked like a stack of parking tickets. When he stood, smiling warmly at us, May started to cry again. Finding my voice surprisingly calm and strong, I explained what we wanted to do.

Edgar drummed his fingers on the desk, not meeting our eyes for a moment. It took him less time than I thought it would. "Let's do it," he said, amazing both May and me. "I'll talk to Chief Dan, but I know he won't have any problem with it because you're going, May. And he respects our school principal here, too; go figure."

I wrinkled my nose at him but our attempt at humour didn't help.

"Can we go today?" May asked, her eyes still brimming over with tears. "I just have this—I can't explain it, but I have a terrible feeling. . ." She crumpled into sobs again.

Edgar put his arm around her shoulders. "We probably should have gone before this. I kept hoping they would turn up and say they'd been on a hunting expedition. I just can't imagine that they're hiding out in the sacred caves. Even Agnes Lake can't be there—she has never gone there on a Vision Quest, according to Chief Dan, even when she has been on quests longer than this. But it's been nearly a month, and I think it was a mistake waiting so long." When May started to protest, he shook his head. "No, I'm not saying that to get sympathy. I've been thinking for a while that we've been too certain that they would not go to the sacred ground. Sorry, May, but Oona had been acting strangely before she left..."

"I know, I even said that myself," May inserted.

"...and Frieda, well, she's an odd duck to begin with. So who knows? And now with no sign of Victor Reeves..."

Both May and I exclaimed "What?" at the same time. I had not given Victor Reeves another thought since Sunday's fire and, with the search of the pond and my self-imposed retreat, I hadn't heard a thing from anyone else, either.

Edgar explained. "After the fire, as you know, we tried getting in touch with him. It seems Evan Fobert hadn't seen him in a couple of days, or so he says. Victor was supposed to be heading to Ottawa to be at a meeting, which he reportedly said he needed time to prepare for. He hadn't specified about when he'd be going, so Fobert claims he thought nothing of the fact that Reeves didn't show up for dinner etcetera. Sounds pretty fishy to me, though."

I was sure Frances would not approve of Edgar's

negativity, but I personally agreed with him where Evan Fobert was concerned. "Sounds very weird," I said. "In fact, everything seems pretty weird at this moment. But what could Victor Reeves have in common with Oona and Frieda—and maybe even Agnes—to have someone kidnap them all?"

"There might not be a connection at all. Maybe the subdivision fire and Victor are completely separate from Oona and Frieda's absences. Maybe Victor has just gotten pissed off and is on a business trip—maybe the women are hunting. But we won't know anything sitting around here." Edgar stood up and grabbed his coat. "Let's go see Chief Dan."

Which is how, about two hours later, just as the noon sun swept away the rest of the clouds and beamed down from above, May, Edgar, Alain, Langford and I set out along Lakeview Road in Edgar's jeep. May and I had not even tried to convince Langford and Alain to stay behind, nor had Chief Dan seemed the least bit perturbed that all these extra people were going to advance on the caves. I could tell when he looked into May's tortured eyes that he was willing to agree to almost anything that might help solve the mystery. At any rate, he had immediately gotten the blessing from the remainder of the Native Council, which made Edgar feel much better. Although legally he'd have the right to search the area, Edgar Brennan was Burchill born.

We parked the car in the provincial park on the other side of Ogeechee Lake. From here, it would be a hike of about four hours before we reached the cliffs near the sacred caves. As I shifted my back pack, I hoped for at least two things: one, that my physical condition was still up to the trek; and two, that the weather would continue the sun-filled, warming trend it had been following all morning. I didn't dare think further ahead than that. We all knew that it would take most of the day to get to the caves; we were all aware of the small tents and sleeping bags that we had rolled into the packs on our shoulders. But the idea of spending the night inside the forest was not one I had yet allowed to sink in.

The first two hours of the hike were straight through the forest on flat land. This was largely untraversed territory; not many ventured this far east of Ogeechee, as most people used the many hiking trails that had been provided by the province and the Native Council. Single file, we hacked our way through the brush, Alain in the lead, swinging his scythe and expertly slicing through the vines that might entangle our feet. Despite his efforts, I found myself tripping fairly often, forcing me to keep my head down to watch my boots as they squished through the barely unfrozen ground.

We tramped along in silence, our bodies slowly becoming used to the high stepping walk that we had to adopt. The distant hum of the highway gradually gave way to birds busying themselves with the signs of early spring; rustles in the distance as animals scampered out of the way of our noisy march; the soughing of the breeze through the brittle limbs of trees. Soon I was engulfed in my new surroundings; away from the noise of the town, focused only on our progress forward.

We stopped in a clearing after about two hours of walking, guzzled down more water, ate energy bars, and met the "call of nature" in our own private tree-sheltered stalls. Covered in perspiration and each with our private fears about what lay ahead, we didn't talk very much.

Langford enwrapped me in an encouraging hug and gave me one of his lingering looks that still, after all these years, can send shivers down my back. I smiled up at him, thinking about everything we have been through together, and wondering what experience would meet us in this unknown part of the forest.

Back in the line, tramping once more through the woods, Langford kept grabbing me from in front, making me laugh until I begged him to stop. Our laughter seemed to loosen everyone up, though, and from then on there were calls back and forth to each other, mostly designed to make all of us giggle. We kept this up, more or less, for two long hours, over land that began to elevate slightly with every step, until suddenly we reached the ridge that overlooked the sacred caves.

The sight of the land ahead silenced us and sent the smiles scurrying away from our faces. We were standing on the edge of a cliff that sloped at a forty-five degree angle away from our feet. But it was not the distance below that caught our eyes first.

XV

Rising above us, about thirty metres high, a wall of rock fanned out in front of us, its ridges and lines shaped into five long fingers, spread and pointing upward. The hand displayed small dark openings, as though the giant rock held a string of marbles across its palm. The light breeze became a wind here, pummeling us from above, tugging at our hair and coats, flinging small bits of dirt at our faces. There was a deep silence; no birds sang, no animals scurried. In spite of the breeze here on the cliff, the other side, where dots of bushes stuck out of the rock face, was frozen and still. No leaf stirred; no squirrel awoke to scold us for disturbing the winter sleep.

The silence roared in my ears, making me feel dizzy. I could hear Langford's deep intake of breath, and sought his hand for comfort. He quickly wrapped his arm around me, as if sensing my imbalance.

It was May who broke the silence. With a sudden, swift movement, she turned sideways and began to crab-walk down the slope. The ground was still damp and slightly frozen, so her footsteps were sure and solid. Edgar and Alain soon followed; Langford and I brought up the rear. No one spoke as we slowly descended the incline, our progress impeded by bushes and vines, our feet carefully ensuring we were anchored before proceeding. A few times I could feel myself slipping and my breath stopped, but Langford was always just slightly below me, his arms ready to halt my fall. The descent seemed to take hours. Heads down, scrambling sideways, clutching and releasing, slipping and regaining purchase, we zigzagged our way through the bushes and stumps and vines that snaked through the trees.

Finally, one by one, we tumbled onto the graveled surface

of the old riverbed. Looking back up at the steep grade we had just traversed, I had a sudden fear of never being able to get out of that valley again. We stood there picking off the debris and mud that clung to our pants and boots, staring around and at each other.

No wonder it was forbidden to come here; suddenly it appeared to me to be a trap. I could tell by the frowns and silence from the others that everyone was feeling much the same way. Again it was May who spoke first.

"This was once a riverbed," she told us, taking on the role of teacher. "Years ago, it would have been covered in muddy water every spring. That's why there are so many small boulders and pieces of rock strewn about. Be careful where you step. The hill that we just came down was something Oona called a terminal moraine."

We all nodded in silence, as if we had come here expressly to learn geography. Encouraged by our attention, May continued.

"See how it slopes up again over here." This time she pivoted in the direction of the rock face. "This section of the cliff made a perfect place to dig caves, because the water couldn't reach the entrances. It's also hard to climb, so that ensured safety, too, from animals and other enemies." Her voice had taken on a childlike quality, and I realized suddenly that she was repeating information her aunt had shared with her when she was a child. I wondered whether May had been to the sacred caves since she had become an adult.

We all gazed upward at the ridge that preceded the ascent to the caves. Although the angle was not steep, the incline was flat, shiny rock. This was the Canadian Shield, a solid core of the most ancient rock on the planet. The combination of granite and gneiss covers most of Ontario and quite a large portion of the Canadian landscape. The portions that seemed to shine were the streaks of hard crystalline minerals glinting in the sun.

"I know a secret passageway, though, that we can use to get up there."

Obediently, as though we were her sedate pupils, the group of us turned in the same direction and followed May along the ancient riverbed. It was more difficult to walk here than we'd imagined, just as May had warned; fist-sized rocks and pointed pebbles continually turned under our feet, causing us to sway and, often, nearly stumble. We walked single file, our arms and hands out to steady from behind, concentrating on the task of walking, listening to the wind whip overhead and dash off into the forest.

The silence down in this enclave made my flesh crawl with goose bumps. I knew for certain that we should not be here.

When May turned toward the rock face, I at first thought she was planning to go back where we'd come from. I couldn't believe she was headed for the gnarl of bushes and branches that appeared at the edge of the cliff. When I looked to my right, I could see the beginning of the woods and the end of the riverbed clearing. This forest was similar to the one we'd come through; but here it was extremely thick, a tangled mixture of evergreen, brush and deciduous, all climbing on top of each other to reach the sunlight. The result was a mass of vegetation that seemed dark and impenetrable.

To our surprise, May parted the bushes and branches to reveal a yawning cave. The odour of dampness and mould, along with a bitter cold, reached out and slapped at us.

"It's very dark in here," May said, her voice echoing back to the group. "Every one of us must keep our flashlights on. Stay close."

I was not happy about going into this cave, I must admit. Even though I trust May completely, the thought of entering this wet darkness was daunting. When we filed into the musty opening, my fears were not assuaged – the walls of the cave almost brushed against our shoulders and we had to lean over, hands on knees, to avoid striking our heads on the roof. The only thing visible was the small circle of light in front of our feet, pinpointing the black, wet rock beneath us. No one spoke.

I began to focus my mind on other things – on Langford, on May, on her Aunt Oona. I imagined myself and May at the edge of the lake, a beautiful fire blazing, while Oona wove her tales about native lore and sang in a soft, melodic voice. I imagined Langford and me, sitting on our balcony at home, the waves lapping at the shore, sipping a Canadian merlot, the setting sun spraying orange over the water; anything but the dank, dark, fetid air around me and the cold, moist walls pressing in on my arms and head.

This path inside the mountain led straight up, although it was a gentle slope for most of the way. Once in a while we had to bend our knees even further and duck-walk through the narrow passageway. To this day, I cannot tell you how I made that slow, torturous journey – every now and then a claustrophobic feeling threatened to overtake me; I would lose my breath and then feel Langford's steadying presence behind me. Once again I would plunge back into my imagination, assisted by the sensation of being almost blind in the dark, with only a spot of light to guide our footsteps.

It seemed to take a very long time before we began to climb further and slowly realize that we could stand upright. A small flash of light ahead soon became a large circle of day. With a rush of relief, we found ourselves standing in a small cave with a mouth that yawned into the sun.

We were now standing opposite to and slightly below the ridge from which we had gazed at these caves some time ago.

It was a strange sensation to look down into the riverbed and up at the forested ridge and realize the sun was still shining and not that much time had elapsed. It was about four o'clock in the afternoon and the sun was hovering over the trees into our eyes.

Edgar stepped to the cave entrance and took his cell phone out of his pocket, glancing at its face intently. We are fortunate in Burchill; the proximity of Canada's capital city results in more communication towers than a town our size would normally warrant. We were also lucky that Edgar's phone had been specially equipped and should be powerful enough to pick up the signal even from this hidden valley.

"I can get a signal if I stand right at the edge," he confirmed, sounding satisfied and happy. "We'll have to spend the night here, though, don't you think, May?"

She nodded, shifting her backpack and letting it fall to the floor of the cave. "Definitely. I don't think we're going to want to take the chance of hiking back through the forest in the dark. And don't worry; there's a way to scramble down without going through the cave again. It's almost impossible to go up, but we can swing down on the ropes." May looked at my face and laughed for the first time in ages. "It'll be okay, Em, really."

Everyone snickered at my expense then, letting their packs fall, stretching and taking deep breaths of the fresh air at the mouth of the cave. Langford kneaded my shoulders and kissed my cheek. I guessed that I must've looked as scared and shaken as I felt.

"This is a good cave for our little encampment, though," Alain said. "It's dry; there's an escape route, not that we'll need it, of course; no animals can get to it from the mouth."

"You're not making me feel any better," I told him.

We spent the next few minutes arranging our packs,

sipping water, munching on energy bars once more, and stretching our bodies for the next leg of the journey, whatever that may be. As soon as May was ready, she began to outline what we had to do next.

"At the back of this cave, there's a sort of rock hallway that leads to the next, and so on, all the way along," she said, pointing in the direction of the rear of the cavern. "We can search all the caves in a fairly short time, although there are some in behind as well. Let's just hope we don't have to go through them, too."

But, I thought, what would we find that would make us not have to search further? Of course, I didn't voice my question.

"Let's go then," Edgar said, his voice betraying impatience and nervousness. He shifted his pack, emptied of sleeping bag, but full just the same, onto his back once more.

May dug in her own backpack and came up with a black bag, which she handed to Alain. Feeling my eyes on her, she looked up and said, "Doc Murphy gave me some stuff. Just in case." Later, I was to marvel at how accurate May's premonition had been.

Alain, Langford and I left our packs behind. We reverted to single file again and stepped from our little grotto into the next cave. This one was larger and damper than the first; huge stalactites dripped from the ceiling. A bird had abandoned a nest on a ledge just by the mouth of the chamber. Someone long ago had sat around a fire here; the embers had charred and drifted into ash mixed with rusty water. Several small rocks were placed in a circle around the remains. The odour was musty and unpleasant. The next cave was small and barely fit the five of us even without our packs. It, too, had been the scene of a fire.

By the time we reached the tenth cave, we had become

accustomed to the same scenery – the remains of fires, bird nests, animal droppings now and then, a fusty smell in the air; the only difference being size in the cavern itself and its opening to the sky. Thus we were utterly unprepared for the sight that met us when we stepped into the eleventh cave.

XVI

This chamber was high and much larger than the others, yet its opening was narrow and let in very little light. Already the sun had dipped slightly behind the trees, so the view was shadowy and dusky.

The odour of mildew and mould had been replaced with something that left a metallic taste in my mouth. It was mixed with feces and vomit and other smells that I could not name. My stomach rolled as my eyes adjusted to the dimness and my mind registered what lay before us.

Two bodies were in the cavern, one to the right of us and one propped up against the wall to the left. Their pasty skin made them look like marble, stiff and inhuman. Blood had poured down the slight incline at their feet and coagulated in a sludge pool. I am thankful to this day that the lighting was so poor; the nightmares afterward would have been even worse.

Their eyes are what haunt me the most – the glassy stare, the filming over, the absence of light and movement and spirit. And most especially, the moment when one of them blinked.

May and Edgar moved swiftly. Frieda was barely breathing, her eyes blinking slowly, as if she were struggling to retain life, a gaping hole in her side. She licked her lips, moaning softly.

"Who did this to you?" May's cry was indignant, angry.

"Walking Bear," she said clearly, plaintively, a lilting tinge to her words, as though she were singing the name. There was one rattling gasp, her chest heaved upward, and then Frieda Roote died.

Edgar turned and hovered over the other body, lying still and prone on the earthen floor, but it was clear that Victor

Reeves was beyond assistance; a round hole in his head spread death and destruction on the wall behind him.

"Look – what's that?" I must admit my voice quavered, with fear and shock, as I pointed at an object close to Frieda's side. Her outstretched arm seemed to be reaching toward it.

Though shrouded in the light and dark that strained very thinly through the narrow opening of the cave, the round curve of the shoulders within the heap of fur and feather gave a clear indication that this mound was real; it was animal, alive or dead.

Everyone turned. Edgar, his gun trained in its direction, crept slowly toward the object. When he knelt by its side and said loudly, "It – he – is still alive, but barely", we all moved forward as though mesmerized.

The bear's head was face down on the cave floor; its fur was matted with blood.

"It looks like it's been beaten and then shot," Edgar said. With his foot, he kicked an object away from the body. To my dismay, I could see clearly that it was a gun. He began to turn the body over.

We all gazed in horror as the fur-covered object became someone we all knew and loved.

"Oona," May groaned, dropping on her knees, too, beside her aunt.

The large headdress had fallen to the side, exposing Oona's grey, taut face. Cleverly stitched and created, the diadem was designed to sit on its human's head, the fur and feathers hiding the face from the onlooker, yet allowing for sight from within. The bear's head was formidable, its jaws slightly open as though the animal were still capable of a threatening growl. The dead eyes glittered as if with anger and ferocity rather than marble. Oona's body was covered with fur and feathers, her hands wrapped in gloves that resembled paws, her boots encircled with what looked like real claws. It was a frightening, incredible sight – Walking Bear, the stuff of nightmares and legends – reduced to a costume in the stark light that filtered into the cave.

Oona moaned and her body quivered. May became at once solicitous and professional – she began to peel away the layers that covered her aunt, exposing cuts and bruises and a dark hole that belied the devastating track of a bullet with its smallness. Kneeling, I tried to assist May as she dressed Oona's wounds and covered her in the warmth of the emergency blanket. We were even able to coax a small amount of water between Oona's parched lips, although her eyes never fluttered nor opened even a fraction.

In the meantime, Langford and Alain set up small flares to lighten the gloom. They discovered a long, wide shelf that had been used as a bed of some sort; there were small pots and bottles, sage and other scented twigs stacked neatly on the natural shelves of the rock outcroppings. A fire had been recently tended here. The cavern looked like the scene of some ancient ritual.

Edgar disappeared into the adjoining cave to lean out of the opening with his cell phone.

Chief Dan Mahdahbee was able to arrange for a native helicopter pilot who would bring emergency workers into the riverbed area. They'd prep Oona and then take her to Ottawa General Hospital. He was attempting to get another helicopter to lift the search party out as well.

When I heard that rescue might be available only for Oona, I admit to being selfishly very nervous that we might have to spend the night in the caves after all, with dead bodies only a short distance away.

While we awaited word from Chief Dan about what might transpire, Langford and I sat in the next cave; Edgar, May and

Alain stayed at Oona's side. Langford and I huddled together in the mouth of the cave, the cell phone held out to catch the signal. We didn't speak, too shaken and shocked to put thought into word. But my mind raced, back and forth, mostly asking why.

Why would Oona do this? How could she kill Frieda, someone she had once loved and nurtured? How could she allow herself to murder Victor Reeves, whom she barely knew, even if he was responsible for the subdivision? It seemed so against reason, against her faith and beliefs, against everything Oona had ever stood for. Why would she dress as Walking Bear to frighten the village? Had Oona lost her mind while none of us noticed? I thought of May's reflections on how strangely her aunt had behaved in the weeks before her disappearance, but I'm certain that May had not suspected the seriousness of her disintegration, or May would've acted. Or Henry or any of Oona's sisters. Someone would have helped her, wouldn't they have?

Or was someone else responsible? And if so, where were they? Why had Frieda claimed, with her dying breath, that the crime was the act of Walking Bear, when the impersonator was, in fact, Oona? Who had beaten and shot Oona? Was it Frieda or Victor who had retaliated and then lost their lives anyway? I figuratively shook my head several times, trying to make sense of my thought patterns and the experience we'd just had. It was so unbelievable, so strange, so eerie. I was having trouble breathing from time to time and tried to focus on the trees, the riverbed, the soft hairs on Langford's hand, the cell phone.

When the call came through, it was as though the lifeline had already been flung from the helicopter to rescue us. Langford was told that Chief Dan's native pilot had been able to secure an army helicopter big enough to carry all of us out, even the deceased. At the landing strip near Burchill, Oona would be transferred to an air ambulance, while the remainder of us would be sent home. Langford and I grasped each other with relief and then went to tell the others.

As we waited for the emergency teams, Langford and Alain made their way back through the caves to retrieve as many packs as they could carry, while Edgar performed his crime scene ministrations and May and I tended Oona.

I should not have been surprised that Edgar had come so prepared, but I was; as a result, I watched his movements with awe. He photographed the scene – a picture of Frieda's body against the wall, stiffening with recent death, blood all over her stomach and thighs, her leg wrapped in enormous poultices and bindings, her face pasty and china-like in the gloom – a picture of Victor Reeves, crumpled on the ground, a flattened paper doll, the blood a thick sea of brown – a picture of the gun, impossibly shiny and violent and frightening even though a hand no longer held it in anger or threat – a picture of the bed where someone had recently lain – a picture of the bear head that had a short time ago perched on Oona's broad, strong shoulders; shoulders which were now another photograph – not of strength and pride but of pain and injury, bloody and crumpled – a picture of the detritus of ritual that appeared empty without the direction of the faithful.

Edgar patiently and meticulously bagged any specimens that he found and obviously deemed to be evidence. When Alain and Langford returned from the first cave, Edgar mercifully covered the bodies with our blankets.

It was completely black outside when we finally heard the loud whirring sounds of the helicopter. The only area the pilot could land in was a couple of kilometres down the riverbed, where the valley opened into an ancient pond that was now parched and bereft of vegetation.

Alain and Langford had retraced our steps through the caves via the tunnel to set up vigil. Now, below us, they stood silhouetted in the fire they'd built and the flares they'd placed all around.

Three people arrived in the cool of the night, just as Edgar, May and I had finished eating our sandwiches and drinking hot coffee from our thermoses. We were feeling somewhat better, but far from comfortable, as we listened to Oona's soft moans and delirious mumbling, none of which was intelligible.

Soon the clang of ropes and hooks filled the cave, as Edgar and I scrambled to secure the ascent of the rescue team up into the cave next to this one. The native pilot was able to nimbly scale the side of the cliff, hand over hand up the rope, like a person half his size.

His sheer mass, the strong, wide shoulders, pleasant round face, huge and capable hands, all served to give comfort and security. "I'm Philip," he announced. "You'll be out of here soon, don't worry."

I felt tears in the back of my eyes and realized suddenly that the shock was deeper than I'd imagined.

Edgar directed Philip to Oona and he was soon a huge presence in the cave of death. They conferred about how to best get her down. It was decided that she should be lowered on a stretcher. By this time, another paramedic had reached the mouth of the cave, helped over the lip by Langford. She was a small, nimble person who exuded confidence and efficiency. She immediately went to Oona, and with May's assistance, began to prepare her for the transfer.

Without realizing it, I had stepped back into the recesses of the cave, trying to allow room for everyone to do their work. When my boot connected with something foreign underfoot, I yelped and leapt back. My flashlight outlined a straight, flat object made of wood and bark, bound tightly together with some kind of leather.

"Look at this," I said loudly, to cover my embarrassment at squealing with fear.

Philip and Edgar came back to join me, and Philip's face broke into a smile.

"This is far better than any stretcher we brought with us," he said. "It's obviously been constructed by a native who knew the old ways."

So in the end, Oona was lowered carefully on ropes and hooks on a device that had been used by her ancestors for centuries. Hand-over-hand, reminding me of my high school days and the climbing ropes in the gym, I went down the rope after May, where Alain, Langford and the helicopter pilot swung us safely to the ground. Next, one by one, tied to the modern stretcher, came the bodies, wrapped and still, looking dark and sad in the moonlight. As much of the equipment and backpacks as could be strapped to the stretcher and the native sled were lowered, then finally Edgar, Phillip and the paramedic lowered themselves quickly and nimbly to the ground.

The helicopter was a huge, old-fashioned green bug with an enormous belly. Inside, Oona was soon hooked up to intravenous and sedated to calm her unconscious ramblings and moaning. The bodies had been placed somewhere below.

Although it was not crowded in our section, the four of us – Alain, May, Langford and I – huddled together in one corner, mostly silent. It seemed to take no time at all before the monstrous machine shuddered to a halt on the ground and everyone appeared to be running from or toward a smaller, more compact helicopter that sat waiting in the night.

Oona was carried carefully and swiftly to the air ambulance. May hugged all of us briefly, kissed Alain, and suddenly she was gone. We watched as the helicopter lifted and, pointing its beam of light, struck off for Ottawa.

XVII

I was sound asleep when I heard the noise below. I tried to awaken Langford, but he was too far away and I couldn't reach him. I lay there, my heart pounding, sweat seeping down the small of my back, wondering why the bed was so enormous, why I couldn't reach him, why those bars were there.

Suddenly the bedroom door swung open and I sat straight up. The creature in front of me was pale and trembling; rivers of blood poured from its gigantic head; bits of tissue and brain and white bone stuck to its face and hands, which were held out toward me.

"I know who you are," it said, the intonation low and growling, close to my ear.

Finally, I found my voice and screamed. Langford turned toward me with a jolt and put his hand on my cheek.

"Honey, honey ... Emily ... it's okay, you're just dreaming."

I opened my eyes in the darkness and the relief streamed through me. I kicked off the blanket to let the air cool my perspiration. Angel placed her paws on the side of the bed and licked my face gently.

"Thank God for that," I was able to say at last, my trembling beginning to subside.

I rolled over and snuggled under Langford's soft, warm arm, against the silky hairs of his chest, listening to the quiet thud of his heart. At my back, Angel leaped gracefully onto the bed and cuddled against me. Beginning to relax in the comfort of both my husband and my little dog, I finally fell asleep once more.

When I am faced with a problem that I cannot solve, I often resort to making a list, sometimes pros and cons, sometimes a simple recording of events. The next day, still exhausted and worried, while May remained in the hospital with an unconscious Oona and Langford retreated to his studio to debrief in his own way, I wrote my inventory.

I began with listing the occurrences and ended up with several journal style entries. From the moment of Oona's disappearance, followed immediately by Frieda, to the appearances of Walking Bear, the fire in the subdivision, the vanishing of Victor Reeves – I wrote it all down from my perspective. Then I went back and started to pull out various details for which I had questions.

The first one glared out at me as something I hadn't thought very much about. Why did Oona race around the tree twenty times before heading for the forest?

This bizarre behaviour has to be connected to the rest of it, I thought; Oona had to have made them deliberately, for a reason. These circles were a message to someone. All the rest had followed from that one obscure communication. What could it have meant? And Walking Bear – had Oona resurrected the legend because she wanted to teach Frieda and Victor a lesson? If so, why had she murdered them? I thought back to May's discourse on the Ojibwa legends that her Aunt Oona had taught her.

The white man had come and interfered with the natural way; they'd taught the natives.greed for things outside of the land and the spirit. Greed had led to the wanton slaughter of the animals and the desecration of the forests. Nanna Bijou's lack of leadership had caused him to be punished for the sins of his followers. Manitou proclaimed that he should have known what was happening, that if his guidance had been effective, he would have known about their transgressions.

I smiled to myself, thinking that Manitou had been talking about "management by walking around" all those years ago.

Instead of patrolling and directing, Nanna Bijou had been one of those leaders who spent all of his time "contemplating" inside his "office".

Thus had Walking Bear been formed—half man, half beast —roaming the countryside searching for those who did not conserve or respect the environment. May had said, "Nanna Bijou, now known as Walking Bear, is said to appear to those who hunt too much or pollute the land. He metes out various punishments, depending on the severity of the transgression." Is that what Oona had been doing? Had she considered Frieda and Victor's sins to be so severe as to warrant their death?

However, there were many legends about the Bear Clan that I had no inkling about, I mused, a little frustrated. How did I know there wasn't another one that fit this scenario better? What was it May had said? There were at least twenty...

And of course, that's when it hit me—twenty legends, twenty times around the tree. Did it mean anything, and if so, what?

I couldn't ask May; she was keeping vigil at Oona's side. Agnes Lake, the only other expert that I knew, was still missing, or, more hopefully, on her Vision Quest. The town and the surrounding forest were by now no doubt filled with crime scene investigators and perhaps even reporters. I knew that the Native Council was going to be heavily involved with the case, to ensure respect for the sacred grounds, and yet to be supportive of discovering the truth. Therefore there was literally no one I could ask.

Then I remembered Peter Smallwood – during the various searches, he had claimed to be steeped in native lore, as he told it, from following his friends in childhood.

I dressed for whatever weather was flung at me that day—

layers that could be peeled off in warmth or kept on in cold. After going out to the studio to speak with Langford, I headed off to the Smallwoods'. I walked swiftly around the corner and over the bridge to Lawrence. The street was pretty deserted; I surmised that everyone was either off to work or gone away to some warmer climate. A few of the children from Burchill Public passed by, probably on the way to Main Street and the various stores filled with goodies.

I turned right at Drummond Street and walked swiftly toward John. By the time I reached the corner, and the Smallwood place, I had peeled off my outer jacket, my hat, and my gloves. The sun continued to melt any leftover snow and the scent of spring was very strong.

Peter and Ellie's house is similar to many of the homes in Burchill, except for the colour of the brick—alternating red and yellow—and several smaller windows along the front and beside the front door. There the similarity ended. The house, placed as it is on the corner of Drummond and John, has an unusually large yard, both at the sides of the house, and at the rear. The Smallwoods have planted a huge number of shrubs and trees, some of which have grown very tall and expansive over the years. Thus their little place looks dwarfed and crowded.

As I went up the steps, one of the branches of a maple tree brushed my shoulder, almost in a welcoming embrace. I reached over to touch the spot and came away with an annoying, sticky patch on my fingers. Sap. This certainly had been an odd winter and now spring. The sap was beginning to run already; some of the trees even sprouted tentative blooms. Yet March Break was not even over and some of the ground still crunched from last week's freakish storm.

In British Columbia, we had gotten used to rain and more rain and cloud, but here in Ontario, there could be every kind of weather imaginable all at once. This winter had been particularly odd and different. This climate was, I thought, so much more interesting and invigorating.

Peter and Ellie's house was completely dark and no one answered my insistent bell ringing. They are both retired, and I knew that they have many interests and often go on day trips together, so I wasn't totally surprised that they were not home. I stood at the end of their walk, staring off into the tangle of their crowded yard. Despite the fact that the trees were mostly leafless, the branches were so intertwined that it looked like a jungle. I reached out and touched a thick, twisted stem that stretched out and flung itself over the branches of a maple, as though choking it. Wondering what kind of plant or tree this was, I rubbed my thumb absently over one of the little nubs that resembled a stunted finger.

I was disappointed and dispirited by my lack of ability to gain the information I wanted, until I suddenly recalled the museum, which is located on Main Street just outside the reserve. I walked quickly, half jogging, reminding myself that I hadn't been keeping up with my exercise lately. I was huffing and puffing pretty heavily by the time I reached the museum and had to remove another layer of clothing. Luckily, the little brick building was alight and the door was ajar in welcome.

The curator is almost as interesting as the collection he's amassed within. His native name is Soaring Bird, so most people just call him Bird. His face is alive with curiosity – his eyes are bright and wide and his aquiline nose and unguarded features make him a handsome man. Bird is what we might have called a "nerd" in the past; he is so wholly steeped in the museum and the history of Burchill that he appears to be disassociated from the present. His speech is infused with curious expressions, stiff formal phrases mixed with slang, and he speaks at such staccato speed that you might think he has an accent. Perhaps it is the daily use of the Ojibwa language of the past that gives him a more difficult time switching to English, which is actually his "birth" tongue.

Bird greeted me with a hearty handshake, delighted to see me, perhaps because I was the only person in the museum, but also because we'd had so many good connections through arranging visits for the school children.

When I told him what I wanted, he was intrigued, but true to form, he didn't ask too many questions. He brought out a huge old book; its leather binding had been softened with care over the years and its delicate pages were filled with calligraphic writing, as well as beautiful sketches scattered here and there, presumably to emphasize or explain.

Bird sat me down in a comfortable chair at his little desk, with good lighting and a cool drink beside me. "My dad wrote this," he said proudly. "He was determined to preserve the stories that his father and grandfather told about our people. Man, our language is such a tangle of dialects! We arrived in this area many moons ago and then took up all the words into our own. Pop was afraid the tales would be lost to the next generations. So he wrote it in Ojibwa and in English. He was a very well educated man."

I ran my fingers lovingly over the soft leather and opened the book. It was well organized, with a table of contents, an introduction, and a dedication to the Ojibwa people of this region. The writing was exquisite, looking more like a piece of art than a translation. Although I could not understand the Ojibwa, I spent a lot of time looking at the formation of the letters, the beautiful accented words, the numerous double vowels. The words seemed to flow, as though every speech was a movement, musical and physical. Whenever I hear Ojibwa spoken, it is a ballet of sound.

The legends of the Bear Clan were all gathered together and, blessedly, they were dutifully numbered. Ignoring my desire to read through all of them, I turned to number twenty. The English was formal yet melodic.

Walking Bear was furious and discontented. The people were worried and filled with unrest. Their spiritual leader had gone long before to a higher plane and had not returned. Walking Bear knew well what could happen to leaders who did not pay attention.

The people continued to wail and cry as the land was abused and usurped. Their animal brothers and sisters were weeping and trembling with fear. Many fled the land and left the people behind without food, covering, or companionship. Those with evil intentions were gloating as they replaced the animals with dead fur and swallowed the land with their greed. Their hands were stained with gold.

The People began to become jealous as they saw their brothers and sisters clothed in finery and surrounded by the best the land could offer. They were in danger of being enticed toward the evil themselves.

Walking Bear knew that action must be his to assert. He sought out the leaders of the Evil Ones and began to whisper in their ears. He set traps for them and confined them while he ministered to their broken and misshapen spirits. They would be set free only when their inner forces were healed and their evil intentions were banished, he told them. Walking Bear began to appear to the people who had been influenced by the Evil Ones, to frighten them back to the ways commanded by Nanna Bijou.

Soon the people heard his message and began to follow the ancient rules. They treated the land and their brother and sister animals with respect. They used only for need, not for greed. The trees began to whisper their gratitude once more. The crops waved happily at the people, pleased to nurture again. The animals returned and settled near the people once more, confident they would not be abused, but protected. Their furs and meat would again be provisions only for life giving. The circle would once again be complete.

The Evil Ones were healed and their intentions turned away from greed. When Walking Bear found the Spiritual One, he berated the leader for abandoning the people.

"You are wrong, Walking Bear," the Spiritual Leader said. "When the people cried out, I answered their prayers. I brought Walking Bear out of his cave. I walked beside you as you healed the Evil spirits. I accompanied you on your patrol of the land. Now I can return to my people, satisfied that my quest has been answered."

Walking Bear nodded his huge head in tribute to the wisdom of the Spiritual Leader and returned to his cave.

I lifted my head from the text and withdrew my list from my coat pocket. Everything fit, according to my own logic, except for the ending. Agnes Lake, presuming she was the spiritual leader of the legend, had disappeared on a Vision Quest; Oona had decided the action was hers to take in the form of Walking Bear.

The subdivision could be the blight on the land. Victor Reeves could be the equivalent of the legendary one who "abused and usurped" the land. Somehow, Frieda Roote must have been doing something illegal, too, which perhaps explained her sudden wealth. Perhaps her transgression had to do with hunting and trapping, since this was what Frieda was renowned for throughout the village; that would explain the part of the legend that spoke of animals trembling in fear and fleeing.

If she had been following the legend, Oona might have kidnapped Frieda and Victor in order to "heal" them. She'd appeared to the people – especially foolish children like Bobby

Mills—in her Walking Bear headdress to frighten them back into following the ancient rules.

But the murders – this was the part that did not make sense. It did not fit with the legend, nor did it match Oona's sensibilities about the sacredness of life.

Telling Bird I'd be back in a moment, I walked outside into sunshine and warmth. I removed my sweater and took my cell phone out of my pocket. Standing facing the forest, the sun glinting off the still-bare branches, I tried to picture May at Oona's bedside as I dialed the number of her own cell phone. She answered at once.

"How is she, May?" I asked first.

May's voice was low, almost a whisper. "Hang on, Em. I have to walk out to the visitors' lounge balcony. I shouldn't really have the cell on, but I was waiting for a call from Basil."

There was a couple of moments' silence, and then May's voice came back, stronger and louder.

"Hey," she said companionably, her tone tinged with affection. "I'm so glad to hear your voice. She's still unconscious. They gave her something to make her sleep on purpose; the doctor said she'd been writhing and moaning and that the only chance to recover would be in keeping absolutely at rest. I've just been sitting here talking to her and reading and singing, just in case she can hear me. She looks so pale and sick and old. Basil's trying to get Henry and the other sisters here. They should see her just in case."

I smiled at May's verbosity. It was certainly obvious that she had needed to talk. "I'm so sorry, May. Is there anything I can do?"

May let out a huge sigh. "I don't think so, but thanks. Edgar's posted a police officer outside the door and he's heading back to Burchill today. Of course they think Oona's responsible for the murders. Frieda all but said so just before she died."

"She can't be," I said forcefully. "Killing for revenge just isn't in Oona's psyche." I told May quickly about the twentieth legend.

She was silent for a few seconds, then, "That's unbelievable. I actually think you must be the most intelligent woman in the world."

As I laughed, I heard someone else's voice in the background. "Hang on, it's Edgar. He wants to talk to you."

"Emily Taylor, I presume. Okay, sleuth, tell me what you've been doing." Though Edgar's voice was attempting to sound hale and hearty, I could hear the fatigue and worry behind the words.

I repeated the story of the twentieth legend. Edgar's response was similar to May's – silence at first, then proclamations of my brilliance.

"I just don't know where that leads us," he said finally. "It certainly explains everything, right up until the murders in the cave. There's something we are definitely missing."

I could barely hear May in the background.

"May's speculating that someone else might be involved, and I would tend to agree with her, although probably no other law enforcement people will. They're convinced here, based on the accounts of our experience, that Oona is the logical suspect. We'll have a lot of investigating to do to prove otherwise. I'm heading out in a few minutes, Emily, to come back to Burchill. Don't do anything else without me. Go home – that's an order. If there is someone else involved, remember that they're still active. Let me handle it when I get back. I'll call Frances, too, to alert her to the legend and its possibilities. Knowing Frances, she will probably want to talk to you. I'll tell her you're waiting for her at home. In the meantime, take down my cell phone number just in case you have any other brain waves."

"All right, Chief," I replied, scribbling the number into my notebook. "I'll head home, I promise." And as it turned out, I really did intend to follow the rules. It was someone else who interfered with my good intentions.

XVIII

"Thanks for letting me read the legends, Bird," I said to him as I returned to the museum to pick up my coat.

"Hope it helped," he replied, turning from dusting an artifact. "A lotta people seem to be interested in this book lately, I tell ya."

I stopped at the door. "Really? Who?"

Bird looked as though he wished he hadn't spoken. He was almost comical in his apron, the duster clutched in his hands, his dark handsome face shining with embarrassment.

"Well, about two months ago, Oona spent a lot of time reading the book. Of course, it's not unlike her to visit here. She spends a lotta time in this here museum, sometimes helping me set things up or write explanations. Oona's well versed in the legends from her own mother and father and grandparents, though, so it did seem unusual that she was so engrossed in my pop's writings, which is probably why I remember that particular visit so well.

"On the other hand, each family fashioned or embellished the legends in their own way, so I guess she was interested in how Papa envisioned them." He shook his head, as if he suddenly remembered. "I am praying for her, man," he added quietly. "She could not have done this thing."

I urged him to keep talking. "You said a lot of people were interested. Who else came to read the book?"

"The day after Oona and Frieda disappeared, Agnes Lake came in. I was real surprised at that, because Agnes never visits, unless she is a guest speaker or something. I always figure she has heard and seen it all in person so doesn't need a museum to remind her. Plus I get the feeling she believes I am caging the spirits by keeping all this stuff under one roof."

He waved a hand over the stacked bookshelves and

display cases. "I figure if I don't preserve these treasures, they will be lost along with everything else we've ... " Seeing my impatience, he stopped talking and cleared his throat. "Anyway, after that, I got a visit from Basil Fisher, Peter Smallwood, and one of those creepy men who hangs around with Victor Reeves."

"You're kidding!" I exclaimed. "All on the same day?"

"No, no, all three were on separate visits. Except maybe...yes, I think Basil was here on the same day as the Reeves guy. I can't remember the timing exactly. I'm sorry, I don't sign people in and out, and the days just...I have to admit, Emily, dates just mean so little to me. It's the past that..."

Again, Bird seemed to get my signal to move on with the story. "All of them wanted to read the legends book. I wasn't too surprised by Peter, because he often comes by. But Basil – he rarely makes an appearance in the museum. I think he's of the Agnes Lake school of thought. That Reeves crony really threw me for a loop though. I hadn't seen him around town myself and I had no idea who he was. Gave me some crap about wanting to understand the ancient ways better so he could reach the native population and explain what they were really trying to do with the subdivision. He never offered his name either and I didn't bother asking. He just seemed so phony."

"What did he look like?"

"Kinda tall, good lookin', blondish hair. He wore one of those expensive suits that high-powered businessmen favour."

That could have described any of the Reeves crowd, I thought, thinking back to the night we'd met them at the Main Street Pub.

"Did he stay very long?"

"Actually, yes, he did. I remember because I was very busy that morning and I was quite irritated. He did seem very engrossed in the stories, though; asked me all kinds of questions."

"What kind of questions?"

Bird rubbed his chin thoughtfully and glanced upwards, as though the answer was written on the ceiling. "Mostly about Walking Bear. Then he wanted to know how headdresses are fashioned and how realistic they are. I briefly showed him the one I have in the back room by way of demonstration. He was very intrigued by it. I explained how the head of the bear is stuffed and how it fits over the shoulders, so the human behind the mask can see through the fur and feathers. It's extremely intricate and delicate, and no one seems to be able to make them any more, so I have kept my grandfather's headdress in the back in a chest rather than up here. I show it only to very interested people. Some day I'll order a display case made that will allow it to be seen but not touched. That will be cool."

I couldn't resist. "Would it be okay for me to see it, Bird?"

"Of course. Hang on a sec." He placed a "back in a minute sign" near the window, then headed for a door concealed beside one of the bookshelves. A large, old-fashioned gold key hung on a hook under the shelf, which Bird used to unlock it.

The passageway led to a dark, musty, windowless room jammed full of boxes, clothing, stuffed animal heads, feathers, horns, books and papers, bits of material and plastic. An old spinning wheel stood in one corner, along with some other furniture that was covered in cobwebs. Bird turned on a small lamp, which threw shadowy light over everything, then went straight to a large chest in the middle of the room.

I stepped up alongside him as he reached down and lifted

the lid. A fusty, rank scent burst into the air, which the remnants of the cedar lining did little to sweeten. A small downy feather flitted upward from the bottom, borne on the draft.

Bird sank involuntarily to his knees. The chest was empty.

Tears slid unapologetically down Bird's shocked face. "It can't be..." he murmured.

I placed my hand on his shoulder, trying to give comfort, though I knew there could be none. "Who else saw this, Bird? Just Victor Reeves' colleague? Who else knew this was here?"

Bird put his head down on the edge of the chest and for a moment I thought he would not answer me. When he straightened up, his face was no longer suffused with shock and agony. He was furious.

"There are not many who know, but certainly enough. Victor Reeves' crony was one of the few outsiders, that's for sure. I am such a fool for thinking he was truly interested. But Agnes, Oona, Frieda, Peter, Basil – they definitely all knew too. And one of them has stolen it. It could be ruined."

Hoping that I wasn't revealing an official secret, I told him about the headdress and costume that Oona had been wearing when she was found. Shocked and upset, he seemed to be far more interested in the state of the diadem than in Oona's health.

"How could anyone have gotten in here, though? You keep the museum locked up, don't you, Bird?"

Bird hung his head. "Everyone knows where to find the key to the front door," he admitted. "And I keep the keys to this room on the hook. I never thought I had anything worthy of a thief's attention. And this IS Burchill for god's sake. Nobody would steal..." His face flushed, because it was obvious that someone in Burchill had, indeed, stolen.

This time, I dialed Edgar's cell phone. After a few rings,

he answered.

"Edgar, it's Emily. Just one more thing. Did you get a good look at the Walking Bear attire? What kind of shape is it in? Is it ruined?"

"Yes, I did get a chance to examine it, actually. The headdress is still in pretty good shape, but the body of the costume is ruined from the beating. Why do you ask?"

I explained about the theft from the museum and before he could admonish me, I offered the information that I had, indeed, been on my way home when Bird had mentioned the bear headdress.

"Ask him what it looked like," the curator urged at my elbow.

Edgar was very detailed. As he spoke, I relayed the information to Bird. A large brown bear's head, its huge shoulders drooped and shaped as a nest for a human's face, long black and white feathers tipped with yellow and red placed in a circle around the bottom of the diadem, a small piece of leather with the emblem of an ink-drawn bear and paw prints...

Bird's agitated voice broke into my relating of Edgar's description. "That's not mine," he said, pulling on my sleeve in his urgency. "My grandfather's emblem was of the bear and the fish. I don't know whose emblem that is." The tears had appeared freshly in his eyes again. "I wished so fervently that it was mine, but it can't be."

Edgar's response was thoughtful. "Then there are two headdresses," he said. "May was right. Someone else IS involved. Emily, I'm in the car heading back. It'll take me about three hours. Go right home and tell Langford everything. Then sit tight until I get there and Frances and I will come over to consider all the facts together. Four heads will be better than two."

I agreed and for once, did as Edgar said. When I jogged into our yard – having shed all my outer clothing except for my t-shirt and track pants – I found Will and Angel playing ball on the front porch. When they grinned up at me, my heart soared with love and gratitude. I wrapped my arms around them both, kissing Will long and deeply, feeling his warm strong body solid and full beneath me. Soon I had let go of Angel and was being cuddled completely in my husband's embrace.

We walked languidly through the door, Angel at our feet, as I told him everything I'd experienced that morning. Naturally, he agreed with May that I was the most intelligent woman he knew, and then he added a few other descriptors that had nothing to do with brains. One thing led to another, until Langford (Will) Taylor and I found ourselves in bed in the middle of the afternoon.

"I love March Break," I said to him later, trailing my fingers down the soft hairs of his chest, feeling the heat of him next to me and through me. A shiver of pleasure zinged its way from my fingertips to my toes and Langford smiled knowingly.

"Feel like doing that again?" he asked.

"Ha! Think you're still seventeen, don't you?" I laughed. "Can you imagine, Will? We have known each other thirty-three years this summer. And I will be fifty years old for god's sake."

"You are still the most beautiful woman in town," he whispered, sending another shiver through me. "I can't wait til you retire and we can do this all day long."

"And you can still turn me into a teenager," I whispered back, licking his lips with my tongue, tasting the warm juiciness of him. I pulled away slightly, looking into his eyes. "Will, do you think we made a mistake changing your name and hiding out here?"

"What makes you say that?" he asked, propping his head up on one hand and looking at me with a genuinely startled expression.

"I mean – it always feels like we're keeping a secret from our friends. I can never be completely myself with May. I'm always conscious of calling you Langford, not Will. I just feel like Vancouver is following us still, having an effect on our lives even now. Lately I've just had this – I don't know—feeling of... dissatisfaction and I think maybe that's at the root of it."

He put his long arms behind his head in a thoughtful pose. "But, Em, if everyone knew, it would follow us even more, I think. It was such a sensational case. The newspapers splashed it all over the place in Ontario too, so everybody probably knows the story. We'd have reporters on our doorstep constantly, trying to see how we're doing. The villagers – maybe not May or Alain or Edgar or Frances – but to the rest of them, I think we'd be curios. I really think it would be worse."

I snuggled into the warmth of his arm, smelled his salty skin, touched the soft hairs just above his groin. "You're right, of course you are. I guess it's better this way." I was silent for a moment, wondering if I would ever feel content and free of the past. "But some day, do you think I could tell May?"

He rolled over toward me, gently caressing my breast. His lips were soft and tender on mine. "I think there will come a day when we will feel safe enough to do that, my love." And then he proved that he indeed was still like a teenager, because he made love to me again.

We had showered, changed, fed Angel, and prepared some food when Frances called. "Ed's home getting cleaned up," she said when I answered. "We thought we'd have some dinner and then come over."

"Don't have dinner," I told her. "Come here for that. Langford and I have already prepared it. Plus we have several bottles of wine that will lubricate the discussion."

"Fabulous!" she said enthusiastically. "Thanks. I could really use a glass of wine, not to mention home-cooked food!"

Thus an hour or so later we found ourselves at the dining room table, wine glasses full, dinner plates heaped, Frances and Edgar's eager faces opposite us and the conversation swirling. It seemed strange to be sitting in our cozy dining room, the night sky clear and star-filled behind us, discussing a horror that most people would never have to face in their lifetimes. Yet all four of us around this table had actually seen far worse.

The central part of our arguments was Oona's guilt. We all took turns trying to theorize how she might have innocently been involved.

"Instead of Oona being the one who orchestrated everything, could someone else have stolen the bear headdress from the museum, pretended to be Walking Bear, and kidnapped all three?" Frances posited.

"That sure would be the way May would like it to play out. It might mean Oona is innocent," Langford said, neither agreeing nor disagreeing.

"But it doesn't explain why Oona was wearing the headdress," I said, hanging onto my own theory. "According to the legend, Walking Bear decided to kidnap the evil leaders to teach them a lesson. He also appeared to the village people to scare them into going back to following the rules. Whoever captured Frieda and Victor might have done so in some misguided attempt to teach them a lesson. I'm still convinced that it makes sense for Oona to have done that. I'm not sure what Frieda's crimes were, but it's obvious what Victor's was—the people of Burchill and Sahsejewon see him as a threat to the environment, a kind of plague on the land. But I do find it impossible to believe that Oona was involved in beating or killing anyone."

"Then perhaps somebody else entered the picture after the kidnapper." Edgar took up the thread of my thoughts. "Someone who stole the Walking Bear outfit from the museum. Bird hasn't looked at it since he showed it to Victor Reeves' colleague recently, so we have no way of knowing when it disappeared. It could have been before or after Walking Bear started appearing. If it was after, maybe this other person gets the idea and decides to take advantage of the situation for something even worse – like murder."

"Not only Oona but Frieda could have done the kidnapping," Frances said. "They both disappeared at the same time."

"Or Agnes Lake," I interjected, reluctantly opening the theory to include more than Oona as Walking Bear. "May said Oona had been acting strangely lately, talking about how she'd kind of missed out on things and maybe she shouldn't have been so goody-two-shoes. Maybe she and Frieda committed some crime together – and it could very well be a crime against the environment. Maybe it's Agnes who is the kidnapper. All of them had visited the museum within the last few weeks."

"That STILL doesn't explain how Oona ended up with the headdress and costume on, but it's a possibility," Edgar said.

"And none of this explains the murders. Why would this mysterious other person kill Victor and Frieda and almost murder Oona?" Frances asked.

"Maybe Oona or Frieda or Agnes had really lost it. Maybe she had metamorphosed into Walking Bear in her own mind. Maybe one of them actually killed the others. Maybe there was such a huge fight they were all mortally wounded. Maybe no one else was involved."

There was a moment of silence and then Frances, Edgar and I looked at Langford's serious face and burst out laughing.

"That's a hell of a lot of maybes in one speech," I giggled.

After a good, hearty, restorative laugh, we were all silent again, thinking about the endless possibilities and twists and turns.

I thought about Agnes, still out there somewhere – was she alive or dead? Was she involved or simply on a Vision Quest and unaware of the tragedy? I pictured Frieda's dying face, Victor's lifeless body, Oona's blood and agony. What had happened in our forest, in those sacred caves? What kind of greed or anger could lead to such wanton destruction?

XIX

He leaned on the frame in the doorway as though they were pals having a friendly chat. His hair was impossibly tidy; his clothes, though casual, had a rich, unwrinkled air that spoke of money; his voice was smooth and quiet. "Got anything yet?" he asked, his eyes boring into the other man's with ice cold aggression, which contradicted the flashing smile.

The other man stood in front, almost protective, hiding her. "I told you, it will take some time. She will eventually reveal the secrets. She just has to know the reasons for doing so."

The answering voice did not change in tone or strength. "How about offering her money? How about a life of luxury and comfort? It worked with the other one, until there was outside interference. It worked with you. Will she go for that?"

The other man's shoulders rounded even more; his face struggled with the urge to weep. He knew he had no real option in this matter, he knew his previous choices had brought him here, but he managed to sound convincing as he retorted, "She isn't interested in material things. She's not like the rest of us. I need more time with her; she's strong. I will find out where the scroll is hidden. I am absolutely certain of it."

"Maybe you're a little too sure of yourself. Don't commit the sin of hubris. Don't forget, there is a life at stake here – one that seems to mean more to you than even money does." There was a solid click as he shut the adjoining door, chuckling.

The man sat for a moment, staring at the beige walls and the nondescript décor. Then suddenly he burst into tears of regret and fear, his shoulders hunched and shaking, his fists ground into his temples in anger and despair.

in that canyon that is mouth
words align themselves in orderly fashion
it is not what they want to say but
afraid of committing themselves
the legends properly fall
scattering about the ground.

She was here, but not here. Her weightlessness allowed her to float over her body, over the lake, the trees, the rocks. She could see the woman in the small wooden hut, breast rising and falling, huddled in the cold under a sleeping bag, wrists red and raw from fighting the handcuffs chaining them to the bed; the woman taking small, pathetic sips from the water tube and in between, crying or sleeping. When she concentrated, when she entered the further plane, she could see the other woman in the white, sterile bed, eyes fluttering, brain waves jumping, there but not there.

She extended her breath and her sight and allowed her spirit to mingle with other souls. She expelled a mouthful of air into tortured bodies. She heard whimpering and sighs. She saw movement and colour. The colours were orange and red and purple and green, ribbons of light, fusion of spectacle. Her mind was at one with Manitou. She could see so clearly.

She drifted for a time, apart from the suffering, silent, still. The wind hummed in her ear and chilled her heated skin. She smiled. There would be a solution, liberation of all, for the Spirit's face was bent to hers, a touch so soft and smooth, a murmur so warm in her ear, the sound of her salvation.

She opened her eyes and cast her gaze upon the man whose cheeks were stained with tears of guilt and fear. Now he would act in the way that was foretold. Her words would give him the gift of understanding. Her eyes called him and he looked into her essence.

XX

We had settled into the living room, brandies and coffees in hand, quietly enjoying one another's company. The night was clear, with an emerging moon dancing its rays on the still water of the lake.

I leaned back in my chair and enjoyed the warmth of the friendship, the comfort of this room and this home we have created. Edgar and Frances are still new to us as friends; there remains a great deal to know about them.

Langford tells me I think too much about that side of friendship – the knowing, the sharing, the understanding of the person. He is very at ease with the surface; his enjoyment is of the moment and the specific time. I wish I could be more like him; I continue to be bothered by the fact that I cannot be truly open and honest about who I am. I have learned to hide so much, to conceal feelings and keep so much of me to myself.

For Langford, this way of behaving comes naturally, whereas for me, for the Emily Taylor of thirty years before, my nature was to share and explore and disclose completely with my friends. For some reason, lately, I have felt dissatisfied with continuing to be the other Emily Taylor. Now, sitting here with two burgeoning friendships, I realized the source of my discontent: I wanted my inner self, the quintessence of me, to be freed once more.

The discordant ring of Edgar's cell phone broke into our soft conversation and my reverie. He spoke quietly and forcefully, already on his feet before the conversation was over. We all looked up expectantly.

"Oona has regained some consciousness," he said, trying but failing to keep the excitement out of his voice. "May would like me to be there first thing in the morning. They don't expect her to get up and dance and talk right away, but I should be there along with the Ottawa police, just in case she does begin to speak." Edgar tugged on Frances' arms and gently helped her to stand. "Here we go again, my dear. I guess I'll drop you off now, cuz by dawn I'll be hopping back into the car."

Frances, sleepy and rested a moment ago, was suddenly eager to leave. We could hear her questioning Edgar as they walked away in the night, no longer lovers, but colleagues; Frances donning her Officer persona once more. We shut the door, Angel at our heels, and headed for bed.

The next morning a brilliant, spring-like sun shone through the windows and energized us all. There was none of the sharp sting of cold in the air; instead it was soft and seductive and smelled like spring. While Langford fairly bounced out to his studio, Angel and I went for a walk around the lake.

Everyone seemed to be outdoors, buoyed by the warmth and promise of green. Children were everywhere, throwing balls in the air, cavorting on swings, tumbling over one another in the joy of activities that winter had prevented. The Burchill students happily called to me and ran circles around Angel, who, once I let her off her lead, went dancing and wiggling and bounding through the park. She had a wonderful time jumping at sticks, nipping at dormant grass, leaping for the balls that some of the kids threw her way.

We talked to all the neighbours, smiled at passersby, and generally felt wonderful. The only cloud that hovered over me was worrying and wondering about Oona and how May was coping. We ambled along the canal, stepping around patches that were still snow-filled, leaping over puddles that gathered as the ice melted and flowed into the deep, concrete ditch that formed the channel.

I can't say whether I planned it or not, but very soon Angel and I – she panting from her antics, my nose red and my cheeks patchy from my body's reaction to inconsistent exercise as of late – reached the native museum. Once again, Bird greeted me affectionately, and then he made a huge fuss over Angel. In answer to my question about his headdress, his face clouded over and he told me what I really already knew – that there had been no sign of it. Bird assured me that it would be all right for Angel to come into the museum; in fact, he entertained her with a ball and a biscuit while I dug once more into the book of legends.

"Is it okay if I copy this legend out, Bird?" I asked, as my fingers traced the lines of the twentieth tale.

"No problemo, Mrs. Taylor. Wait until you see this modern convenience."

He led me into his office at the front of the museum, where a photocopier, a fax machine, and a computer gleamed in the corner, incongruous but necessary. It took only a few moments to photocopy the legend, both Ojibwa and English, and then Angel and I took our leave of Bird.

He looked saddened and somehow not as enthusiastic about the museum and the artifacts; I had no idea how much the bear's headdress had meant to him. I patted him lightly on the shoulder and tried to reassure him that it would be found undamaged.

"I am certainly hopeful that you are correct," he said, his formal words bumping up against one another, his handsome face worried and doubtful.

Angel trotted happily back up the pathway, her tail lifted, her nose down, buoyed by her treat from Bird. We were coming around a bend in the canal when we saw the dark-clad figure arise from the bench in front of us. A low, guttural growl from Angel forced me to pull back on her leash.

I bent down to reassure her. "It's Basil, don't be afraid, silly girl," I said, and then straightened to greet the squat, round individual who stood before us. "Basil, are you all right? Did you hear that Oona has regained some consciousness?"

He sat back down on the bench, huddled inside a thick wool cape that must have been overly warm, looking old, as though he had lost his energy, his will to keep going.

"I have heard," he replied, his words clipped in the way that many of the Burchill-born people speak. The influence of British and Native combined to give many of the older inhabitants a stilted, formal speech pattern.

I really have no idea how old Basil is, but he must be at least seventy, so he grew up in a time when the Aboriginal and British influences were both struggling to take hold. Basil is Henry Whitesand's best friend, thus I knew his connection with Oona was strong, and that he must be grieving, but he continued to appear more distracted than worried.

I sat down beside him, concerned by his lack of response as much as by his appearance. "Are you all right, Basil?" I repeated.

"I am sick in my heart, Mrs. Taylor." He paused, drew in a breath and looked at me, his round black eyes ringed with lack of sleep, his glance lackluster and sad. "But let us not speak of that."

His words had such finality that I couldn't reply. I sat there for a few moments, watching Angel poke through the bushes behind us, sniff our feet, and generally occupy herself quietly. I thought of the subdivision fire and the kidnappings. Did Henry and Basil know more than they were letting on? Was Basil's general apathy a result of guilt? Then Basil spoke again.

"You have been to the museum." It was a statement, but

it was tinged with curiosity.

I happily took the opening to fill the awkward silence. "Yes, I've been back to reread the legends – you know, the ones that we've all been so interested in."

He glared at me sharply, but I kept going, pulling my scribblings out of my pocket. As I did so, I noticed a red welt on the thumb of my left hand, which, as though aware of the observation, began to itch.

"I photocopied one of them – number twenty, to be exact. I'm not really sure why. I just keep thinking that we must be missing something." And perhaps you shouldn't be telling that to this particular man, a voice said in my head, but it was too late now.

Basil took the sheets from me and read them very slowly. As the minutes ticked by, I began to wonder if he was deliberately stalling. Then suddenly, absurdly, he began to laugh.

"Crow Wing is such a lazy one," he said. I must have looked completely baffled, because he added, "Come, I will show you."

He got up and began to head toward Mahdahbee Craft Depot. When I hesitated, he called over his shoulder once again, "Come." Thus Angel and I obediently followed.

The depot was vacant, as is the norm for this time of year. Later in the spring, it will be filled with the crafters, delivering and shelving their wares, or designing and sewing right on the spot. In the summer, the depot provides the product for the shelves in Mahdahbee Department Store. Here, the tourists always find gifts and souvenirs that are different, unique, and made by hand in Sahsejewon.

Right now, though, our footsteps echoed on the old wooden floor and the shelves were mostly bare. I could hear the murmur of voices in the back room, which is the direction in which Basil led us.

Angel sniffed the air, the floor, our feet once more, then trotted proudly at my side through the store, her tail a question mark.

Basil opened the door to the back room to reveal Chief Dan Mahdahbee and Joseph Overland. They were sitting in rocking chairs, smoking stubby, pungent cigars. All around them were stacked the foundations of crafts that would be sold this summer – cedar and birch bark, feathers, fine thread and paper, lacy twigs dried and stiffened, delicate stones, paints and brushes and other tools for creating.

I shook hands with Chief Dan and with Joseph, whom I know only vaguely. His children attend the private native school and, although he is prominent on the Sahsejewon Council, I have not been in his presence very often. He is a tall, thin man with thick black hair and large brown eyes. His hooked nose and pocked-marked skin keep him from being handsome.

Basil explained our presence. "Mrs. Taylor has been looking at the legends that Crow Wing wrote out, trying to make sense of the mysteries of Burchill," he told them.

In response, Chief Dan and Joseph both gave the same uproarious laughter.

I was beginning to take this personally. "I really would like to know why this is so funny," I said, my voice peeved and exasperated. I almost put my hands on my hips in my favourite Principal attitude.

Chief Dan moved a pile of paper from a chair and motioned for me to sit down. "Sorry, Emily. Let us fill you in." He tapped his cigar into an ashtray and seemed to settle down for a long story. "We Aboriginal people are actually quite class conscious when it comes down to it," he began.

"No different from any other people," I opined.

"True. But we often don't acknowledge our own prejudices yet criticize everyone else's. Anyway, Sahsejewon is a unique case. Our people claim to be Ojibwa, when in actual fact we are a combination. Long ago when the Hurons and the Ottawayans asked for help against their enemies, the Ojibwa clans united and answered the plea. After years of warring, many of the tribes really became intertwined, though the Ojibwa culture was mostly dominant."

I shifted on the stiff, uncomfortable chair, trying very hard to pay attention. The red welt had spread down the pad toward the bend of my thumb and was very itchy now; I began to wonder about poison ivy and tried not to scratch it. I concentrated on Chief Dan's lecture once more.

"But the Ojibwa traditions that grew up around Sahsejewon and Burchill have many differences. We are largely from the Bear Clan and have often refused to be called Ojibwa, which was a derogatory name given by enemies of our people. Probably the most revered name is Anishanabe, which means the "original people", but we Sahsejewon inhabitants cannot really lay claim to that, since we evolved into our own little category.

"Our legends, though, have many similarities to the Ojibwa legends, and to the creation stories from the Anishinabe traditions. It always comes back to the land, to our connection to the earth and the spirits of the animals and trees and plants. They are filled with lessons about stewardship and balance. Our songs and prayers and dances are all centred on trying to walk the sacred way – the way of healing, compassion, creation rather than destruction." Chief Dan leaned forward, his eyes full of the energy of faith. "Thus we laugh, Emily, when we read Soaring Bird's father's interpretation of the written legends. The Oral Tradition is so much richer. It has level after level of meaning and morality.

So many lessons are taught and they are complex and multilayered."

"That Crow Wing was a lazy one," Basil interjected, repeating his assessment. "He made all the legends almost sound the same. I didn't read that number twenty, but I bet it sounds like all the rest."

I recalled the legend of Walking Bear that May had told me and compared it to legend twenty. Basil was right; they were very much alike.

"Crow Wing was Soaring Bird's father?" I asked.

"Yes," Basil answered. "His white name was George and he was a very lazy man. Now his son is lazy too."

"Basil," Chief Dan said softly, admonishing without being harsh, "Soaring Bird means very well. He has done a great service to our people by preserving the traditions, and that was due to George's work in trying to put everything into writing. The Oral Tradition is no longer conserved in this busy world. Even my father saw many of the lessons being lost and wrote out a lot of the Oral tales. And since the themes of the stories are very similar, it stands to reason that the legends will sometimes sound the same. What does Bird's twentieth legend say exactly?"

Basil said nothing, though I was tempted to remind him that he, too, had read through Bird's book very recently. Instead, I handed my sheet of paper over to Chief Dan. He read it carefully and, without a word, got up and went to a shelf in the back of the room. He brought back a large, leathery, photo-album sized book, which had bits of yellowed, crumpled paper and edges of pictures sticking out all over. He laid it carefully on the table in front of him and opened it to the first page.

I could see that it was filled not only with Ojibwa words and writings, but also with hieroglyphics. The lines and the tiny pictures raced throughout the pages like sheet music.

"You see, Emily," Chief Dan said, continuing his lecture kindly, "a great deal of our language was not easily translated because our ancestors used hieroglyphics. George did not spend a great deal of time on these, unfortunately, which is why Basil is so disdainful." The Chief ran his stubby fingers, flashing with diamonds and gold, over the pages until he found the one he wanted. "This is the Twentieth Legend. You see how it is mixed with some written language and some pictorial language. But I still believe I can fill in the missing pieces for you, even if I cannot read it exactly. We can compare the Ojibwa, the English, and add in the hieroglyphics as well. That should give us as complete a story as possible."

I sat down beside him, with the copies of Bird's legend opened next to Chief Dan's book as a comparison.

"First of all, look at this mark above the story. It is supposed to be a lesson for the future, not the present. In other words, this tale was told down the ages as a prediction, or a warning about what might happen unless there is intervention," Dan told me, making his way through the page with his eyes and his fingers, as though partly feeling his way.

"Look here where it says 'the people continued to wail and cry as the land was abused and usurped'. There is a great deal more explanation in the Ojibwa translation than in George's. As well, there are pictorials to go with it." He was silent for a moment; his lips moved noiselessly as he transformed the pictures and Ojibwa writing into English for me to understand. "This tells us that an ancient secret will be torn away," he said slowly, his words stilted as he tried to give the tale meaning. "I believe this is saying that the secret will be stolen. It has something to do with a scroll on which the secret is written. The sacred grounds will be excavated, defiled to even greater extent, unless the scroll is recovered."

."Are the sacred grounds the caves?" I asked.

"Not necessarily. In fact, probably not. All of Burchill and Sahsejewon would have been considered hallowed, just as we Aboriginals continue to believe that all of the earth is meant to be revered. The caves were reserved for burial and none of the translations in any way reference those rites. But some secret will be kept from the people, which will cause the earth to be violated and mistreated to such a degree that the Original People will be forced to move away unless someone does something. In turn, even the animals will flee, just as it says in George's translation." Once again, Chief Dan was silent as he translated.

I suddenly realized that I had been scratching my thumb again and looked down, startled. The red rash had spread to the base of my finger and was tracing its way over the pad of my hand. It was excruciatingly itchy. I had to see Doc Murphy, I thought; this must be poison ivy.

"There is a lot more detail in the Ojibwa about how hunting will become rampant and how conspiracies will abound to take over the land completely, until no Original People will be able to live there. The descriptions of how the land is dug up and defaced are pretty strong." Again, he translated in his head before speaking it aloud. "There is also a great deal more information about the English sentence, 'Their hands were stained with gold'. There are probably several interpretations, but the Ojibwa is a little clearer – there is a connection between the scroll, the land, and the gold. Perhaps money exchanges hands, or maybe there is actual gold found on the land. It's not that specific. Either way, though, the transactions are illegal and immoral, and result in the land being 'swallowed ... with their greed'."

Again, he was silent as he read, his thick fingers flashing with diamonds and gold as he traced the letters, the Ojibwa vowels, the pictorials. I wonderful briefly about this man; about the apparent contradiction between his native roots and the wealth that he flaunts.

"This section is very interesting," he said finally, and he read aloud, "*The People began to become jealous as they saw their brothers and sisters clothed in finery and surrounded by the best the land could offer. They were in danger of being enticed toward the evil themselves.*" Chief Dan looked up at me, his eyes lively with enthusiasm as he explored the story. "There's a dire warning in the Ojibwa and in the hieroglyphics: someone in the village – can't say how many – but there are people who have betrayed others and who are destined to bring disaster upon everyone unless they are stopped. It looks like they will even bring ruin to themselves, because in turn, they are duped and betrayed.

"When I read this part, from George's English translation, and look at the Ojibwa, they match almost completely," he continued thoughtfully, and read loud, "*Walking Bear began to appear to the people who had been influenced by the Evil Ones, to frighten them back to the ways commanded by Nanna Bijou'.*" He paused again, thinking. "But this doesn't seem to reflect what has happened. Walking Bear has appeared to many people, some who are clearly innocent of any wrong-doing."

I thought about the appearances that occurred over the weekend to anyone out walking near the forest areas; I thought about our own encounter with the apparition. Something didn't quite make sense.

Chief Dan went on, reading George's English translation, then going into more detail. "*He set traps for them and confined them while he ministered to their broken and misshapen spirits,*" he read. "The Ojibwa and hieroglyphics support this translation, stating that Walking Bear does confine the evildoers, but in the Ojibwa part of the tale, some of them will heal and some will not. The pictorial translation goes on to warn that unless the secret scroll is discovered and the wicked ones who have not changed their ways are driven from the land, the sacred spaces will be ruined forever. There is a lot more detail about how Walking Bear must heal the sinners, turn the people back to their previous good behaviour, and how he must replace the scroll that contains the ancient secret." His large finger pointed to a picture that appeared to be hands crossing. "This hieroglyphic suggests that the scroll must be put back into the right hands, rather than into a secret place.

"There are more descriptions of the land and the animals and how everything may be able to return to the rules of balance and protection. Although it's all written as a prediction of the future, it doesn't foretell what happens in the end. Walking Bear could be successful, or he could not. And..."

At his hesitation, I prompted him. "What?"

"Either way, before everything is finished, there will be bloodshed."

I thread myself one hour to the next,
sorrow riding me like a pack of wolves

She used his pain and his guilt to probe his mind. He saw clearly what she was doing, but he allowed it to happen, having no idea where it might go, except that the suffering had to end. She could feel him, at last, put himself in her hands. His head bowed toward her; he listened with his heart.

"I will lead you to the scroll," she whispered, her tongue dry against the inside of her mouth, her words slurred with thirst.

"Why?" He wanted to be able to explain it to them, she realized, for he was far too weakened to be able to convince them on his own any longer.

"I cannot allow more death or suffering. I do it in exchange for life."

He nodded, knowing this was something the man would believe. He went to the door and gave the code. When it was opened, those cold hard eyes almost unhinged him, but he straightened his shoulders and reminded himself that he was a fairly good actor. Those days in the summer theatre could carry him through...

"She wants to show us where it is," he stated, his voice louder than he'd commanded it to be.

"How did you do it?" The man's eyes had flickered momentarily with greed and hope and he knew the man was hooked, even though the look had become guarded and icy once more.

"She's sickened by the death and suffering," he said. "I described it all to her. I told her how she would be responsible for more. She doesn't think a piece of paper and even some land is worth more of the same." He was whispering now, the door slightly closed to prevent her from hearing. "She's been taught to preserve life, after all. I knew it was just a matter of time before she was worn down. I told you I could do it."

The man's composure – that thin film of civility and humanity that was painted on him like a showy layer of varnish – melted with lightning speed. Suddenly he was a wild, ferocious, untamed animal whose only desire was to rip his prey apart. Though the other man was taller, rage made the aggressor appear gigantic and much stronger. He grabbed the cowering man by the shirt collar and pulled his face down so that they were almost nose-to-nose, close enough for the spittle to spray between them when the man spewed out his anger.

"You weakling bastard. You'd better be telling me the truth and you'd better come through, or I will take such pleasure in tearing you and the women apart slowly and painfully. Understand me?"

It was not so much the words as the power of wrath that made the victim tremble and break out into a sweat that ran down his back like fingers on a piano keyboard, ringing out a song of disaster.

XXI

Chief Dan, Joseph, Basil and I all looked at each other, fear crossing each of our features by turn.

"The bloodshed has already happened," I said. "Does this mean that the rest of it has come true too – everything about Walking Bear, about the secrets, about the land...? How does it all fit together with Oona?"

"And Victor Reeves and Frieda," Basil added. "Not to mention Evan Fobert."

"Evan Fobert?"

"He went to the museum," Basil answered me.

"Is that why you went and looked at Bird's legend book, too?" I queried, unable to help myself.

Basil was silent for a moment. "Yes. I saw him enter the museum. I waited and then gently got Bird to tell me what he had been scrutinizing. Ever since Henry had the fight with Victor Reeves, I have been overwhelmed with a terrible feeling. I started following all of them, Evan Fobert included. I kept thinking that something was going to go horribly wrong for people I have known and loved, and now it has. The legends told us so. And somehow, I just know those contractors are at the root of it. I..." he hung his head for a moment, and we all waited, breathless. "I guess I was hoping that it really was Walking Bear come to rescue us." Basil looked, at that moment, embarrassed and ashamed.

My mind began to form imaginative connections. Who had set the subdivision fire? And thinking about the fire, did Basil's shame mean he was involved in something more than simply picking a fight? Was Chief Dan somehow involved, to protect his own gold? Evan Fobert. Victor Reeves. Oona, Frieda. How did they all fit together?

The incredible, stinging itch of my hand forced me to stop

my wild ruminations. I had to see Doc.

I thanked Chief Dan and Basil, said good-bye to Joseph, and, with Angel happily following at my heels, I headed over to Doc Murphy's place.

When we first moved to Burchill, I was amazed to find a true country doctor living in the town. Ron Murphy is a skilled, well-informed physician who has chosen to stay in the village even though he could easily have had a more lucrative position in the city. As they say here, he is Burchill born and therefore loyal to the community. He works well with the Aboriginals and has incorporated a great deal of the wisdom of the elders and the medicinal practices of the Ojibwa into his methodology. I just hoped he wasn't too busy today to see me without an appointment.

Doc Murphy lives on Brock Street in a house referred to by the locals as "Mill's House", dating back to the 1800's when the family who owned the mill built it and lived in it for many decades. Coincidentally, his nuclear family home, which was also previously owned by the same family and known as "Mill's House 2", is still occupied by his mother, to whom he is very devoted.

Doc's wife and two sons seem very happy to have their home melded with the doctor's office; perhaps it is because Ron is always near no matter how many hours he works. Maire often helps out with the clients and the paperwork. In fact, it was Maire who opened the office door to admit me.

She is a tall, large-boned woman whose beautiful eyes and smooth, pale skin do not betray her age. Maire still has her melodious Irish accent behind her words and when she is happy to see you, her eyes 'smile'—just as the song says.

"Emily!" she greeted me. "Come in. How are you?"

She opened the door and I entered the waiting room, where the comfortable chairs were all empty.

"I was actually wondering if I could see Doc," I told her. "I've come up with some kind of rash and it's driving me nuts. I'm sorry I don't have an appointment."

"You came at a really good time, as you can see, Emily," Maire laughed. "Ron is just getting caught up on some research he has been doing and hadn't scheduled any appointments for the next hour and there haven't been any emergencies."

I started to apologize. "Oh, I'm so sorry – I could make..."

"No, no, he'll be glad to see you," she interrupted. "Come on in."

Maire walked ahead of me and opened Doc's office door. He was sitting at the desk, head bowed over a huge textbook, nodding off in the sunlight that poured through the large side window. His wife put her hand on his shoulder and laughed softly.

"Looks like you need an interruption, eh, Ron?"

Doc looked up, startled, blinking his eyes at us, embarrassed. "This is such boring stuff," he admitted, chuckling. "Emily, how nice to see you! And you are right, honey, I badly needed a distraction. I absolutely HAVE to get through this and maybe a break is what I need to get my batteries recharged. Have a seat, dear patient."

He patted the big leather chair next to him and I obediently sat. Angel curled at my feet, tired from all the walking and running and sniffing.

"How about a coffee and a cookie to distract both of you?" Maire asked. "I have a fresh batch of each. I might even have a dog biscuit handy."

All three of us responded in the affirmative, so Maire disappeared through the connecting door into their home.

Between cookies, deliciously spiced coffee, and a few soft barks and tricks from a little dog satiated with treats, Doc looked at my hand, pulled a giant medical book from his shelf, and hummed and hawed over the predicament.

"Have you ever had dermatitis before?" he asked me.

"I have to admit I don't even know what that is, so definitely not," I answered.

"It's a skin rash that's usually the result of an allergy," Doc explained. "Since you've never had it before, I'd venture a guess that it's something you've been in contact with recently that you've never touched before. It usually takes a day or two to break out, depending on how severe the allergy is. When did it start?"

"I think just this morning," I said, trying hard to remember the exact moment my thumb began to itch. "But as to what I could have come in contact with – well, considering all the places I've been in the last few days – I couldn't really say. What sorts of things would cause it?"

"Well, most common at this time of year would be some sort of tree, or plant, or bush. Trees would be the best guess, since most plants and bushes are kind of hibernating right now."

I thought of the trips through the woods that we'd made recently, but the timeframe seemed wrong. Doc was still looking at his book.

"People have different kinds of allergies, but I'd say it must be something that's not very common around Burchill. Otherwise you'd probably have come down with this shortly after moving here. You're so often outdoors, not only with Langford, but with the school kids."

I thought of trips to the museum, the reserve, the craft store, the woods, the canal. Could it have been something in the museum? If so, why hadn't I caught it before this?

"The good news is that the rash can be controlled with medicated cream. I'll write out the prescription for you and you can go home and put it on right away. I know the itch is probably driving you crazy."

"Any way of finding out what I'm allergic to, Doc?"

He turned and smiled a little grimly. "Hate to tell you, Emily, but aside from sticking you with needles to test for everything under the sun, the best way will likely be when you touch the thing again. The second flare-up will probably happen almost immediately and be somewhat worse."

"Oh. Great."

Doc laughed at the expression on my face. "Don't worry. This cream will do the trick the next time, too. You'll see. Thanks for waking me up though."

I laughed. "You're very welcome – glad I could oblige. I'd wager you'll have a good fifteen minutes before your head's down on that desk again."

Angel and I left Doc laughing. We trotted down Main Street to the drug store and were soon armed with cream and instructions for use. I immediately slathered my aching hand with the cool substance and sighed as it reached through the rash and soothed the raging itch. We were heading home, tired and hungry, when Frances pulled up in the patrol car.

"Emily! Just the person I wanted to see. I've got a hunch," she said, holding the door open.

Angel and I hopped in, with no idea of what was to come.

death is the major strength
with which to emerge from this cocoon of bondage
we say "forgive us our trespasses"
forgetting that death lurks at every opportunity

She wanted to let go. The cool breeze had beckoned her and she saw and heard the sea beyond, calling to her. The small birds sang, the sun warmed her skin, her loved ones smiled. She knew it could be so easy. She would simply lie back, sink into the feathers, be enveloped in soft arms, breathe without pain.

She had looked into the eyes of Charles Nabigon, welcoming, dreamy, affectionate, and she whispered to him, Running Wolf, I come to you once more, I put my searing body in your cooling embrace, warm my cold heart in your love, die to live in your circle forever. He nodded, his smile broadening, the lines of his last illness gone from his handsome face, his hands strong and open to her again. Beside him, the children were alive, they could walk and talk and respond. They reached out for wife, lover, mother. She let the life go from her body.

It plowed into her like a punch, the fist strong and powerful. The breath surged inside her once more, forcing her chest to expand and her body to jerk upward from the bed. She tried to fight it, to resist, to return to the quiet and the sea and Charles. But when she saw through the cloud that surrounded her, when she tasted the breath whose strength poured through her, she turned instead to the other face, the other arms who pulled her by the hands and forced her upward. It was not peaceful or welcoming or silent; it was a rough and torturous path, but she knew she had to do it; she even willed her own muscles to respond to the call. She had to do this. She opened her eyes.

XXII

I couldn't help but laugh, though it was more from relief than mirth. "Frances, you won't believe this, but I was going to rush home and call you."

"As a matter of fact, I would believe it. I really think there is something to this cosmic intelligence thing." Frances cleared her throat, as though she'd revealed too much, and changed the subject. "I've been doing a lot of thinking about Oona and Frieda. What about you?"

I told her about the visits to the museum and the craft store, about the missing pieces of the legend. "I seriously think that Oona was leaving a message when she ran around the tree and pointed to the twentieth legend. There is something that we have not paid enough attention to. I think we should go look at Oona's place again."

"Great idea. I'm supposed to be off duty today, so let's go exploring. Oona still hasn't said a thing, so all I'm doing is mulling everything around in my mind until I feel obsessed."

We dropped Angel off with Langford, who, although not keen on my driving away with Frances, didn't try to dissuade me. I pulled on rubber boots and a windbreaker and I was ready for an adventure.

We decided that searching through Oona's small house was a priority. Since the cabin was never locked and Oona invited anyone to visit at any time, we knew we'd have no problem explaining our presence if anyone ever asked. Although it had already been searched, and it was a very small space, we both had an intuitive feeling that there was some clue we'd all missed. Armed with the information about the secret scroll, we agreed that it should be looked at with a different perspective.

The sun had continued fingering any snow or ice left

under crevices and behind trees. As it melted, the water made little rivulets everywhere, causing me to be happy I'd put on my hiking boots. Through the hush and sway of the breeze in the woods, we could hear birds tentatively heralding spring.

The little cottage looked sad and abandoned even from the outside. Normally, there'd be a puff of smoke rising invitingly and often the sound of Oona humming or singing along with her old radio. I felt a rush of grief and sent a prayer to whatever spirits controlled her life.

"I keep thinking positive thoughts for Oona," Frances said as we headed for the front door, startling me with her perspicacity. Maybe she was right about cosmic intelligence. "Even though I don't know her well, I admire May so much. I don't want May to suffer."

"Ditto," was all I was able to say, touched by the feeling in Frances's voice.

The cabin door was firmly shut, which looked so unusual that it gave the whole frontage a different appearance; the shack was now forlorn and dark and abandoned. Frances strode confidently ahead and pushed open the door, which swung inward on creaky hinges. I followed her petite frame into the cottage and heard her shocked gasp before I saw the reason for her reaction.

Although I knew from past experience that Oona didn't have much in the way of material things inside her tiny home, I was also aware that everything had been neat and clean and that all things had had a place. The disorder and mess into which I stepped was shocking and disgusting. Tea bags, boxes of cereal, sugar, salt, sauces, catsup, spices and other kitchen items had been turned upside down and emptied all over the floor, the counter, the table. The single cot had been upended, its mattress sliced and its insides strewn about like a box of cotton.

Frances and I stood still in the middle of the room; the rays of the sunshine picked out the vandalism the way a magnifying glass would highlight the dirt on a windowpane. I sucked in my breath through clenched teeth and felt my heart begin to pound. I knew what this kind of violation did to your soul; I was briefly glad that Oona would not see her little shelter desecrated in this way.

Frances's voice was clipped and hard; she was every inch the police officer once more. "Obviously they want something from Oona," she said, getting out her cell phone. "Marty, I'm at the Nabigon cottage. Can you send someone out? I'm going to search around a little and then leave. I'll try to get in touch with Edgar too, but in the meantime I'd like one of the volunteers to get out here and bag up anything interesting. Probably not much use dusting for prints, but they could do that here and there too." She paused and listened for a moment. "But won't you be putting in a double shift?" She smiled. "Got it, Marty. You're the best." She hung up. "Marty's almost finished his shift but he doesn't want to trust this to any of the police volunteers. He's an amazing guy. I think he'll fit very nicely into Burchill once we get him full time."

"Do you think that will happen?"

"Depends on how the subdivisions go. If there are more people, we'll need more help." Snapping on gloves, Frances began to move around the hut, her eyes bright with observation. She handed me a pair of gloves. "Look at things, Emily," she said to my unspoken question about what I should do, "and then you can pick them up if you think there might be something underneath. Just try to memorize where they were and put them back as close as possible. It's not like the murders were committed here or anything, so you don't have to be too precise. But Marty will want to photograph the place when he gets here."

We began to move around the cottage, looking at every little thing, picking papers up off the floor and replacing them. We were silent and tense; it felt cruel and awkward to be wandering around the mess, adding to the destruction instead of fixing it. I tried hard to concentrate, to emulate Frances as she employed her trained powers of observation to pierce the secrets of that room.

Ironically, it was I who found the picture, curled up under the table as though flung there and dismissed as unworthy of consideration. It was a photograph of Oona and Frieda, taken very recently by the look of both women. I thought it was odd that Oona had kept it or even posed for it; she didn't like images and she certainly seemed to have lost a great deal of her affinity for Frieda. Although, I reminded myself, there had been many new contradictions in Oona's behaviour and perhaps this was one of them. For no reason other than curiosity, I turned the picture over, and in black pencil, etched into the silvery white paper of the photo, was the drawing of a scroll.

XXIII

When Edgar arrived in the hallway, May was huddled in Alain's arms, leaning against the wall. Through the open door Edgar could see the doctor and two nurses working around the bed, leaning over Oona with machinery and urgency, and his heart sunk. Poor Oona, he thought, after all this suffering, she isn't going to make it.

Alain nodded and shook his hand; May didn't turn her face toward him, but her hand, too, reached out and squeezed his. Edgar couldn't help but feel a spark of jealousy, seeing in the close unit of these two people something that he wished to have with Frances.

Just then, the doctor came back into the hall. "She's stable again," he said, his voice abrupt and business-like. "But I must tell you honestly that I don't know how long she'll be that way. She's very tentative." He gave a nod that simulated some understanding and strode away.

The nurses finished straightening the sheets and making Oona comfortable once more before they took their leave, giving far more sympathy and support than the doctor had. Oona's face was tight and pale, her long dark hair with its shots of silver framing her contorted, lined skin. She was no longer twitching; her lips were closed and dried with spittle. Even her breath barely raised the sheets that covered her still body.

May let out a whimper of anguish and clutched at one limp hand that lay motionless at Oona's side. This woman had been her model, her strength, her guide. May put her face down on the bed and wept, while Alain stood close to her, his hand on her shoulder, connected to her grief through his love.

Edgar stood at the window, feeling helpless and angry. The world went on below them, cars parking, trucks delivering, people walking, running, talking. He didn't know what sound made him turn back to the bed, but when he did so, he witnessed Oona's body as she jerked upward as though pulled by an unseen hand or a spring pushing from underneath. A tortured breath dragged through her pleading mouth, then expelled again as she dropped to the mattress. May had stood up and all three of them stared in fear and amazement.

Once more, a surge of oxygen seemed to force itself into Oona's gaping mouth and then her chest began to rise and fall, her face filled with lifeblood, the lines of her countenance held outlines etched with animation instead of demise.

In front of a stunned audience of three, Oona Nabigon opened her eyes.

XXIV

Somehow, we kept coming back to the tree and the circles. Oona had provided the messages – for whom, we weren't sure – and we had to figure them out. Perhaps the message wouldn't have been so cryptic for someone else, but Frances and I were confused.

I called Langford on my cell to fill him in on what we'd discovered. He was less than comfortable with my involvement.

"Emily, isn't this for the police? Shouldn't you step aside now?"

"We're not doing anything dangerous, honey. Honestly." Later, I would certainly wonder just how honest I'd been, or whether I had truly just been very naive. "We're checking out territory that's already been scoured by the police – just looking at it from the perspective of this new information. Frances won't let me stay if she thinks it's going to get dangerous."

I could tell that he thought this last statement, at least, was true. "Okay, my love, keep me in the loop. I'm still in the studio. It's going well. Angel's sound asleep. I think you really tuckered the poor little thing out."

I laughed. "You should have seen her! She ran and jumped and sniffed all morning. No wonder she's tired out. I promise I'll keep calling, Langford, but not too much. Get those paintings done. I won't be long." Famous last words, indeed.

Once Martin Michano had arrived with his equipment, Frances and I headed out on foot toward the tree and Bahswaway Pond, which was a relatively short distance away. The sun was still very high in the sky, continuing its pleasant assault on the hidden bits of snow and frozen ground. Our feet stuck into the mud in places but we happily plowed through, our inner child excited by both the adventure and the promise of spring.

There wasn't much to see at the tree any longer; the message that Oona had left had long since been obliterated. We circled it nonetheless; not speaking much, both of us busy with our own thoughts.

I wasn't entirely comfortable with Frances yet; her changeable nature and various moods were still difficult for me to understand. I have to admit as well, that I am used to being the one in charge and I was having trouble keeping my opinions to myself. Thus I was a little quieter than usual.

I followed Frances as she headed around the pond and into the woods, biting my tongue from asking all the same questions over and over again. Why had Oona wanted the twentieth legend to be read? Was the message about the scroll or about Walking Bear or both? Who was Walking Bear? For whom had the message been written? Why had someone killed Frieda and Victor and tried to kill Oona? Where was Agnes Lake?

Luckily for Frances, I kept repeating these mantras in my head only. She was preoccupied, her eyes wide, her mind busy translating everything that she was seeing, trying desperately to unravel the mysteries.

We weren't far into our trek when we got the biggest message of all – one that would lead us into a situation that neither of us was prepared to handle. Hidden under a bush, scarcely out of sight, we found the bear headdress.

"This has not been here very long," Frances said, as we gently pulled it out into the open. "I'd bet several hours at most. Somebody wanted it to be found."

"I agree. A message without a doubt. But what's it supposed to tell us?"

"Good question." Frances straightened up. "I'm going to call in reinforcements." She grinned, the witty young woman shining through for a moment. "Just like in the movies." She listened at the cell phone for a moment, but she had not called the person I'd expected. "Chief Dan. Emily and I have found another bear headdress. We need your expertise." She was silent for a moment as the Chief spoke. "Sure. Bring them along. We'll meet you at Oona's cottage."

A diadem is a lot heavier than it might look. I wondered how anyone could walk around with a headdress like this one over their shoulders for hours at a time. Between us, with several rests, Frances and I lugged it back to Oona's and set it on the tiny doorstep.

Luckily, Martin Michano was still there. He began to snap pictures immediately after Frances had filled him in.

Deposited there in the sunlight, the headdress was displayed for more careful scrutiny. Once again, I was staring at a large brown bear's head and shoulders; a round opening for eyes and part of a face; long white and black feathers with red and yellow tips circling the diadem; a small piece of leather with an ink-drawn emblem. This time, though, it was also covered in leaves and twigs – and the emblem drawing was of a bear and fish. This must be Bird's headdress, I thought. Other differences were spots of sticky stuff and the small stubs on some of the twigs. The little nubs looked familiar and I wondered where I'd seen them.

As we waited for the Chief, Frances and I drank the bottles of water Marty had so thoughtfully brought along. He had completed the photography and quickly left to make his way home at last.

Frances and I sat on opposite sides of the diadem, in thoughtful silence, enjoying the sunshine. It was beginning to disappear over the trees and, knowing fickle nature, I wondered what we might expect for tomorrow's weather. That was when my hand began to itch.

Thinking it was simply time to put on more cream, I glanced down at my hand and was shocked to discover that the irritation had spread. My entire hand seemed to be pink and throbbing; the rash was heating up my skin, ready to break out in the little red pimples. I couldn't help but exclaim, "Holy shit," whereupon Frances looked over and made the same exclamation when she looked at my hand.

"What the hell is it?" she asked.

"It's an allergic reaction – it's called dermatitis," I told her. "Doc said I must be allergic to something I touched recently that..." I was silent for a moment, suddenly struck by the memory of a tiny stub sticking out from a twig.

"What?" Frances prompted.

"I think I know where I got this allergy," I said slowly, walking back to the diadem and pointing. "See that little stub? It looks like the twig has a thumb or something?"

Frances looked down carefully. "Yes, I see it." She squatted and brought her finger close to—but not touching, I noticed – the small gnarl of wood.

"Well, I just remembered where else I've seen one of those. The Smallwoods' yard. I've never seen any tree quite like it. Doc said I probably touched something unusual, some plant or tree that's not common around here. And it was the day after my visit to Peter and Ellie's that I broke out in the first rash." As I spoke, I was frantically reaching into my pants pocket and spreading the cream all over my hand this time. "Plus – do you think that sticky stuff could be sap? Because if it is, there is a damaged tree in their yard that was oozing it yesterday."

This time, Frances touched her finger to the sticky substance and sniffed at it. "Could be," she said. "It doesn't have much of a scent, but does smell a little sweet."

"Do you think Peter could have taken the headdress?" I asked her, because I was busily jumping to conclusions.

Frances rubbed her chin thoughtfully, probably scratching in sympathy with the ministrations I was going through as we talked. "I have no idea. But it sure looks that way from this bit of evidence. We could be jumping to conclusions" (little did she know, that's exactly what I'd already done) "and I don't like to do that – however..." I could tell she was really mumbling to herself, uncertain about what this turn of events could mean.

Just then, Chief Dan drove up in his big black car – I have no idea about cars, but I do know that the Chief changes them often and they are always large and shiny – with Bird and Basil. Bird leapt from the back seat and ran to the headdress. Frances barely kept him from pulling it into his arms.

"That is mine, Officer Petapiece," he said, sounding petulant and angry.

"Okay, Bird, but calm down, we need to be sure, and as it might be evidence in a crime, we have to be careful. You know that, right?" Frances put her hands on his shoulders and looked him directly in the eyes.

Grudgingly, he nodded his agreement, so Frances dropped her hands. "Now, Bird, walk around the diadem and tell me how you know it's yours and if you see anything different."

Bird did as he was told, while the rest of us looked on, silent. He walked around the headdress, carefully scrutinizing it. I noticed that Frances had taken out her little notebook.

"I know it's mine by the emblem," he said slowly. "The feathers are pretty much the ordinary kind we use. But most of the twigs look like the ones I used. However" he squatted and pointed, careful not to touch it, "some of these have been added. You see, my grandfather had worn it so often that a lot of the original twigs and leaves had fallen off, not to mention what's died since then. I replaced a lot of them last year, but they had grown brown and dry. So these green leaves and these twigs are new." I noticed that he pointed to the twigs with the tiny stubs. "And – it's got some kinda gooey stuff on it. I hope they haven't ruined the fur."

Frances finished off her notes. "Okay, Bird, thanks. I'm going to ask the Chief to lock it up for now. It'll be safe and probably not used in court, but you never know. I don't want to take chances. I have to be thorough so not only will we catch whoever is doing this, but also get them punished for it." She was stating the obvious, I thought, but Bird's face was still suffused with anger and petulance, and Frances needed to be clear with him.

Bird's countenance showed very obviously that he wanted to argue, but felt cornered. Basil, who'd been unusually quiet the whole time, helped him load the headdress reluctantly into the massive trunk.

Chief Dan stayed with us.

"I don't think you should do anything else about this," he said to Frances. "Maybe you should wait until Edgar returns."

I could tell that this statement was the wrong thing to say to Frances. Her body language immediately showed her irritation. "I'm an officer of the law, Chief Dan. I think I can operate without consulting Edgar each time."

The native leader obviously didn't understand her statement in the context in which she'd said it. "There is somebody very dangerous and very clever doing all of this," he went on in his formal, thick-tongued way, which, right now, made him sound patronizing and condescending. "They have made good use of legends and of beliefs that our people have held for many years. They are causing the legends to come true. If that is so, there will be more bloodshed. I do not wish it to be yours. You should have Edgar here. He will know how to handle this."

He turned on his heel and left, leaving Frances blushing as though she were a child who'd been scolded. I would have found her reaction funny, except that I could tell she was really quite angry. I realized that Frances had to deal with this kind of attitude on a regular basis. She was a woman doing a largely male dominated job.

"He didn't mean it in a condescending way," I said quietly. "He's really very kind. He's just being protective."

"He wouldn't dare say the same things to Edgar, Emily," she retorted, her demeanor formal and authoritative once more. "Would you like me to take you home? I'm going off to the Smallwoods' and I certainly would agree with the Chief that for you, at least, this might get dangerous."

I remembered my promise to Langford, but the memory was a lot less insistent than my curiosity. "I'll go with you, Frances. I can show you the tree with the nubbly twigs and the maple tree with the sap. We can see if Peter and Ellie are home again. I don't think there should be anything dangerous in that."

at the end of this
long day something
has stirred in me, some
huge sadness walked
across my body.
Water across pebbles holds
more substance than all of me,
even the smell of water is
recognizable, I am that raw.

The woman's breath was becoming shallower. In the recesses of her mind, she knew that she should force her lungs to expand, to take in the oxygen, to continue to receive the life-giving air. But the nights had been too long and the days too torturous. She no longer wanted to live.

The mice had raced over her face and hands and feet, their little claws feathery and light, their fur brushing her skin and causing it to itch. A spider had crawled into her hair, wiggling and tying its threads from her to the wall. Some time during the night, an animal had dug its way into the hut, from a window or a hole beneath, she was not sure. It may have been a raccoon or a rat, but she could feel its malevolent presence in the hut. It did not come near her, but she could hear it moving in and out, building a nest or amassing weapons against her, she did not know.

Her hands and feet had ceased to tingle; she had no feeling in them at all. She could not rock back and forth on the hard bench; she lay still and defeated, trussed like a load of wood, just as stiff and inanimate.

Her lips had swollen and the skin was puffed and cracked. She had no more liquid inside her mouth to ease the tightness. Her tongue was heavy and engorged inside her throat. She was not even concerned about the pain now. She felt limp, hopeless, numb. All that remained was the breathing, in and out, even when she tried to suppress it. Shallower now, ragged, but automatic, still there, continuing to make her poor heart beat, her body to suffer the heat, the cold, the insects and the animals. No real thought entered her mind now, but before that, she had prayed. *Just let me die,* she had whispered to the night.

XXV

By the time we got to the Smallwoods', the sun was beginning to disappear and a chill had set in. I was glad I'd worn layers of clothing, because by now I had everything on – sweater, jacket, and even gloves. Frances threw on her police issue jacket and some dark leather gloves as she got out of her car and headed up the walk. She was still quiet, but I thought it was more in thought than in anger, as her shoulders were not as stiff and her colour had gone back to normal.

Most of the villagers seemed to be ensconced in their homes. Children had been called in for dinner and very few people were still walking the streets. It was a soft time of day; muted and calm, resting before the shadows of darkness enclosed everything. There was an air of regret – our beautiful spring-like day was almost over and who knew if that gift would be offered again soon?

Peter and Ellie's home remained the same as before—deserted and dark. Once again, I was struck by the size of the yard, by the immensity of the trees and shrubs that crowded out the house and one another. I showed Frances the maple, its angry scar with the trace of sap beginning to push from the bark; I pointed out the gnarled branch that had shoved its way over and under all the other branches and trees, its little nubbly fingers twisting and turning and even escaping through holes in the fence. Frances had no idea to which tree the branch might belong either; it was difficult to trace through the jungle and the twigs did not resemble any tree that was familiar to us. Convinced that this was the source of the misery of my itchy hand, I didn't go near it.

"This is a strange corner," Frances said, her hands on her hips, hair tousled, as she looked left and right. "It's almost deserted. No one could actually see into this yard, or even see the front door from the sidewalk."

I remained quiet, trying to follow her thought patterns. When she didn't add anything else, I said, "I wonder where Ellie and Peter are. I know they travel a lot, but neither of them mentioned a trip when we were together during the hunt for Oona."

At that moment, we heard a dog bark very near by. We both turned to see Mary Jo Samuels, pulled along on a leash by a huge black mutt, coming up the sidewalk toward the Smallwoods'.

"Hey!" she said pleasantly, her face lighting up. "I'm surprised to see you both, but happy, too." She wrapped the leash expertly around the fence post and the dog happily sniffed through the brush at the edge of the walkway. "Are Peter and Ellie home?"

"Have they gone on a trip?" Frances countered.

Mary Jo's freckled nose wrinkled up in bewilderment. "No, that's what's so odd. Nick and I were the ones who went away last week. We were only gone from Sunday to today and we didn't want to take Shug" a nod to the dog cleared up who Shug was – "so Ellie said they'd come and walk her every day and feed her and water her. But for the last two or three days, they didn't do that. Thank goodness Shug drank out of the toilets and pawed her way into the food bag. Otherwise..."

We all looked at Shug, who was snuffling and snorting in the weeds and undergrowth. The bags of fat hanging down from her stomach area swung with her movement, making me think that she probably wouldn't have starved. However, it was still puzzling.

"So, did someone else report it to the police before I did?" Mary Jo asked.

At first I didn't understand the question, but Frances did

instantly. "Actually, no, Mary Jo. That's not why we're here. But now that you've told me, I'll file a report for sure. Thanks."

It was clearly a dismissal, so Mary Jo untied Shug and started back down John Street toward her place, which I knew was on Lewis. "You'll keep me informed, won't you, Officer Petapiece? I'm really worried about them. They love Shug and wouldn't have left her like that. I think something's happened."

"I'll let you know, Mary Jo," Frances said absently. She was distant again, thinking perhaps, or concerned, or mystified, or maybe all three.

I wondered if Frances would call Edgar now. It seemed to me that she was delaying talking to him in order to prove that she could handle it. Standing on the corner waiting for her to decide, I looked off down the street and saw Frieda's house. It was really within a stone's throw, right at the corner of Drummond and Lawrence, and I wondered how well Peter and Ellie knew her.

Impulsively, I said, "Let's go over to Frieda's house. It's right there. We could look around for anything that might give us a clue about the scroll. It seems to be the only thing we have to go on."

"Great idea, Emily. In the meantime, I'll call Edgar and tell him about the Smallwoods."

She talked on the cell phone as we walked down the street in the twilight. I thought of calling Langford, too, but knew he would still be painting until the light disappeared entirely. And besides, I knew he would want me to come home and I didn't want him to say it. The sense of excitement and adventure had pumped up my energy and I simply could not resist carrying through with the mystery. I absolutely had to be in on it. I was afraid Langford's doubts would raise

Frances's fears again and she'd force me to go on home.

I realized Frances had been quiet, listening, for quite some time, her eyebrows raised. When she'd ended the call (not, as I expected, with "I love you" but with "I'll check in later" and a click of the cell), she turned to me and said, "Oona Nabigon is conscious again. She's opened her eyes and is struggling to say something. The doctor wants to give her a sedative, but May is insisting that Oona be allowed to speak. Edgar said they might know everything in a little while, so we could go home."

Before the disappointment could sink in, she added, "But let's still go over to Frieda's. It can't hurt to have a look around her property. Maybe the door will be open again."

We couldn't help it; we both chuckled.

Frieda's house is similar to the Smallwoods' in style and size. However, the brick is all one colour, a sort of reddish brown. Contrasting white door and window frames, a Victorian screen door, and beautiful landscaping made the little home extremely attractive. Lovely evergreen bushes and spreading maple trees surrounded it.

I knew that Frieda had paid a considerable amount of money for this house, even though it had not been refinished inside. She had been planning to have it redecorated; had even bought the paint and hired Burchill's favourite handy man to do the job. Now I could imagine the paint cans gathering dust in the basement, never to be used. No one was even sure who Frieda's beneficiaries would be. The whole situation made me feel suddenly guilty and sad, as if I had been getting a voyeur's perverse pleasure out of her tragedy.

Frances went up to the front door and looked through the stained glass window. She could see only shadows and edges, so she moved to the picture window on the left side. The inside of the house was dark and deserted. "Well, no open doors I'm afraid," she said, going back to the front and opening the screen.

As she did so, she turned to face me, her hands on her hips, her body leaning on the door. Suddenly, she disappeared from view as she tumbled inward. At first, as I stepped quickly forward, I assumed that the door had been unlocked and ajar and that her leaning had simply propelled her into space. Until, of course, I saw the man with the gun.

The lake shines in its silver
and I am held in its peace.
The solitude of cloud envelops me
and I am its child.
The earth entwines me
and I praise its goodness.

Light streamed ahead of her as she walked along the pathway. Below her, she could see the rooftops of the little town, could see the roof of the home where her body lay waiting. Ahead, she could hear the voice of the one she needed. She continued to walk, the *peetwaniquot*, the cloud, gently drifting toward her as she continued along her path.

As she walked, she reached out for the woman shackled to the bed, gently coaxing her heart to beat, her breath to continue, in and out, oxygen flowing throughout her body.

Now she could see him below her and she was pleased; she knew his face was suffused with understanding; knew that he felt her presence in the breeze and in the sunlight. He would know where to find her.

She returned quickly along the pathway. Allowing herself to drift slowly downward into consciousness, she began to feel the softness of the shawl on her shoulders, the firmness of the floor beneath her body. She heard the voices, frightened and bewildered, but not defeated. She encouraged her energy to surround them, even as her body continued to lie still.

When they stood up, their whispers excited and hopeful, a smile curled around her face even as her eyes remained closed.

XXVI

For most people, violence is something they've experienced only on television or in the movies. In my life, I have had first-hand knowledge of that kind of terror far too often. I am not a courageous person; in fact, the moment I saw that gun and the twisted hatred etched in the man's face, my body reacted with a heart pounding flush that raced through every limb in an instant. When I was yanked roughly forward into the house, I was trembling and faint.

All the regrets of the day rushed forward to block my consciousness: I could only see Langford's face and hear his admonitions and his warnings. I wished fervently that I could be back home with him and Angel.

We were divested efficiently and roughly of our cell phones and Frances's gun. Dazed and breathless, I was pushed onto a chair in the near-empty living room, with Frances sitting cross-legged and trussed at my feet, the barrel of that ugly gun just a few inches away from her head.

In my frightened silence, I could hear Frances continuing to talk as she confronted our assailants. It was a shock to my system to realize just how brave Frances Petapiece really was.

"I am an officer of the law," Frances said to them, her voice affronted but reasonable. "Don't do this. The consequences are not worth whatever it is you plan to achieve. You will be caught. There is absolutely no doubt that when you involve a police officer, you will be hunted until..."

One of the men stepped forward and cut her off with a slap to her face that resounded through the room like a cymbal. "Shut up, Officer Petapiece. Your psychological babble won't work. We have every contingency covered, or we wouldn't have opened the door. Your persistent snooping could have ruined everything, but as it is, we will put the opportunity that has been gifted to us to good use, believe me."

I was staring up at his face, trying to reconcile this violent, angry, sleazy man with the smooth-talking, ever-so-polite, suave "suit" that Evan Fobert had been when I first met him. His voice was still polished, his jacket unwrinkled and expensive, his blond hair perfectly coiffed. But his face, instead of handsome and unlined, was cruel and unsightly, mirroring the filth that obviously lived inside him.

My head felt as though a huge weight had been placed there: the weight of violence in the past, the weight of guilt, the weight of fear. A huge regret crowded my chest with the beating of my heart; I wanted my husband, I wanted to feel his arms around me, see his face, touch the soft hairs around his neck. I couldn't offer any help to Frances; I knew what could come of this evil and it seemed that she did not. Instead, she sat even straighter, despite being on her rear end on the floor. She appeared to be even more aware of her surroundings, even less fearful. Did I know something she didn't, or was it the other way around?

"Listen, Fobert, why didn't you just go and find some other land where there wasn't as much resistance? Why chase after some phantom scroll to secure ownership? Canada's full of land. Why didn't you go find another spot? Now you're responsible for two deaths – maybe three – and you're contemplating more. Is this really worth it?"

Evan Fobert had stood smiling as she spoke, almost as though he were indulging a child. When Frances had finished, he actually laughed out loud.

"You think I'd do this for an empty piece of land? Really, Officer Petapiece, I thought you were smarter than that." He turned and picked up a leather tube. "And the scroll wasn't a phantom, my dear. Here it is in my hands. Where it will soon disappear. We can't have this turning up in the wrong places, you see." He fingered the tube as though it were a swatch of silk. "That land, my esteemed police agent and school principal, is literally a gold mine. Never before, particularly in this part of the country, has a vein this large been discovered. It is, without exaggeration, worth billions. You thought Victor Reeves was going to desecrate the land with his subdivision? Wait until we begin to scrape the precious stone from under those trees!"

The legend, I thought – it was going to come true. I shivered, remembering the section that warned of a great deal of bloodshed.

"And how do you propose to explain our deaths?" Frances demanded.

"Well, we actually have all that worked out, believe it or not, Officer. We are quite the planners, aren't we, boys?" Evan looked at the other two huge men who seemed to fill the small living room. "I'm tired of conversation right now, boys, and we have a few things to do to set the stage. Put them in the room with the others."

Grinning, the big man behind my chair yanked Frances and me to our feet and, with a thick black gun pointed in our direction, he walked us down a short hall to a closed door. Shoved from behind, Frances and I stumbled into the room, silenced by shock and the rough push that landed us both in the middle of the room.

This was obviously a bedroom or a den that Frieda would never get around to redecorating. It was empty of furniture; the hardwood was rubbed down to a faint blond colour; the walls were dark beige. Full paint cans and brushes still in the packages were piled in one corner. The window was boarded up; the only light was from the last lingering fingers of today's bright sun poking through the small opening at the top.

In a corner of the empty room, a man sat huddled by a small, prone figure. Neither of the people looked up; they appeared to be frozen into mannequins with shock or fear.

There was an echo as Frances spoke.

"What the hell is going on? Who are you? Who is that?" She pointed past the hunched figure to the body covered in a multi-coloured shawl, grey hair sprouting above the colourful blanket.

The man seemed to collapse in on himself. He landed heavily on the floor beside us, his legs splayed out in front of him, head down. His tall frame looked gaunt and crooked; his blondish, thinning hair was brittle and unkempt; dark circles under his blue eyes emphasized the lines of his face. He gaped up at us, his visage filled with shame and distress.

Peter Smallwood looked years older than the man who had regaled us with stories of his youth as we tramped through the woods only a few short weeks ago.

"It's Agnes Lake," he finally said, after clearing his throat several times and failing to push the words from his mouth at least twice. "She's...fine, really. She's just weak from the visions. She...hasn't been on a quest for this long before."

I could see that Frances did not believe him. She crouched down beside Agnes and gently turned her toward us. The older woman's eyes were clamped shut; she made no movement. Frances leaned over and listened to her chest, then felt for the pulse at her wrist. She nodded involuntarily, looking back at Peter and me.

"She IS okay," she said, her tone one of astonishment. "Her heart is beating very strongly and nice and slowly. Peter, why are you here? Tell us what the hell is going on and what these idiots plan to do." The last was said with all the authority of a police officer who knew she had the suspect in captivity.

Once again, Peter had to clear his throat and wait for the words to surface from somewhere deep within his personal torture. When he finally spoke, he did so in a rush as though speech would abandon him before he got the story out.

"They're going to kill us and then blame it all on me." He sounded pathetic and self-pitying and, as if knowing how it sounded, he amended his tone immediately. "And in a way, it is all my fault. It started when Frieda went to Victor Reeves and told him about a secret scroll. The scroll apparently gave ownership of Victor's subdivision land to one of the Original People. Not only that, the land held a gold vein that had never been mined. Frieda told him that she could find out where the scroll was hidden and she promised to sell it to him. Reeves got some expert to come and verify Frieda's claims about the gold and then supplied Frieda with a great deal of money to find that scroll.

"Frieda knew that the scroll had something to do with Oona, but Oona didn't even know anything about it. As soon as Frieda started questioning her, Oona got really suspicious.

"When Oona couldn't get Frieda to tell her where she'd gotten all her money and why she was so interested in the old legends all of a sudden, I guess she decided to become Walking Bear.

"Frieda had been over-trapping, too, and with all her new money, she'd been shipping furs out like crazy and making even more money. I don't really know what happened with Oona, but I think she had this idea that she could change Frieda in some way. And I do think it kind of worked.

"The minute Frieda was gone, Evan Fobert came to me. They...somehow they knew about my gambling debts. No one else knew just how desperate I'd become, even poor Ellie. They also knew that I was more familiar with the old legends than most. He convinced me to follow Oona and see what I could find out about the scroll and the ownership of the land.

"I was able to follow Oona to the sacred caves; it seemed to me that she had become...I don't know, almost not caring if anyone saw her. But when I listened in, I knew Oona and Frieda weren't interested in anything to do with the land; they never mentioned the scroll or the gold. They were genuinely making friends again and Frieda was regaining her spirituality. Oh and yah, I forgot to tell you, Frieda had accidentally walked into a bear trap and injured her leg badly, so Oona and Agnes were healing her."

Frances stopped him. "Agnes?"

Peter nodded his head. "While all this was going on, Agnes had entered her Vision Quest. She came upon Oona in the woods and tried to convince her that this way of changing Frieda was wrong. But Oona would not back down, so Agnes kind of – she supervised in a way and helped with the healing."

I thought about Legend Twenty, not only about Walking Bear and his mission to isolate the evildoers in order to heal them, but also about the Spiritual Leader. *"You are wrong, Walking Bear," the Spiritual Leader said. "When the people cried out, I answered their prayers. I brought Walking Bear out of his cave. I walked beside you as you healed the Evil spirits. I accompanied you on your patrol of the land. Now I can return to my people, satisfied that my quest has been answered."* The fact that Agnes Lake was here, a prisoner and a victim with us, filled me with terror, for it appeared that evil had won.

"Fobert also talked me into becoming Walking Bear, too, to keep people frightened and distracted and so I could look around under cover," Peter continued.

"Somewhere along the line, Evan Fobert decided he was going to get rid of Victor Reeves. They'd had some kind of falling out and Reeves threatened to fire him. Fobert was having none of that now that there was a lot of money involved. So...his henchmen took Victor out into the woods and – they left him there.

"Poor Oona...she...I think by then she was in a different space...she seemed to think she really was Walking Bear. She dragged him into the cave, too, thinking she was meant to heal him and stop the subdivision." Peter's voice broke again. I could see the tears running down his cheeks.

"In the meantime, you were out there in Bird's bear costume, scaring the villagers and following Oona," I prompted.

Again, Peter nodded. "Yah, though Oona was doing some of the Walking Bear stuff, too. As I said, I think she really began to believe she was Walking Bear reincarnated by Manitou. She began speaking Ojibwa again with Agnes and Frieda. She was happily living the old ways in the cave. She had no idea of what was swirling all around her."

"How did Fobert and his gang find out where the sacred caves were, Peter? Did you take them there?"

Peter's head drooped further. "Yes. I did. I...if I'd known...I like to think..." He stopped for a moment. "I took them there and they went in and they...I thought they were just going to take Victor back out, having taught him a lesson, and convince him to play nice. I didn't go into the cave with them. When I heard the gunshots, I tried to help, but they kept me back. I knew all was lost then. I knew I was completely gone, that Ellie would never forgive me."

"Did you burn down the subdivision?" Frances asked.

"No, Fobert's own people did that. They wanted an excuse for not rebuilding in that area, because they discovered the biggest vein of gold is there. They took Victor out into the woods on the same night, so it served as a distraction, too."

"Why didn't you come to us after they killed Frieda and

Victor Reeves—and almost killed Oona?" Frances demanded.

Peter's tears gushed forward; his nose was running and he didn't bother to wipe anything away. He looked and sounded both weak and pathetic and I felt a rush of abhorrence for him at that moment. "They came to my house and they took Ellie captive," he whimpered. "I am such a loser, and Ellie is so good and kind. All I've ever done is spend her inheritance and run us into debt and all she has ever done is love me." He lowered his head entirely and wept for a moment. "They also had Agnes. I...about the only good thing I did was save her from being killed in the cave. I told them she was a shaman and that if anyone knew where the scroll was, it would be her."

Frances drew some tissue from her pocket and forced it into his hand. We both looked away as he blew his nose and wiped his eyes.

"I ransacked Oona's house and tore apart this one looking for that damn scroll. I couldn't find it. They took Ellie somewhere out into the woods and tied her up in a hunter's cabin, threatening to let her starve to death or be torn apart by animals if I didn't find a way to get that scroll. I don't know where she is...I looked when I could, but I don't know where...those huts are always being ransacked and rebuilt in different locations..." Peter seemed to resolve himself not to break down again. He lifted his head and looked at both of us.

"Eventually, Fobert started believing me about Agnes; that she would know where the scroll was and that she would tell me, especially once she found out about Ellie. I convinced them to let me stay with her and question her. And she did tell me, as I knew she would.

"It was hidden under the tree that Oona had raced around. Frieda had found it right before Oona disappeared, but she'd decided she didn't trust Reeves and the boys. It was pretty symbolic that she buried it under that tree, but I assume she knew that. I think Frieda always, on some level, loved Oona.

"They let me go and dig up the scroll on my own. They knew it would look strange if someone saw me with those men, but that my presence alone near Oona's place or in the woods would go unnoticed. And they knew, of course, that I would never put Ellie's life before mine. So I left the headdress where I knew someone would find it. And I searched around for Ellie. If I could've found her, I would've come to you, Frances, I really would have. I left Chief Dan a clue, too, but I don't think he's gotten it yet, or maybe he just hasn't interpreted it the way I meant him to."

We were silent in the little room, each with our own thoughts. My mind was racing with the information – all the little pieces of the puzzle that had flown together, all the hideous betrayals, the greed that had led us to this place. I couldn't imagine how these people expected to get away with any of this. It seemed like madness to me. Did they really believe that they could set Peter up to be the culprit? I couldn't see Edgar accepting any of that as the explanation. And yet, as Peter had said, his actions over the last few days certainly made him not only look guilty, but he also did actually share in the blame. Maybe Edgar wouldn't believe it, but could he prove otherwise?

Frances got to her feet and tried yanking on the plywood covering the window.

"I already tried that, Frances," Peter said morosely. "They used huge nails to seal it shut. I could barely budge it. I also tried making noise. These old walls are so thick and those bricks, they just seem to muffle the sound. Besides, they'll hear us if you start kicking or screaming or pulling down that board."

Frances ignored him and continued pulling on the board, so I went to the other side of it and yanked as well. There was a tiny creak as it gave somewhat, but not enough to make much of a difference. When I stretched up and cocked one eye to the crack, I could see the darkening shadows in the yard, make out the trees bordering the lawn.

"No one could see us from the street," I said, "even if we could get our hands in there to signal someone – which we can't."

Frances turned away, her face flushed with anger, and listened at the hallway door. "What the hell are they doing out there? I can't hear a single sound."

"They're just waiting until night," Peter told her, again in that defeated, self-pitying tone. "That's when they'll stage whatever scene to make me look like the sole culprit. We will probably shoot each other or something, Frances."

I almost burst into hysterical laughter at his last sentence. "This is ridiculous," I hissed, keeping my hysteria at bay with great difficulty. "This can NOT be happening." My shoulders shook with silent laughter. Peter and Frances stared at me as if I'd just gone insane.

"Emily, I know it's something we'd normally see in some stupid movie, but you have to hold it together, hon, or we're finished for sure."

I looked up at Frances, tears rolling down my cheeks that had begun as laughter and were now turning to tears of dread and frustration. "I'm sorry. I'm just..."

"I know." Frances tugged on the door handle, which did not budge an inch. She walked over to me and put her hand on my shoulder. "It's insane. It's so insane and so awful that we absolutely can't let them get away with it."

I nodded my head, drying my tears on my sleeve, and

straightened my shoulders. She was right. I had to keep my resolve. I had to get back to my husband. I turned back to the window and squinted out, more to have something to do, and a reason to turn my back as I composed myself, than to look for rescue. To my astonishment, I could see dark shapes moving across the lawn, in and out of the periphery of my vision.

"Frances," I said urgently, trying to keep my excitement down to a whisper. "Look."

I handed over the small opening as though it were a telescope. When Frances turned around after peering through the opening, her body was rigid with excitement. "I can't see who they are, but there are more of them than that bunch out there," she whispered. "Maybe Chief Dan got your message after all, Peter!"

It was amazing how that statement caused a sudden and rapid transformation in Peter Smallwood. When I think back to it now, I believe it was this turn of events that got him through everything, and might even have prevented Peter from committing suicide. He had done at least one thing right. He was suddenly on his feet, scrabbling at the wood, peering through the tiny slit, anxiously whispering to us about what we should do next.

"We have to warn them," he said. "We have to signal to them that we are in here and stop them from being hurt."

"Or going away," Frances added. "That probably explains why no one is moving out there." She jammed her thumb in the direction of Evan Fobert and the two huge men who accompanied him. "They're keeping their eyes on the activity outside, ready to do something drastic if they have to. And of course Chief Dan wouldn't try to break in or anything. He will go through the yard and try to look into the house, but he won't come in unless he sees something wrong."

I had been looking around the small room, at the paint cans, the drop sheet, the brushes, the old curtain rod standing in the corner. All waiting for a decorator's hand that had been stilled. "I've got an idea," I said, cementing my thoughts as I spoke. "We can take that drop sheet – somehow attach it to the curtain rod. Paint a message on the drop sheet and shove it through the cracks – there – and there." I pointed to the small openings that we'd been able to make at the top of the board. "They just might see it and even if they can't read it, they'll know it's a signal."

Frances and Peter's faces lit up. "Excellent plan, Emily. Let's do it."

"What will we say?" I asked. "What will the message be? We can't just say help. They won't know those men are out there with guns. They'll walk into a trap."

"I've got a suggestion," Peter said.

We pried the lid from one of the open cans, tore open a package that held a thick paintbrush, and slathered a huge DANGER on the drop sheet. The paint was a shiny bright green, a colour that seemed inexplicable, something I would never have used inside my home. But for our purposes, it was perfect, almost glowing in the dark as we slapped it on.

Peter was able to stab a hole in the cloth with the end of the curtain rod. We held the right side up as he threaded the left end of cloth through the opening, poking and prodding, coaxing it through, the curtain rod becoming heavy as it carried the drop sheet across the window, getting caught on the board here and there. It seemed to take hours as we shoved and nudged the cloth along. But at last we had most of it threaded through, the curtain rod poking its head out at the other end. Peter was able to force the curtain rod all the way through, then we were able to rest it on the board where it hugged the window frame. We left it there and waited.

It was not long before we heard the sounds at the front of the building. There were popping noises, like fireworks, and I knew I was hearing gunfire. The shouts were a meaningless racket because we could not understand a single word. We could hear boots and running feet in the hall. The little house seemed to tremble under the violence that was ravaging its insides.

Frances and Peter and I huddled around Agnes. I am ashamed to say that all I did was pray. The god that I ignored most of the time received a litany of promises, regrets and entreaties from me during those minutes in which we had no idea what kind of scenario was playing out all around us. Agnes' slow breathing, her warm, motionless body, kept us focused and calm as we waited. The energy that appeared to emanate from her was patient and certain; her god had already answered.

When someone began to jiggle the door handle, we all peered with terror in the gloom of that small space. My heart raced and pounded; I could feel Peter and Frances stiffen with fright.

"Peter? Are you in there?"

It was the voice that broke us. Chief Dan's strong, deep, clipped tones surrounded us and brought the tears to our eyes. Peter sprang to his feet, followed by Frances.

"We're in here, Chief. We can't open the door." It seemed an inane thing to say, but Chief Dan responded immediately.

"We're coming in, Peter. Stand away from the door."

A loud ripping noise, the shattering of the wooden frame, and suddenly the light from the hallway splashed in on us, along with a refreshing burst of air.

The first faces we saw were those of Chief Dan and Basil Fisher. Their large, comforting frames filled the doorway as they embraced us all, talking incessantly, questions flowing from them about how we got to be there. We were all speaking and moving at once. But when Chief Dan knelt down beside Agnes, the room was immediately silent.

"Shaman," he said, "wise one, awaken. It is over."

Agnes Lake stirred first and then sat up, her back ramrod straight, her face serene yet alight with joy.

"I knew you would come, old friend," she said to him, placing her hand on his cheek. "I knew you would hear me."

The talking began once again; the delirious chatter was more mine than Frances' or Peter's, but the questions kept coming and getting answered. I was dizzy with relief and anxious to call Langford.

In the living room, Evan Fobert and the two others were face down on the floor, hands cuffed behind their backs. Martin Michano was talking rapidly into his cell phone. Burchill's two other new officers, Ron McNeil and Helen Jackson, stood over the captives. Everyone was ignoring Evan Fobert's muffled and frantic attempts to speak.

Somewhere at the edges of my awareness, I saw Barry Mills and Michael Lewis, our police volunteers. Henry Whitesand, as well as several other members of the Native Council, hovered in the house and outside in the yard. Doc came charging through the front door at one point and threw his arms around me, asking if everyone was okay.

The circus of voices and people came to order when Frances and Marty pulled Evan Fobert up to a sitting position. Frances squatted down in front of him, her face severe, her eyes bright with anger.

"If you tell me where Ellie is, I might be able to talk to the judge about how cooperative you were," she hissed at him through closed lips. "No deal making, no promises, no hesitation. Now."

Evan Fobert was smart enough to know when he was defeated: there was no hesitation; nor did he beg for mercy. He simply told her. Immediately, the three men were thrust to their feet and placed in the various police cars that surrounded the house. Chief Dan, Barry, Frances, Peter and several other of the Native Council members were gone in short order, heading for the woods where Ellie Smallwood lay suffering. Marty and Michael remained in the house, talking on phones and writing notes.

I stood outside in the twilight with Doc, Agnes, Henry and Basil, watching the parade of vehicles race away. It seemed that most of the neighbourhood had come out, too, including Mary Jo and Nick Samuels as well as Maire Murphy. Very soon, the tall figure of my husband leapt from our car, along with a small dog who raced into my arms before even Langford could get there. A huge, reassuring embrace was all the lecture he gave me; his eyes told me that he had questions that could wait until we were alone.

Henry and Basil were solicitously looking after Agnes, even though Doc had reassured them of her completely good health. As they took her by the arm to guide her toward Basil's car, Agnes turned back to come and stand by my side. Her hand was warm and silky smooth on mine.

"Child, do not linger in the past," she said, her voice soft, her eyes clear and wise. "Come to see me soon, Emily. I can help."

Once again the tears sprang to my eyes; I was startled and touched and amazed by her perspicacity. All I could manage in response was to nod my head. Langford and I were both quiet as we watched her walk away with her two friends, politely refusing their assistance as she stepped carefully down the sloped lawn toward the car.

Angel sat close beside me, her beautiful little head lifted so she could keep her eyes on me. The fact that I'd been gone far too long, along with Langford's fearful response to my call, had been enough to make her very nervous. I kept bending down to reassure her and pat her head.

Later that night, when questions had been answered, and Langford had spoken his mind, when forgiveness had been granted and reassurances made, our lovemaking was slow and tender and fulfilling.

XXVII

The next morning, the weather had changed dramatically. Instead of sunshine, clouds had gathered menacingly over Burchill; the wind was whipped up into a frenzy, blowing old withered vegetation in swirls through the streets and lopping the heads off little plants that had blossomed prematurely. The temperature had dropped so drastically that the townspeople who'd put their winter woolies away had to drag them back out again. Hats and mittens and winter coats were donned once more if they needed to venture outside.

Those of us who had been involved in some way in the "Walking Bear affair" (as it came to be known) were asked to gather at the police station.

Langford and Angel stayed at home; the little dog was fast asleep at my husband's feet when I left. The painting that had absorbed Langford's mind lately was a stunning replica of the view from our bedroom window; the colours were silver and blue with touches of golden and red sunlight as it hovered just above the horizon and fingered the water. The perspective was from our balcony, so the viewer was in direct line with the waning sun. Below, on the lake, two white swans floated cheek-to-cheek as though dancing; their frame suggested a heart. At the moment, he is calling this work Ogeechee, but as soon as I gazed upon it, I suggested that the title be, Devotion.

I walked to the police station, clad in scarf and hat and mittens and my big ski jacket. Buffeted by the wind and the debris being tossed about, my face was chapped and red by the time I reached my destination. As I pulled off my gloves in the reception area, I was glad of the heat that wafted out from both the furnace and the people gathered in the foyer.

I was relieved, too, to see that Doc Murphy's cream had begun to work, for the rash on my thumb and palm was dried and far less itchy. At that moment, I saw May.

We flung our arms around each other and stood that way for a long time, both of us in tears.

"How is Oona?" I asked, pulling myself apart from my friend and looking into her tear-filled brown eyes.

"She's getting there," May answered. "She's eating a little on her own, sitting up a lot of the time, and talking. At first she was pretty incoherent, and she kept saying strange things, but eventually she was able to recognize us, and tell us what had happened. The doctor said she might be able to come home soon, as long as she has care. Henry is going to move her into his place for a while, and Alain and I will help when we can. Doc said Maire offered to come by every day."

"Count me in, too, and Langford. We'll all take turns," I told her, squeezing her hand with my good one. Only then did I look around at who else was gathered in the room.

Edgar stood at the front, talking to Frances, Marty and Chief Dan. The Burchill Regional police officers and volunteers were scattered amongst the Native Council members, everyone seeming to talk at once. Only one of the major players in the drama was missing – Peter Smallwood. Under the watchful eye of the Ontario Provincial Police, he had been allowed to maintain a vigil at Ellie's bedside in the Ottawa General Hospital. Charges, I presumed, would soon be laid.

I glimpsed Agnes Lake, sitting on a chair near the front of the room. Wrapped in a beautiful coloured shawl, the Shaman's small body looked elegant and relaxed, straight grey hair, tied with a red ribbon and piled on top of her head. I went immediately to her, and, squatting beside her, I placed my hand on hers. She smiled serenely at me; her sharp brown eyes seemed to pierce my inner thoughts.

"You will speak with me today," she said, her voice raised

only slightly at the end, making the statement more of a command than a question.

I nodded, letting go of her hand, and straightening up in front of Edgar. When the tall, usually reserved police chief saw me, he reached out his strong arms and pulled me into a huge hug. "You're in this again, eh, Emily? I think I'd better give you a badge."

I laughed. "Better talk to Langford Taylor before you say stuff like that, Chief Superintendent Brennan."

Edgar released me with a smile and I went back to stand with May. He waited for a few more people to arrive, including Basil and Henry, and then he called us all to have a seat and to come to attention.

"All right, we've got a few items to attend to, everyone," he said, his voice authoritative and strong. "All the individuals involved have made statements; they've been typed up and they're ready to be signed this morning. But I thought we might all fill each other in on how everything unfolded – just so each one of us – especially myself and my team of officers, as well as the Native Council – have as complete a picture as possible.

"Before we do that, I'd like to commend everyone involved, especially Frances, Marty, and Chief Dan, and all the other officers and council members. The tragedy was bad enough, with the deaths of Victor Reeves and Frieda, but it could have been so much worse. A special thanks to Emily Taylor and Agnes Lake as well. Without their influence, the outcome would not have gone our way. Anyhow, let's get going, and I'm sure each of you will see that, without certain parts being played, the result would not have been as positive as it was."

With fits and starts, back-tracking and forgotten insertions, the entire story did at last emerge.

Knowing that Oona and Agnes Lake would have the knowledge necessary for tracking down the scroll, Frieda had begun her quest by attempting to get back into Oona's good graces. Oona, suspicious of her old friend's motives, pretended to go along with Frieda, even drinking with her in the pub and talking about amassing more wealth, something that was anathema to her true philosophy. But trust did not exist in their relationship any longer, so Frieda, in turn, did not have complete faith in Oona's statements. Their friendship continued to deteriorate.

Oona was aware of the legend and the existence of a scroll; her suspicion of Frieda's true motives had been inscribed on the back of that picture in her cabin. Perhaps she'd drawn the scroll as a symbol of Frieda's greed, or maybe she was exploring her own thoughts and feelings. We were never to know, as Oona's memory, even later, was sporadic.

Once she had recovered her ability to speak, Oona confirmed that she had had no real proof that the scroll was not just a legend, and she certainly could not believe that it had been found in her cabinet. However, Agnes verified that Frieda had admitted, in the cave, that she had found the scroll tucked in the corner of an unused cubbyhole in Oona's hut.

Frieda had no trust for Victor Reeves, either, and was not prepared to give the scroll to him immediately. She kept it with her at all times, until she went into the woods to follow Oona.

"My guilt would not allow me to take it when I went to find her," she told Agnes. "I hid it under the tree, the tree that Oona used to mark her trail."

In the meantime, Oona decided that she had to act. The legends were strong with stories of Walking Bear and how he intervened to prevent the land from being ravaged. She believed that Frieda was somehow involved with Victor

Reeves; she knew for sure that her old friend had been given money by his organization. She was just uncertain about the reason, although she was aware that Frieda had stepped up her trapping operations.

Oona fetched her father's bear headdress, fashioned boots and mittens from bear claws, and began to set a trap for Frieda. She knew that only Frieda would be able to follow the trail of Walking Bear that Oona laid out. After all, Frieda had been Oona's star pupil. She deliberately pointed to Legend Twenty through her circles around the tree, knowing Frieda would immediately connect to Walking Bear. Oona had counted on Frieda's innate childhood superstitions to keep her off balance and to entice her into going deeper into the forest.

It was a dreadful irony that led Frieda right into the jaws of a real bear trap, pinning her to the ground in agony, slicing through skin and bone and damaging her leg almost beyond repair. Yet Oona began to see this occurrence as almost a blessing; Frieda was forced to rely on Walking Bear for her comfort, healing, and sustenance. Oona's spiritual experiences with Frieda in the cave, and her old friend's transformation, pushed Oona into another plane: she began to believe that she had been destined to become Walking Bear.

When Frieda and Oona disappeared, Victor Reeves was convinced they had absconded with the scroll. He believed that Oona had persuaded Frieda to sell the information to the highest bidder.

According to Peter Smallwood, Reeves was a greedy, condescending and evil man, who had made enemies even of his employees and partner. He continued to berate Evan Fobert on how he had handled the situation with Frieda and the scroll. The moment Frieda disappeared, he gave Fobert the ultimatum that he find her or, as controlling shareholder, Reeves would remove Evan from the company before any profits were realized.

Evan Fobert went on a fact-finding mission: he read through the legends; he discovered Peter Smallwood's gambling weakness and recruited him. He encouraged Victor's inherent animosity toward the natives, spurring him on when he began to insult them, such as when he fought with Henry. Evan Fobert wanted no one to mourn Victor Reeves' loss and he wanted plenty of suspects, for Evan Fobert planned to be rid of his partner one way or another.

At the same time as we were gathering in Burchill, Evan Fobert and Peter were being questioned separately in the vast chambers of the Ottawa police station. Peter, despite cautions from his lawyer, was laying out the story, determined to set things right, his brow beaded with sweat and his eyes bulging with the stress.

The officers sat opposite him, one of them operating the tape recorder, the other gazing into Peter's face, his eyes daring the prisoner to lie. To the veteran policeman, Peter Smallwood was a spineless, selfish man who had placed other people in danger to make his own problems disappear. He was surprised to witness a demonstration of strength of will that carried them through the tedious details of the grilling.

"When I reported what Oona and Frieda were doing in the cave, Fobert decided they would take Victor Reeves out in the woods, too, to be taught a lesson." Peter hung his head, then lifted it again, not daring to slip into weakness once more. "I really, stupidly believed that no one would be seriously hurt. I actually thought that Evan would scare the shit out of Reeves and that would be that."

Fobert, held in another room with his own lawyer and interrogators, was at that moment, probably inadvertently, corroborating Peter's assertions. "At first," Evan said, "I thought Victor would give in. He was never very brave, he was always whining and I really thought he would stop threatening me, would change his ways. I just had to show him that I had the upper hand, what I was capable of."

The police officers in this room reacted differently to this prisoner; Evan Fobert was an arrogant sociopath who believed in his right to acquire whatever he wanted, no matter who got hurt in the process.

"But I was wrong. Victor is a stubborn son-of-a-bitch when he wants to be," Fobert went on, as though his partner were still alive. "Even after hours in that horrible cave, Reeves was only more determined to take away my stake in the gold strike. If I'd let him out after all of that – well, it was either kill Victor or he would have killed me. I really didn't have much of a choice. If he'd only listened and learned his lesson."

Evan Fobert shook his head sadly, unaware of the disbelieving looks from the other people in the room. The skewed thinking that could allow a man to kill another over gold that didn't even belong to them in the first place was a symptom of someone who cared about no one but himself.

The female police officer, leaning over the table and watching with satisfaction as Fobert grinned stupidly at her, spat the words at him in staccato speed. "Your men are telling a bit of a different story, Mr. Fobert. They claim you sent them into the cave to kill Victor, not to persuade him to change his ways." Her tone was sarcastic and pointed. "They say you instructed them to remove Frieda; after all, she still had the scroll. When the woman in the bear outfit jumped on them, trying to prevent them from taking Victor and Frieda out of the cave, they had to beat her into submission. Then suddenly the injured woman, the one with the splint on her leg, had leapt up and attacked them too. Your poor, picked-on thugs, they had to pull out their guns and start shooting to subdue two women."

Evan Fobert stared at her, then gave a grunt and a sneering smile. "You just can't get good help these days," he quipped.

Once he had begun, Peter Smallwood couldn't seem to stop. "I was terrified when I heard those gun shots outside the cave," he told them, his voice shaking with the memory. "I had to go in; I was so afraid they'd hurt them. I...the blood, Oona and Frieda..." It was some time before he could continue.

Peter convinced Fobert's men that Agnes' status as a spiritual leader meant that she would have wide knowledge of the scroll and the legends and therefore she would be useful to Fobert. Frieda and Oona appeared to be dead; they realized they needed Agnes.

The criminals subsequently ensconced themselves in Frieda's house, keeping both Agnes and Ellie captive as collateral and inducement for Peter's co-operation. They tore the place apart searching for the scroll, convinced it had to be inside Frieda's home. When they couldn't find any trace of it, they had Smallwood search the village, Oona's hut, the museum, and the caves for any sign of or clue about the scroll.

Meanwhile, the community learned from Agnes that, though she had initially not approved of what Oona was doing, the Shaman observed that Frieda was genuinely transforming. Once she was physically and mentally healed, Frieda had the potential to be a spiritual and benevolent person. Victor Reeves' arrival in the woods made Agnes extremely nervous and she once again tried to persuade Oona to stop. By then, however, Oona was "under a spell".

"It was similar to a Vision Quest, I think," Agnes said thoughtfully. "Oona began to believe that she had truly evolved into the persona of Walking Bear."

Agnes, mindful of Legend Twenty and her role as Spiritual

Leader, decided that she had to stay with Oona and guide her to eventually release both of them.

"After the shooting," the Shaman told us in quiet, mournful tones, "I had to transport into my mind. I couldn't deal with it at first. I could not think about what I could do to end this evil."

Peter Smallwood hadn't known how to cope, either. "At first, Agnes remained in a trance, refusing to speak. I was having a hard time convincing Fobert not to beat her. I begged her and begged her, whispering into her ear. Finally, when she did speak, she told me exactly what to do."

Agnes told him to go at once to the scroll's hiding place and where to leave various clues for the police and Chief Dan.

"I put the headdress in the woods near Bahswaway," Smallwood continued. "Agnes was certain that Bird would not stop looking and that he would likely be the one to find it and that he'd tell Edgar right away. I left a piece of Agnes' shawl on Chief Dan's porch. Agnes knew he'd recognize it – they all have special quilting and buttons that are all different from each other."

"Why didn't you simply come and tell Edgar or Chief Dan what was happening to you?" one of the officers interrupted, unable to hold his patience any longer.

Peter replied slowly, his words thoughtful and spaced. "I really believed that I was always being followed by one of Fobert's men. Agnes told me I could explain dumping the headdress in the woods as a distraction because Bird was calling too much attention to its loss. The police might start the searches again and maybe they'd find the bodies, so I was letting Bird find it.

"Before I left it in the woods, though, Agnes told me to take it home, reinforce it with Buckthorn twigs and cover it with maple sap. She knew these things can only be found in my yard. Buckthorn trees are not native to Burchill, you see," he explained. "And maple sap doesn't spill from any other tree so early in the season, except from my maple; it was struck by lightning a few years ago and has dripped almost year-round ever since. Agnes said that Edgar would know right away that these clues were from me and it's true, Edgar often comments on the Buckthorn and the quirk of that maple tree. Of course we didn't know that Edgar had left Burchill to stay with Oona in the hospital."

Peter had told Fobert he was going to search Chief Dan's property for the scroll when the native leader was away; dropping the piece of shawl on the porch had been furtive and quick.

"I figured I could explain everything and they wouldn't know I was actually leaving a trail. I was so terrified they'd see me talking to anyone, especially Edgar or Chief Dan, and that they'd kill my Ellie." For a moment, he couldn't speak, his eyes filling with tears. "Agnes was right when she figured that Edgar or Frances, but especially the Chief Dan, would interpret the signs correctly and come looking for us in the right places.

"But I really thought that the only way to secure our release was to turn over the scroll, take the payment they had promised, and disappear from Burchill."

"Mr. Smallwood," the same officer exploded with annoyance. "Don't you know that they would never have let you go anyway?"

Peter was silent for a moment. "I am such a coward, Officer. I know my thinking was twisted. I was confused and terrified. Every decision I made was terribly wrong right from the very beginning. The only good thing I did was to listen to Agnes."

Back in Burchill, Edgar was reassuring us that Peter's

testimony against Evan Fobert and his men, along with his co-operation and part in apprehending them without further victims, would probably ensure a lighter sentence. And despite Peter's faults, his weaknesses and offenses, it appeared that everyone in that room at least, was relieved.

Once Chief Dan found that piece of shawl, he alerted the police. Fortunately, Martin Michano had not gone home as he'd said he would, but had returned to the station, anxious to develop his pictures, and it had been he who answered the Chief's call. He was the one who first put together the clues about the headdress and the shawl. When he was unable to reach Frances on her cell phone, he called in the other officers and the volunteers. Chief Dan gathered the Native Council members and met Marty at Frieda's house.

In between thinking about all the twists and turns of the story, I was suddenly very alert to two words: Buckthorn twigs. I remembered the pointy little thumbs on the tree outside the Smallwood property and covering the bear headdress. Now I knew what I was allergic to! No more Buckthorn for me in the future.

Without our signal at the window, Marty admitted that he would probably have doubted the Chief's conclusions and forced everyone away from the property.

The native leader, however, looking over at Agnes, said that he had felt her presence on that shawl, and in Frieda's house; but without that signal, he might have charged in, unaware that armed men would have been waiting for them. A small silence met his statement; it was as though an intimacy had been shared in public that caused everyone to feel embarrassed.

Basil Fisher's deep voice broke into the quiet. "What was on the scroll?" he asked, something all of us were anxious to find out.

"I'll let May tell you that news," Edgar said, gesturing for her to come forward.

May stood in front of us all, her face flushed with excitement. "It seems that the land which has been claimed by the Crown all these years actually belongs to my Aunt Oona," she said, her voice shaking a little with wonder and promise. "My uncle Kenneth Nabigon, Oona's husband, inherited it from his ancestors. Kenneth, ill with cancer at such a young age and having lost his only children, had a will made that ensured Oona would inherit everything. For some reason, he never told her about the land.

"The scroll is quite old, but authentic, and had been registered with the Crown a very long time ago. No one ever bothered to research it properly, even when Victor Reeves applied to the government to buy the land. It seems the registration was lost in some misplaced files and never retrieved. But it will be now! And won't they have egg on their faces for failing to follow the proper processes?"

The whole room burst into the kind of laughter that results from the rush of happiness at exacting revenge – this time on a faceless bureaucracy that had not shown any kind of willingness to look into Burchill's entitlements and complaints; recorded voices who had told the townspeople over and over again to follow the proper processes.

The laughter was also a release of emotions and lasted long enough to bring tears to many of the eyes in that room. It was joy at the thought that Oona, whose husband and children had died so young and whose life had not been easy—that Oona, who had been a champion of the land since she could talk—would be the one to lay claim to the disputed property. It was relief that no more blood would be shed; that the greedy and the weak had been thwarted.

May continued once it was quiet again. "As for the gold

deposit, and Victor Reeves' claim that the expert he hired found something worth a great deal of money—all of the papers have been handed over to a geologist. She will research the claim and let us know. She did caution us that very large strikes are rare this far south in the Canadian Shield, but she also said it's certainly possible. But we'll cross that bridge when we come to it, and of course, whatever the outcome of the investigation, it will be up to Oona to decide what to do with the land."

Once May sat down again, Edgar never did get the crowd under control, nor did he try very hard. Everyone got to his or her feet, slapping each other on the back, shaking hands, hugging, crying. We all experienced a great deal of catharsis, a kind of healing, and we took our leave slowly. At the door, May offered to drive me home, but I looked back at Agnes.

"No, thanks, May, I think I'll walk Agnes home," I told her.

My friend looked closely at me, knowing there was something I wasn't saying, but she hugged me and did not ask questions. Agnes and I bundled up in our winter woolies and began to walk up Main Street toward Sahsejewon.

Above us, angry clouds punched the air and sent a cold and piercing wind flying into our faces. We pulled scarves and collars up to protect our cheeks. Our bodies were buffeted like sails as we drove ourselves through the gathering storm. By the time we reached Agnes' cozy little home, large flakes of snow were doing cartwheels over the lawns, freezing on any part of our flesh that we hadn't managed to cover. We both puffed and sighed as we landed in the small entranceway, stamping up and down as we divested ourselves of our heavy clothing.

Agnes' home is a beautiful log cabin that had been built by her grandfather. Every log was carefully placed without nails or screws and remain in their natural state. The ceiling is at least twelve feet high. Inside the open, large living area is a huge stone fireplace, which Agnes quickly lit. One corner of the room is dedicated to the kitchen; a modern bar has been built around the refrigerator and stove, with stools for sitting and talking while food is being made.

It was not here that I went, however; Agnes motioned me to one of the wingback chairs in front of the fire and I gratefully followed her direction. A lovely soft fur was folded on the seat and I tucked it around my legs, feeling safe and warm and comfortable. After everything that had happened, I almost felt like falling asleep, yet I was alert to Agnes' movements. I looked around the room as she puttered silently with a kettle and cups.

There are so many artifacts in Agnes' home that it could have been part of Bird's museum. Beautiful furs, soap carvings, decorations designed in wood, feathers and dried flowers together in various arrangements, a large natural walking stick, baskets and clay pots, all in various shapes and sizes, dot the room. But it doesn't look crowded or overstuffed; it feels wide open and spacious yet warm and welcoming.

Agnes sat in the chair next to me and handed me a large mug. It was a hot, steaming liquid, sweet and tasting of mint, and I sipped it gratefully. Agnes tucked her feet under another fur and we sat companionably for a few moments, both of us staring into the red and blue flames of the fire. Then, without notice or introduction, Agnes began to tell me a story.

"There was a young man who was very sick when he was young," she said. "He was so ill and weak that the young man spent most of his childhood inside his hut. He could only watch as the other children played with sticks and ran around the village. His mother and father would bring him out on a chair to watch the celebrations. He was never able to partake of a shawl dance or a plea for rain.

"When he was older, he began to sit outside for long hours. He had to merely watch as his peers went out on their quests for vision that would bring them into manhood. His own manhood was reached only in the confines of the village. He spent many hours at the forest edge, watching the animals, observing the plants, following the flights of the birds.

"When the boy reached beyond his teenage years, a miracle happened. A new Shaman was anointed in the village. This Shaman was a great friend of the young man's father and began to spend a lot of time with the youth. They spoke of the many attempts to heal his illness and discussed new methods that may be helpful. The young man, having spent all of his life observing and studying, began shyly to share his learning with the Shaman. The Spiritual Leader returned his trust by sharing all his own knowledge with the boy. Slowly, under the Shaman's watchful eye, the young man began to get better. Soon he was well enough to walk through the village; then to the river; then to the next village for the great shawl dance.

"The young man began to join with the Shaman in healing others. After several years, he was well known in the village and even in the villages beyond as a gifted healer. Even the Shaman would tell others that the young man had surpassed the Teacher in his abilities. The youth was happy at last, that he had attained good health, and that he was able to help others do the same. But the Shaman could tell there was something bothering him.

"'Son', he said – for the Shaman had begun to think of him as his own – 'tell me what troubles you.' At first, the young man was reluctant to tell his mentor what was wrong, for he was so thankful to the Teacher and did not want to sound petty or ungrateful. But soon he knew he had to ask the question, or it would fester inside him and ruin his new and happier life.

"'Teacher,' he finally said, 'Kitche Manitou is good above all others. I am grateful for the gift that I have been given. But when I was a boy, and even when I was a young man, I had to watch as many of our villagers died. If I had been well, perhaps I could have saved them. I could have been using my gift so much earlier. Why did Kitche Manitou strike me with illness and prevent so many of the People from being healed?'

"The Shaman was quiet for a moment. When he spoke, he covered the young man's hand with his and looked straight into his eyes. 'But have you not seen Kitche Manitou's plan, my young friend?' he asked. 'If you had not been ill, you would not have spent all those hours studying and observing. You would not have learned from the plants and the birds and the animals. You would have been the same as all the others, learning only how to run and jump and dance and hunt. Your gift developed only because you had the opportunity to watch how the plants grew; to learn which ones healed the animals and which ones were poisonous; to see how the birds used certain leaves to make their nests and keep out their enemies.

"'Even more important, you would not have had the time to know yourself. You spent long hours with your inner self, understanding who you are, coming to terms with your limitations. Now you must learn to accept and use your powers. You must know that your gift for healing would not have been given to you without your past. Your present has allowed you to use the gift; in your future, you must continue to spend time observing and learning and never allow yourself to be lost in bitterness about the past. For let me say this again, without your particular past, you would not have your particular present or your particular future.'

"The young man went on to become an old man, replacing the Shaman when he went to the other world. He never forgot the words of his mentor and friend. He never regretted his past but continued to use it for the good of the People. He became a Healer so strong and powerful that he was known by all the Ojibwa in the area.

"He told the story of his past to his children, his protégé, and anyone whom he healed. He taught the People never to become bitter about their lives, but to learn from their past experiences, and to turn them into good. And because of his teachings, the village continued to prosper and the People were as free from illness as they could expect to be."

When Agnes' voice became silent, I could hear the crackling of the fire and the sound of tiny ice pellets hitting the log walls. Tears flowed down my cheeks, unchecked and irrepressible, but it wasn't from unhappiness that I wept: it was from a great release, a kind of forgiveness; a shedding of a heavy cloak that I had worn around my shoulders, one that bent me over and occupied my physical and spiritual being. I felt free and lifted by her words, by the lessons of the Shaman, especially the one sitting beside me.

Agnes turned in her chair and placed her hand on mine, looking directly into my eyes. "Let it all go, child," she said. "Learn from it. You have so much goodness. Do not be afraid to share that who you are is because of where you have been, what you have suffered. Remember that your present is a result of that past. And so will your future be."

That afternoon, as the Ontario weather turned vicious and dumped a final winter blast of snow and ice upon Burchill, I told Agnes Lake everything. In between my tears and her gentle questions, I revealed all that had happened to me and to William, my beloved husband, my talented and tender

Langford.

I told her how I longed to be closer to May and how afraid I was to tell her who we really were. Agnes cajoled the old Emily back, the one who is optimistic and open and emotional, the one who'd built walls of mistrust, who'd become just a little distant. May and the people of Burchill had begun to chip away at the wall I'd built around me; thus my feelings of insecurity and fear had resurfaced. The shaman, though she never really gives advice directly, helped me to see a pathway through.

That afternoon, Agnes Lake set me free.

XXVIII

On Saturday evening, the last weekend before March Break ended, the town was still buried under a foot of snow. The sun had been out all day long, glittering and sliding over the ice, but nothing seemed destined to melt for a long time. Snow ploughs had been up and down the streets; people had dug out their driveways and made pathways up the sidewalks. Children and adults alike had spent all day making snow people or throwing snowballs or dragging sleds up hills and racing down again. Now, as the sun began to disappear behind the lake, most of the villagers settled in for an evening of indoor activity.

Langford had built a beautiful fire in the dining room fireplace, which stood beside the floor-to-ceiling windows, where the mounds of snow glistened outside. I had set the table with all the lovely dishes and glasses and napkins that I seldom ever use. As I stood in the doorway to gaze upon how lovely everything looked, I vowed to use the good stuff more often. The waning sun brought an amber light into the room, which made it look even more comfortable and welcoming.

We had bought plenty of bottles of our favourite wine, and as we waited for our company to arrive, we both sipped from the nectar of the gods in big, wide, made-for-red-wine glasses. Soft music played in the background and Will and I floated around the house happily contemplating playing the perfect hosts. Angel looked up now and then from the carpet in front of the fireplace, but she merely blinked at us, seeming to laugh at our antics, and did not move from the comfort of her warm spot.

When the doorbell rang, we were as giddy as newly-weds entertaining for the very first time. Our company came in laughing and hugging, their faces all red from the walk over, their excitement about an evening with us almost as palpable as ours. May and Alain were happy and rested; the lines had gone from my friend's face and, as she shared her aunt's continuing progress, the relief made her eyes sparkle.

Dinner was a huge success. Both Will and I had contributed to the delicious dishes that we served; our guests were more than appreciative. Several bottles of wine disappeared and, by the time we had special coffees in our hands, whip cream dripping over the sugary edges, the laughter was loud and we all somehow found hilarity in everything.

It was only then, after a look exchanged between Will and myself, that I began. "May and Alain," I said, "we have a story to tell you about our past."

About the Artists

The Author

Catherine Astolfo is a retired elementary school principal who is now living her dream of writing full time. In between, she has been assisting her children in running their film production company, Sisbro & Co. Inc. "Victim" is the second book of a series of four featuring Emily Taylor. For information about the first book, "The Bridgeman", and more to come, check out www.sisbro.net.

The Poet

Merci Fournier began writing poetry nearly twenty years after emigrating from England. She has been published in several literary magazines and anthologies in North America and Australia. As well, Merci has a chapbook, "The Baker's Wedding", published by Southwestern Ontario Poetry Press, and a broadsheet, "Marzipan", published by Underwhich Editions. To get in touch with Merci or to explore more of her poetry, contact her through www.sisbro.net.

The Visual Artists

Carly Smith drew the cover and the illustrations for each of the native chapters. She lives near Ottawa and is currently studying architecture at Carleton University. Carly's amazing artwork can be seen at The Brookstreet Hotel in Kanata. Through her website, www.artishard.net, Carly not only displays her art but encourages others to join in the creative process.

Helen Duplassie is also an educator whose dream of creating art has blossomed since she retired. Helen drew the map of Burchill for both The Bridgeman and Victim. As well, she crafted the drawing of the footprints around the tree for this book. Her beautiful artwork is displayed through Beaux Arts in Brampton (www.beaux-artsbrampton.com). To find out more about her art, email her at helendu@rogers.com.

ISBN 142511546-2

9 781425 115463